RAPTOR

RAPTOR

DORSEY FISKE

A Tom Doherty Associates Book 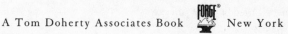 New York

RAPTOR

Copyright © 2000 by Dorsey Fiske

This book is printed on acid-free paper.

Design by Jane Adele Regina

A Forge Book
Published by Tom Doherty Associates, LLC
175 Fifth Avenue
New York, NY 10010

www.tor.com

Forge® is a registered trademark of Tom Doherty Associates, LLC.

Library of Congress Cataloging-in-Publication Data

Fiske, Dorsey.
    Raptor / Dorsey Fiske.—1st ed.
      p. cm.
    "A Tom Doherty Associates book."
    ISBN 0-312-87263-1 (acid-free paper)
    1. Policewomen—Fiction. 2. Female friendship—Fiction. 3. Serial mur-
ders—Fiction. 4. Police artists—Fiction. 5. Rape victims—Fiction. I. Title.

PS3556.I81463 R3 2000
813'.54—dc21

                                                              00-034723

First Edition: October 2000

Printed in the United States of America

0 9 8 7 6 5 4 3 2 1

To Margaret, with thanks for her help with a super idea;

and to Jo, Ellen, Pat R., Marty, Pat and Tom, and Stella.

Acknowledgments

With thanks to Doris and Stanley Budner for their invaluable assistance with the book's publication; to my agent, Liza Dawson, a pearl beyond price; and to my editor, Melissa Ann Singer, for her discernment, persistence, and charm.

RAPTOR

Mid-August

HEAT. Fever heat. The city is sick with a fever. It sprawls, steamy, inert, sunk in tropical torpor. The weather has been hot for weeks. It feels like years. The thought of the city in winter, covered in snow, is a pipe dream, a shimmering fantastic impossible vision. It is hard to believe there has ever been snow in the city, hard to believe the city has ever been cool. There is only the heat, a malign smothering force which hovers, relentless, over the buildings and the vacant lots.

People shuffle listlessly along the city streets. It is too hot to pick up their feet. It is too hot to move. Those who can afford it exchange air-conditioned cars for air-conditioned restaurants for air-conditioned houses. Those who cannot sit panting on their front stoops, languidly fanning themselves. The air is heavy with unshed water. Black beads of tar ooze from the softened asphalt of the streets. The dog days of August have arrived with a vengeance.

The row of brick houses on Broom Street is new—only a couple of years old—and cheaply built. Several of the air-conditioning units have been defeated by the unrelenting heat wave; and even though it is nighttime, the interiors they were installed to cool are hot as bake ovens. The inhabitants have raised their unscreened windows in a vain attempt to capture a breath of air. Near an open window someone is playing the Neville Brothers. The notes fall like leaden weights, muffled by the thick atmosphere. Drums dully thump-thump-thump, Evan Neville's high pure voice cuts through the murk like a knife, singing about heat—emotional heat. About fever in the morning, fever at night. Like tonight.

He crouches, waiting in the dark, a deeper shadow among the shadows. He is dressed all in black: black jeans, black sneakers, black T-shirt, black gloves dangling from jeans pocket. He saw her leave several hours earlier. It was still light then and he was dressed differently. He keeps track of her movements; sometimes he is a delivery man, sometimes he hands out flyers, sometimes he is just a passerby headed for the neighboring park. But tonight he is dressed for business. Real business.

Her house is at the end of the row. The windows in the second-floor front bedroom are open. So is the kitchen window: ideal for a quiet entry, he notes. The night is deathly still with no breeze stirring. He had thought of waiting inside for her return. But the house is small and there is a chance she might see him. Sometimes he attacks in the early evening, but he prefers to catch them asleep. That way there's no time for them to call 911. There is the risk that she might close and lock the kitchen window when she gets home, and he likes an easy entrance. It leaves fewer clues. But he is patient. Patience is the secret of his success. If he can't get in tonight, there will be another opportunity. There always is.

A young man and a girl—*the* girl—approach, moving listlessly in the envelope of heat. They stop at the front door of her house. They are quarreling. He listens intently, leaning back invisible in the bushes.

"Come on," the young man says. "Don't be such a prude."

"It's too hot."

"You've got air-conditioning. I'll heat you up, it'll cool you off." He laughs at his own wit. His laughter is an intense, slightly hysterical jangle of noise. He has had a lot to drink.

"I said no. I told you, the air-conditioning's gone bust. It's too hot even to ask you in for a drink." She sounds slightly relieved as she says this.

Despite his less than sober condition, her companion sees his chance and seizes it. "If it's that bad, you'd better come back with me."

"I said no," she repeats, annoyed. "Look. It isn't that I don't like you. I just don't want to sleep with you. Not now."

"That's not the way you acted last Saturday," he says insistently.

"Saturday was . . . I had too much to drink last Saturday. Anyway, we didn't. We nearly did, but we didn't."

"What makes you so sure? You were high as a kite," he teases her.

There is a pause. Then she says, "We didn't. I know we didn't. I didn't pass out."

"I wish we had," he says, his voice low and amorous.

There is a silence. The listener holds his breath. *Damn*, he thinks. *The son of a bitch is going to queer it for me.* He grits his teeth as he sees the two separate shadows meld. Then,

"No," she says again, but her voice is tentative. "Not tonight. Please. I have a lot of work to do this week. I can't let myself get tired. I shouldn't even have taken time out to go to dinner with you. I have to concentrate on this case I'm working on. You know, the one I told you about."

He takes hold of his opportunity. "Well, how you going to get any sleep in that hotbox? You said the air system's broken. Look, I won't touch you if you don't want me to, but you'd better come back and sleep at my apartment." He takes his keys out of his trousers pocket and waves them in front of her invitingly. "You can have the bed," he says. "I'll take the living room sofa. And stay there. Scout's honor."

She hesitates. It is a tempting prospect. Even with the electric fan and a cold shower, she won't get much rest. But he makes the mistake of supposing he has won and puts his hand on her arm, touching her breast as he does so.

"No, I . . . Thanks, Tom, it's very nice of you to offer. I really mean that. And some other time . . . It was a wonderful dinner, wonderful evening. It's just this case. The firm is counting on me to pull it together by the end of the week. I can't let myself get distracted."

He can tell by the sound of her voice, which has traveled the road from uncertainty to firmness as she says this, that the time for changing her mind tonight is past. But he can't help asking her, "How you going to get any sleep in this weather? With no air-conditioning?"

"I'll manage." She is determined not to go with him. Their kiss has made it clear to her that even with air-conditioning, she won't get much sleep at his apartment.

"Well, then . . . What about Friday? Your case be wrapped up by then? Dinner after work?"

"It has to be. I said it would be. Sure, I'd love to."

"Great. We'll celebrate." He moves in for another kiss, but she dodges and inserts her key in the door.

"Terrific. See you then. Six o'clock, same place?"

"Right."

" 'Night. Thanks, Tom. Super evening."

The lock of the door clicks and she is gone. The alcohol has slowed Tom's reflexes. He shakes his head to clear it like a dog coming out of water and stands uncertainly for a moment or so, then mutters, "Shit," and shambles off.

The figure hidden deep in the shadows does not move. He will wait until the girl has taken off her clothes, turned off the lights in the house, climbed into bed, and gone to sleep. Even in this heat, even without air-conditioning, she is bound to sleep at first. The heat is like a drug. It drains the energy from people, knocks them out for a few hours, then it wraps itself around them like damp felt, smothering and waking them. But in a few hours it will be too late for her.

At first he hears a variety of night noises—the muffled sound of footsteps on pavement, the heavy drone of an engine as an occasional car passes along the city streets, the sharp yelp of a dog. Then there is unbroken silence. The watcher has not moved from his niche in the shadows. The lights in the house he is watching—the lights in all the nearby houses—have been extinguished for almost an hour. It is time.

Warily he moves over to the kitchen window, which she did not bother to close and lock before she went to bed, and climbs over the conveniently low sill. A beam of light from the streetlamp casts a cold glitter on the blade of a knife that hangs on a magnetized holder beside the window. It has a wintry gleam that is strangely attractive in the sweltering night. He snatches it up to see if it is as cold as it appears, and tests the edge with his finger. It is razor honed. It gives him an idea. It may be useful when he gets upstairs. It will serve as an artful persuader. He has never thought of using a knife before.

The idea pleases him. His method has been to hit the recalcitrant ones until they can no longer resist. But the knife is a far more elegant solution. He does not enjoy inflicting damage as much as he enjoys the fear in their eyes, their knowledge that he can do anything he likes to them, their realization that he holds absolute power in his punishing hands, the power of hurting, the power of life and death. When he hits them too much, too hard, they do not feel it after a while. They are no longer frightened, they are too numb to feel. But the knife! The knife will evoke a flicker of fear, a glitter of pure icy terror at the back of her eyes, a reflection of the sliver of steel he wields in his hand. And afterward, when she is filled to the brim with all the fear she can hold, he can use the knife to release it. In the blood. A river of blood, a torrent of blood. If he wants to. If he chooses.

He gazes, entranced, at the thread of shimmering light that runs along the edge of the knife blade. He wonders why the idea of using a knife has not occurred to him until now.

TOM IS SITTING AT THE BAR IN DUGAN'S IRISH PUB ON DELAWARE AVEnue, staring down into the third glass of bourbon he has had since leaving Janet. He is awash in alcohol, but fortunately heredity has endowed him with a hollow leg which still supports him, despite his overindulgence. On his way home he passed Dugan's and saw by the lights that it was still open, so he decided to make a quick stop for a glass of something as a sop to his injured feelings before returning to his empty apartment. One glass has turned into two or three, and he is beginning to think that he gave up on Janet too easily. In retrospect he realizes that as he left, she was just beginning to weaken. But it is almost

one in the morning. Only a few diehard drinkers are still loung-
ing at the long old-fashioned mahogany bar, and the bartender
has taken to looking significantly at his watch. Time to go home,
Tom thinks to himself mournfully. Home to a lonely bed. Of
course, he might make a swing past Janet's place—it is not far
away—in case the heat has kept her awake. Maybe she's
changed her mind, with the heat and all. Pretty thing, Janet; a
real knockout. Tall, slender, long strawberry blond hair, bright
turquoise eyes. He wasn't just putting a letch on her, he thinks
virtuously, he's beginning to feel really serious about her. That's
why he wants her to get a decent night's sleep.

But as the bartender pointedly begins to turn off the lights,
Tom comes to the reluctant realization that no matter how al-
truistic his motive, it is too late to bang on Janet's front door.
Besides, he has a job to go to tomorrow, too. Time to roll on
home. He waves amiably at the bartender. " 'Night all," he says,
and wanders out the door.

THE WATCHER EASES HIMSELF ALONG THE LITTLE HALL OUTSIDE THE
kitchen. Slowly. Each foot testing the floor for noise, gradually
adding a little more weight and a little more weight, until he is
certain that the boards will not creak loudly enough to be heard
upstairs. In the small sitting room a fan whirs, blurring any
other noise. He has drawn on his gloves so he will leave no
fingerprints. In his left hand he holds a flashlight the size of a
pen with a pocket clip which serves as the switch. It casts a coin
of light in front of him, just enough to enable him to see where
he is going. In his right hand he carries the knife he found in
the kitchen, blade upward, and every so often he caresses the
edge of it lovingly with his thumb. His eyes flick back and forth,
from knife to light beam, back to the knife again. He cannot
keep from looking at the knife blade for long. It excites him
more than anything he has ever seen. He cocks his head upward.
Was that a sound upstairs? Silence. Satisfied, he tests the first
step of the staircase gently, gingerly, with his foot.

TOM FINDS HE IS AMBULATORY, BUT ONLY JUST. He is fairly steady on his feet, but in the dark the streets of Wilmington are strangely misleading to negotiate. Clouds driven by a night wind sweep across the sky, and he blames his difficulties in navigation on the pixilating moonlight. However, eventually he reaches his apartment building on Rodney Street, a rambling renovated dwelling festooned with gingerbread that originally housed a large and prosperous Victorian family, now turned into six reasonably commodious apartments furnished with all mod cons.

Tom reaches into his right hip pocket for his house keys. They are not there. Annoyed, he slaps his pockets in a search for them. No luck. He swears and puts a hand into each pocket, turning them all inside out, and finally in desperation inspects the interior of his billfold. Nothing. He grovels on the ground along the path that leads to the porch, paying special attention to the perennial border, but they are nowhere to be found. He seats himself despondently on the steps, resting his aching head in his hands. Where the hell, he asks himself, are his keys? He finds that as soon as he allows his mind a little leeway it begins to wander, but with an effort he manages to force it back on track.

Keys. Took them with him? Door to apartment locks on its own, might have left them inside. God! Never get in. Wait! On his way out, remembered he hadn't checked mailbox, went back into foyer. Dropped them there?

He goes onto the porch and peers through the clear glass sidelights that flank the front door. A lamp in the hall is still lit, but he cannot see the glint a bunch of keys would make, either on the floor or on the low table in front of the tenants' mailboxes. He turns the doorknob and pushes, but the door is incontrovertibly locked. Frustrated, he shakes it; and when this action produces no result, he sits down again to try to think where he could have dropped his keys.

THE WATCHER HAS REACHED THE TOP OF THE STAIRCASE. It was a slow ascent. He is a cautious man. Caution has saved him from capture more than once. And being thwarted only whets his appetite for the next attempt, makes it more exciting, gives the game an added spice. Anticipation is part of the thrill. The thought of the look that crosses their faces—first surprise, then sheer disbelief, then the slow hideous realization that this is real, not one of those nightmares that make the sleeper wake thanking God that it hasn't really happened, that it was only a dream after all. Then fear, the stark unreasoning terrified comprehension of what is to come. That is the best time. After it is over he always feels the inevitable letdown. Until he begins to plan the next one.

While he is climbing the stairs, he feels a rush of air and hears a faint metallic clatter which grows louder as he nears the second-floor landing. At first it startles him; then he realizes that she must be running an electric fan in the bedroom as well as the one downstairs. All the better, he thinks; she will be less likely to be wakened by any noise he may make.

On his way up he balances lightly on his toes. The flexible rubber soles of the canvas shoes he is wearing make very little noise, even at ordinary times. At the head of the stairs the door to her bedroom is open, as he was certain it would be. He takes the precaution of switching off his penlight, though its slender focused beam would be unlikely to rouse the sleeper. But he no longer needs its assistance; enough light from the moon and a nearby streetlamp filters through the filmy curtains at the open windows to show him the way. Despite the fan whirring in the room, it is stifling in this narrow shoe box of a house, but he does not notice the heat. Now that his hour is upon him, he is cold with purpose, like chilled steel. Like the blade of the knife he is holding.

The double bed is set sideways to the bedroom door. The light from the windows discloses the form of the sleeper in a disordered nest of bedclothes. She wears nothing—it is too hot to bother with a nightgown—and her pale flesh is pearly in the dim light. Her lack of clothing disappoints him. He likes to see the horror in their eyes when he makes them take off their clothes; he likes to watch the way their hands tremble while they are undressing.

———

TOM GETS UP AWKWARDLY FROM HIS SEAT ON THE PORCH. He cannot remember how long he has been sitting there. But he thinks he knows where he left his keys. He remembers taking them out in front of Janet's house when he was trying to persuade her to come back to the apartment with him. He must have dropped them there. What a bore. He'll have to go back now to find them, or he won't get in. But he's tired. Why not wait till morning? No chance of breaking into his apartment—it's on the third floor, and he's not in the mood for mountain climbing—but he can take a catnap on the porch till dawn, which isn't that far off now. He settles his back next to a pillar and closes his eyes. Then a thought strikes him. By now poor Janet will be hot as the devil. *She* hasn't spent the last hour or so having a drink (or two, or three) in a comfortably air-conditioned bar. She has been fruitlessly trying to get some sleep in a house so blazing hot you could probably bake pizzas in it. By now she'll be pleased and grateful to be carried off from her tropic inferno to an agreeably Arctic pad. He won't try to get in bed with her, he thinks piously, oh, no, not he! She needs her beauty sleep for the day ahead. But when she realizes how pigheaded she's been, how thoughtful he is, how sensible it is to stay at his place until her air-conditioning is fixed, then maybe tomorrow night . . .

The thought energizes him. He gets up again and moves off creakily in the direction of Broom Street.

BEING A CAREFUL MAN, THE WATCHER HAS CONSIDERED THE PROBLEM OF the open windows in the bedroom. He knew that was the room he would find her in, because of the light showing there before she went to bed. He has decided that he will make her close them once she is awake. All the windows in the little house are open except those in the downstairs front, so there is no point in taking her into another room. Besides, the next house in the row is vacant, with a For Sale sign planted in the handkerchief-sized garden in front of it, so even if she manages to scream before the windows are closed, it's doubtful anyone will hear. In any event the humid night air dulls sounds so they seem faraway and dreamlike, particularly to people who are sleeping.

On padded feet he moves next to the bed. The flashlight is in his pocket now, but the knife still glitters in his raised right hand. With his left hand he covers her mouth and roughly shakes her into consciousness. Her rose-gilt hair catches the faint light that emanates from the windows. It has a warm gleam, unlike the chill of the steel.

She does not want to rouse into the hot dead air; he can feel her lips mutter protestingly against his palm. But despite her reluctance she begins to wake, and panics as she finds she cannot breathe because his hand is blocking her nostrils. Her eyes fly open. Even in the half-light he can see they are brilliantly blue.

He places the point of the knife so it pricks the delicate skin of her throat. "If you scream, I'll kill you," he hisses. "I'll slit your throat to the bone."

She stiffens. Clearly she has got the message, so he removes his hand from her mouth. The knife, he thinks triumphantly, was a masterful move. It delivers an instant message. It makes him feel powerful, more powerful than he has ever felt before. From now on he will always use a knife. It gives him more time to see the fear, to smell the fear, to taste it. A frisson of pleasure ripples down his spine as he watches the pupils of those blue blue eyes grow larger and larger from the terror seeping into them, until her eyes look nearly black.

"I'm going to rape you," he tells her. "And if you make a sound, I'll split you like a barbecue chicken. With this." He takes the knife away from her throat and shows it to her. He waits for the full realization of what is happening to flower inside her. Her eyes widen. Her mouth forms an O of fright. She starts to scramble out of bed, but he pushes her back.

"You aren't going anywhere," he informs her. He holds her down on the bed, sets the knife on the floor where she can't reach it, unfastens his trousers, and rapes her.

———

Tom's progress along the night streets of Wilmington is erratic. He is not as drunk as he was, but he had been very drunk indeed. He squints at the street signs he passes to make certain he is going in the right direction, since between the night, the heat, and the booze, the terrain seems strangely unfamiliar. It is only a ten-minute walk from his place to hers, but in the dark it seems much farther, since now that he has got the wonderful idea of being Janet's knight-errant, he is impatient to carry out his quest. At long last, however, he rounds the corner next to her house. The streetlamp provides a source of light that evokes a small answering gleam on the ground beside the front steps. It catches his eye and he gets down on his knees to inspect it hopefully. What luck! His key ring. Now he has access to a sanctuary where he can take his damsel in distress. Gleefully he picks up the keys and carefully, lovingly, stows them in his pocket.

The Watcher has finished. For the moment. He picks up the knife and ponders what he will do next. She watches him, thoughts skittering frantically back and forth inside her mind like mice terrified by a cat. He places the point of the knife on the tender flesh of her stomach, and she cannot repress a squeak of fright.

"Shut up," he tells her conversationally. "Or I'll gut you. Like a fish. Ever seen what they do to fish?" He prods her with the knife and she bites her lips, locking them together with her teeth to keep from screaming. Rape, then, was only the beginning. What else will she have to endure? Is there any chance for escape? She is certain he is going to kill her. Eventually. She feels that to be killed at once would be a blessing. The black-garbed figure stands between her and the door to the hall, and she is wearing nothing that would serve as protection against attack with the knife. Her flesh shrinks from the thought of the knife. It will rip and rend and shred her flesh. If he did not have the knife, she would try to slip past him. Once down the stairs... But it is the dead of night. There is no one on the street to help her. And he has the knife.

He moves away from the bed, his eyes fixed on her. His

attacks have never been in the middle of the night before. They have been early in the morning before his victims were awake or in the forepart of the evening, when he was worried about an interruption, when he had to be quick, when he lacked the luxury of time. Now that he has so much time, it is like having an entire birthday cake all to himself. He has time to spare for whatever he may choose to do; he has the leisure and the power to experiment. And he has the knife.

In his delight over the potential of the weapon he picked up by chance on his way into the house, the Watcher has forgotten about the open windows. They are recalled to his memory by a muted shout from the street below.

"Janet!" yodels Tom. "Oh, Janet, your swain returns. Come to the window, my lady fair." Tom has decided upon the method direct to summon Janet from her unquiet bed. Not for him the doorbell or a pounding on the front door.

When they hear Tom, Janet's face and the face of her attacker wear strangely similar expressions. Both hearers are completely astonished. An instant later the Watcher's expression turns to one of naked fury. A wild hope assails Janet. She opens her mouth and screams as loudly as she can, a scream that reverberates in her own ears, crashing inside her skull like an echo of itself.

"Help, Tom! Help! For God's sake help me!" she screams and, still shrieking like a calliope, rolls off the bed, rolls under the bed in an attempt to avoid the knife.

The Watcher, enraged at this unexpected unsettling of his plans, rounds the promontory of the bed and kicks out at her as the readiest means of assault, then seizes a projecting foot and begins to drag her out from under the bed with one hand, the blade glistering evilly in his other fist, waiting until enough of her is exposed for him to make good use of it. But the bull-like roar that floats up through the bedroom windows and the thumping he hears on the door below make him decide quickly that flight is a wiser option.

"Janet! For Christ's sake! What's wrong? Hold on, I'm coming!"

The agreeable haze of alcohol cushioning Tom's brain has

evaporated at the ring of terror in Janet's voice. The small house vibrates with the blows he is raining on the flimsy door with his sturdy shoulder, hammering away at it like a battering ram. He has almost made up his mind to break out the mullions of one of the front windows when the lock gives way and the door flies open.

Shouting, "Janet! Janet! Where are you?" at the top of his lungs, he races up the stairs which the intruder ran down only seconds ago; and stops at the bedroom doorway when he hears a voice—unrecognizable, if he had not known it must be Janet's—say, "Here. Here I am."

She crawls out from under the bed, holding a sheet which she has pulled down and decorously wound about her. He helps her to stand, putting his arms around her to keep her upright. In a small shrunken voice she says, "Thank God!" and bursts into a deluge of tears.

MY JOB IS NO PICNIC. I don't mean the drawing part of it, which is challenging and rewarding. Or the detecting part, which never fails to give me a Sherlockian thrill. What bothers me are the people I have to talk to in order to produce the sketches I make. It's not that I'm an unfriendly type; I like people. That's the problem. I feel so desperately sorry for the ones who have been hurt. And for the ones who are still frightened. Sometimes I can almost feel their injuries as if they were my own, because I have to talk to them as soon as, even sooner sometimes than, they can bear to remember.

I'm a police artist by trade—well, to be precise, a police detective, with criminal sketches my specialty. It ain't art, but it's a living. In my spare time I work on the sort of daubs that I hope will make me a household name long after I'm moldering in the grave; but so far no museum, let alone the most modest of collectors, has come knocking on my door. In the meantime I earn the rent for my garret, along with cash for my canvases and crusts of bread, by delineating the unlovely features of malefactors—what are known in equally unlovely police jargon as perps, for perpetrators.

But though I should prefer—understandably—to be known as the newest successor to Gauguin or Monet, or maybe Berthe

Morisot or Suzanne Valadon, my paying work is not all drudgery. It can be immensely satisfying to produce a recognizable face, one that gets its owner arrested and convicted after he has committed a particularly vicious crime.

A word about my methods might be in order. I employ a judicious combination of the psychological and the suggestive. I'm rather proud of the system I use, which is my very own. Well, to be perfectly honest, it's an amalgam of other people's methods, one that seems to work for me. At least I've produced some winners that way; or it might be more accurate, from the criminals' point of view, to say losers. I try to wear something that doesn't look too businesslike; that day it was a short-sleeved pale yellow linen suit the shade of clotted cream. First I talk to the witness in a way calculated to make him or (in this case) her relax as much as possible. I make tea or coffee with my electric kettle, or get sodas, and I break out some outrageously delicious (though unexpectedly healthy) chocolate chip and pecan oatmeal cookies that I make for the purpose. Sometimes I play something restful like Mozart, or maybe the Pointer Sisters—whatever the witness prefers—on a tape player I keep in a corner.

We talk of this and that, I give her time to unwind, but every so often I slip in an innocuous little question. Like "Do you remember what shape his nose was?" or "Were his eyes close together or far apart?" or "What kind of hair did he have?" Sometimes the witness replies reflexively, without time to think the answer over. When someone does that, I'm pretty sure I'm getting something. So as I jot down my questions and the answers, I doodle idly on my pad as if I were just marking time; and when I've asked all the questions I can think of, I finish up the sketch I've been making and show it to the witness—just a preliminary one, of course.

Then, once I've gotten everything I can winkle out of the witness with questions, if I need to I show her those photographs of facial characteristics that most police artists depend on. But I've found that though sometimes photographs clarify, they can also confuse a witness. On the whole I get my best results with the tea-and-sympathy question-and-answer method.

I wasn't looking forward to the interview with Janet Davies.

It was only two days after she'd been attacked; and I've found that, for those who are subjected to it, rape tends to be the most upsetting of the violent crimes. I suppose that's because it is so personal and so intentionally vicious. I mean, you can argue that a mugger may not have meant to hit his victim, that hurting him was an accident resulting from the robbery, but rape is never an accident. No way. So it's one crime that is impossible to explain away to yourself. And—I've thought about this a lot—the really dreadful thing about being hurt by someone else, as long as you don't sustain permanent physical damage, is the knowledge that he did it on purpose. Particularly if it's a total stranger, someone who just picked you out of a crowd for the hell of it, out of pure dyed-in-the-wool nastiness.

Anyway, there I was, sitting in my little olive-drab-painted cubicle—government issue pigment, hardly the most cheerful color known to man, and one I would change in a flash if only the PD would let me—waiting for Janet Davies to make her appearance. When she walked into my office, she was looking pretty battered. She had a real shiner, the result of a kick the rapist had delivered when she hid under the bed, which had developed to the point of black-and-purple iridescence, like an overripe banana. She had milk white skin that provided an un-believable contrast to the bruise. But as if to counteract the im-pression made by her injury, she wore a snappy summer outfit—white linen trousers and a lime silk shirt tied at the waist, the collar flipped up under a black linen jacket. Her newly washed red-gold hair was tied back with a crisp black grosgrain ribbon, and a scent redolent of hyacinths and lilies and jasmine—the same, I realized, that I was wearing—wafted about her. She was bandbox fresh, as if she were thumbing her long elegant nose at her attacker and saying, "See? You haven't made a bit of difference." But of course he had.

I liked her as soon as I met her. She was amazingly resilient, considering what she'd been through. The police officer who brought her up to my office was Jacko Benson, a special favorite of mine. He's young and cocky, fresh out of Police Academy, with a face full of caramel-colored freckles and a carroty cow-lick, and he's a good kid. He's pretty new at the job, which accounts for his cockiness, and he was treating her as if she were made of spun glass. It was his first rape case. He was one of the officers who had answered the call, and I could tell it had shaken him.

"Here's Ms. Davies, Kate," he said to me. "Ms. Davies, Police Detective Marbury."

I've taken back my maiden name. It makes sense, since it's the name I've been used to for most of my life. The fact that I have annoys Harry; but after all, we are divorced, even though we still see a lot of each other. It's one of those cases of can't live together, can't live apart, I suppose. I adore Harry, but while we were married there were times when I wanted to kill him. And, he has not infrequently informed me, vice versa. Now that he just turns up off and on, for the night or the odd weekend, our relationship stays on an agreeably even keel.

"Call me whatever you like," I said, smiling at her, "but I prefer Kate."

"Thanks," she answered. "I'll call you Kate if you'll call me Janet."

The preliminaries concluded, Jacko took himself off, and I seated her in the shabby but supremely comfortable armchair I bought secondhand on Third Avenue when I was living in New York and pretending it was Paris. Janet's eyes fell on one of my watercolors—I do my best to blot out as much olive-drab wall as I can with some of my paintings—a picture of rain falling on water. That's all it is, though it's large for a watercolor, two by two-and-a-half feet—just slender gray lines of rain, angled slantwise, making patterns on the surface of a dull pewter sheet of water. I find it soothing, which is why I've hung it there. I hope the witnesses do, too.

It's hardly surprising that I was pleased when Janet stared intently at it for a moment without speaking, then said, "I like that. Really like it. Did you buy it in Wilmington? Who painted it?"

She was the first person in that room who had asked me that question. I felt absurdly flattered and rather shy, and said, "I did."

"Of course!" she said at once. "I'm sorry. I ought to have

realized." She looked at it again, and added, "You're very good, but of course you know that. You're bound to know, if you can paint like that. It didn't occur to me that a police artist would be a real artist, too, if you know what I mean. Oh, God. I hope I'm not being rude."

"Sometimes I wonder if I am," I said. "A real artist, I mean. Thanks for the compliment."

"No question about it. I minored in fine arts in college—not that that means much, but it did give me an eye for what's good. Useful when I become a partner in the firm and have to start an art collection where I can stash my ill-gotten gains. I'll corner the market in Kate Marburys—that is, if there are any left to buy." She laughed. It was a good laugh to hear. To be able to laugh, especially at yourself, less than two days after being raped, is no mean feat.

I explained my procedure to her. She was genuinely interested in the methods I use. "Would you like some music while we work?" I asked, "and if so, what? Beatles? Springsteen? Ronstadt? Mozart?"

"Mozart, please," she said at once. "It's so restful. And healing. *The Magic Flute,* if you have it. The music washes over you like a delicious warm lilac-scented bath. It always makes me feel relaxed and clean. I know I need to relax, and I need to feel clean again. That's almost worse than the fear. I keep taking showers to wash the filth off; I feel as if I'm scrubbing all my skin away. I didn't feel frightened while it was happening, so much as revolted. It was *disgusting,* like having a wino throw up on me in the New York subway."

I put on *The Magic Flute,* and we both sat for a few moments without speaking. She'd gotten the music right—the clarity and purity and radiance of it made it seem as though a world crusted with dirt and crime was merely a bad dream, and it was the ideal world of Mozart's music that was the reality.

"You're a lawyer, aren't you?" I asked her. I find it's always a good idea to begin on an oblique line, to get a feel for the way the person I'm interviewing lives, what his/her life is like.

"Yes," she replied. "I'm with Duncan, Henry, Williams, and Meade. They've been fantastic about everything, by the way—

offered me a paid leave of absence to give me time to recuperate, and said they'd assign someone else to wind up the case I'm working on. But it's nearly finished, and I figure the best cure is work, something to take my mind off what happened. It's not as if I were sick, for God's sake!"

She gave a toss of her head, as though she were throwing off all the troubles and uncertainties she'd just been saddled with.

As we discussed her work and the daily pattern of her life, I discovered that we had several friends in common. Not surprising. Wilmington's a small town. She had just mentioned a lawyer I know in her firm who happens to be black. This gave me an opening, so I asked, "Did your attacker have the same complexion as Knotts Fisher?"

"No," Janet replied, without hesitation. "They both have light skin, but Knotts's is paler. Actually, it's hard to be sure Knotts is black until he tells you, but it seemed to me that this man— this little creep, I should say; a *man* doesn't commit rape—was definitely black."

I made an unobtrusive note on my pad. "Describe his nose as best you can," I requested.

She closed her eyes in an attempt to visualize her attacker's face. "Narrow at the bridge, but the nostrils were wide and flattened."

"If this becomes too difficult for you at any point," I told her, "let me know, and we'll put it off to another day."

"No," she said, opening her eyes to look at me, eyes the exact shade of the turquoise with which the ancient Egyptians glazed their faience. "I'm okay, really I am. I want to help catch the son of a bitch; it will make me feel a whole lot better if I can help. And I want him to get caught before he rapes someone else. If Tom McIlvaine hadn't come back and heard me scream, I'm quite sure he would have killed me." She gave a shiver all over her skin, like a horse trying to rid itself of flies. "I saw it in his eyes."

"His eyes—close together? Wide set?"

"Pretty average as far as location goes, but a little on the small side. And mean. A cold obsidian gaze, like a snake's. Oh, and bushy eyebrows. I remember thinking they looked like a pair of caterpillars. Woolly bears, but without the stripes. That was a strange thing to think, wasn't it? I suppose I was trying to take my mind off what was going to happen."

"But useful," I said, jotting down a matched pair of caterpillars in the outline of the face, which Janet had already described as squarish with broad cheeks. "Anything unusual about the shape of his ears?"

"I couldn't see them," she responded. "They were covered by his hair. It was in a sort of Afro cut, but fairly short. Not one of the really spectacular kind."

We worked together on the likeness for some time longer, with effervescent music pouring over us as if it were spouting up from a fountain in a green garden, until I felt that I had dug everything out of her that was there to be unearthed. She had remembered a surprising amount of detail, and I had a feeling it was all accurate. Perhaps because of her legal training, she was both perceptive and precise, with a retentive memory. I told her so.

"I'm glad I've been able to help," Janet said. "I had such a brief glimpse of his face that I was afraid I wouldn't be any use. I mean, while I was being raped I kept my eyes closed and tried to imagine I wasn't there. I only really looked at him just before Tom called out and I screamed. I don't think it was for very long, it just seemed a long time because I was frightened. But it's funny. Right now his face is like a snapshot fixed in my mind. I only have to close my eyes and there it is, as though it's been filed away in a drawer marked Rapist." She shuddered. "Useful, I suppose, but I hope it will fade eventually. Now that I've told you, it can't be too soon to suit me."

"I'm sure it will go away," I answered. "But I must tell you that at the moment your photographic memory is tremendously useful. There." I sketched in a few last lines and held up the pad so she could see what I had drawn. "How's that?"

She stared at the paper with her limpid blue gaze. "It's frighteningly like," she said at length. "It's so familiar it scares me."

"Does it remind you of anyone you've seen anywhere else?"

She continued to look at the sketch I had made. "No," she said. "I can't think of anyone else who looks like that. You've got the Afro just right. But then you've got everything right. Do you paint portraits?" She looked around at the pictures on the walls of my office. "I don't see any."

"Sometimes I do. But I don't hang them here; it might mislead people I'm interviewing into remembering something incorrectly, like those photos used by police artists that I told you about. As a matter of fact, I was thinking I should like to paint your portrait someday, if you're willing. You have that incredible Renaissance coloring. I fancy myself something of a colorist, and I'd love to try my hand at it."

"Thanks. I'd like that. Someday." She hesitated, then looked down at her hands, which were clenching and unclenching in her lap, and said, "I know it's stupid, but I just keep thinking, if only I'd closed and locked the kitchen window. If only I'd gone back and stayed the night with Tom McIlvaine. He offered to put me up because my air conditioner wasn't working. If I had, then . . ." She looked over at me. "I feel so—so *grimy*. I feel as though it's going to be months and months before I feel clean again. And then there's . . ." She swallowed, and dropped her voice so that it was almost a whisper. "There's AIDS."

God, I felt sorry for her. Poor kid. One minute the legal case she's working on seems like the most important thing in the world, the next she's recovering from a vicious attack and hoping like mad she hasn't been given a fatal disease.

"Look, Janet," I said to her. "You've been fantastic about all this. But give yourself a break. We can't be sure till the DNA test results are in, but I can tell you that except for the knife, which is a new nasty little wrinkle, and some difference in timing, the attack on you bears all the marks of a serial rapist we're tracking. To our knowledge, he has attacked at least seven other women in the past couple of years, and the sketch you and I just collaborated on tallies with the descriptions given by the other women he's raped. If he's the one I think he is, it wouldn't matter if you'd locked your window or spent the night somewhere else. We're certain he stalks the women he rapes. If he hadn't gotten into your house two nights ago, he would have broken in another time. He prefers an easy entry, but he's been known to break a window and pick a lock. Moreover, if he'd broken in some other night, there might not have been anyone to hear you scream. I know that what you went through was terrible, but if it had happened at a different time, you might have been dead afterwards."

Janet's naturally pale skin grew even paler. "Has he killed someone? I don't read the local paper. I'm in corporate law," she apologized, "and it's as much as I can do to get through the *New York Times* and the *Wall Street Journal* every day."

"No, he hasn't yet, luckily; but he's beaten all of them, and he's been growing more and more violent over the series. And we're really worried about his use of a knife in your case. It seems as though he picked it up casually on his way in, since you told us there's a knife missing from your kitchen; but now that he has used a weapon like that once, it's very likely he'll keep on using it. I said that it's going to take some time for the DNA test results to come back from the FBI lab, but I'm gut sure it's the same man. Sorry—creep, in your much more appropriate vernacular. Oh, speaking of DNA results, has anyone told you about the DNA test for HIV?"

Janet had recovered her equilibrium. "No, what's that? I've never heard of it."

"It's called PCR for HIV, and it's relatively new. It's expensive compared to the standard AIDS test, but it's ninety-nine point seven percent accurate and you only need to take it once—at least twenty-eight days after possible exposure. With the other tests for HIV, you have to wait for three months, repeat after a year, and keep repeating for as long as forty-two months, to be sure you haven't been infected."

Janet sat quiet. "Thanks for telling me about it," she said after a moment. "That's wonderful news. And frightening, too, if you know what I mean. It means I'll have to prepare myself to take the test sooner than I thought. But what a relief if it works out!"

"Yes," I agreed. I felt a lot of sympathy for Janet. Bad enough to have to cope with the physical and emotional injuries resulting from a brutal sexual attack, without being forced to face the possibility of having contracted a lethal and incurable disease, the scourge of our age. But she was incredibly game.

"Lucky me," she said, and meant it. She gave a courageous and lopsided grin, its lack of symmetry due to the kick that bastard had given her. "I could do without the black eye, as well as a few other things, but you know something? It's great to be alive. I always knew it was, but now I really know it is, if you get my drift."

I did.

CHAPTER 3
Late August

THE WATCHER SITS IN HIS FAVORITE CHAIR LOOKING AT THE ELEVEN o'clock news on television. The news is boring. There is nothing about him. The Janet Davies rape is dead as a doornail; fresher news has taken its place. He turns off the set in disgust. Pity he didn't have more time to work on her, he thinks angrily; pity he didn't use the knife on her a little. Then the media wouldn't have dropped the story, *his* story, so quickly. The story would have had legs, it would still be headline news. He always makes it a point to follow media coverage of his exploits; he savors his cleverness, the way he foils his trail. They won't catch him, he thinks smugly to himself. There's no way they can find him.

His wife sits on the sofa, going through her mail—mostly catalogues. She loves to read catalogues. She says they are more relaxing than reading novels. She likes to try out perfume samples, the kind that is sandwiched between two leaves of an insert meant to be peeled open so the section impregnated with scent can be rubbed on the skin. The Watcher can hear the rustle of paper as she flips through the pages of one of the pamphlets. A moment later she gets up, stands beside his chair, and leans over him with her hand in front of his face.

"Smell," she orders.

Startled, he breathes in, and for an instant he is a little boy again. Then he sees red, as if a scarlet curtain has descended over his eyes. It terrifies him. This is the wrong time, the wrong place. His heart begins to pound from the sudden rush of adrenaline.

"What the hell is that stink?" he shouts furiously.

The intensity of his response surprises her. "What's the matter?" she asks him. "It's perfume. It's called Ravie. It came in the Saks catalogue."

He half rises in his chair. "Wash that goddamned stuff off," he tells her. "Now!"

"Why? I like it. I thought I might buy some."

"Wash it off. It smells like garbage on you. It's disgusting. Don't ever put it on again."

"It couldn't smell like garbage. It's been around for ages. If it didn't smell good on skin, they wouldn't still be making it." She presses her inner wrist against her nose and sniffs. "It smells great," she tells him indignantly. "It smells like jasmine and lilies and . . ."

His nails dig deep into the palms of his hands as he fights to keep himself under control. He mustn't, *mustn't,* he tells himself. Not here, not her. He'd get caught. *Just calm down,* he says silently.

"I told you to wash it off, for Christ's sake!" he shouts at her.

"All right, all right! Keep your pants on." Highly offended, she stalks into the kitchen, and a moment later he hears the sound of water running.

He breathes a sigh of relief. It had been a near thing. He had almost spun out of control, but he had managed—just barely—to keep his head, even though they were alone, the two of them, with no one to interrupt. And he doesn't want to hurt her. She is his protection. He goes over to the kitchen door and watches her dabbing at her wrist with a paper towel. She is close to tears.

"Sorry, honey," he tells her more gently. "I just hate the smell of that stuff. It does something to me. Promise you won't wear it again?"

He drops a kiss on the top of her head and, mollified, she says, "Sure I'll promise, if you hate it that much. I'll stick with

Obsession. I really like Obsession, but I was beginning to get tired of it, so I thought I'd try something else."

"Obsession smells great on you," he tells her, giving her shoulder a squeeze. "You stick with Obsession, okay, hon? I tell you what, I'll buy all your perfume for you from now on."

"That's sweet of you," she says, surprised and disarmed by his sudden generosity. "Thanks a lot, baby. Why don't we go to bed now?"

"It's not time yet. I'm not sleepy," he objects.

"I wasn't thinking about sleeping," she responds archly, with an inviting tug at his shirt.

But he isn't interested. His brief rush of rage has exhausted him, and left him thinking about only one thing. The next one. The next one, with a knife this time. He wants to sit alone peacefully and plan.

"Hey, honey, not tonight, okay? Big day at work today, I'm bushed. Sorry. Tomorrow night, I promise."

She pouts at this rebuff, but goes off to bed alone meekly enough, first giving him a good-night kiss on his forehead. After she has left the room he sits in his chair for a long time, thinking.

CHAPTER 4
Early September

NOW AND THEN I ASK MYSELF HOW, AFTER A CAREFREE YOUTH MISSPENT in New York and the capitals of Europe, I managed to end up in stuffy old Wilmington, Delaware—hardly the center of culture, God knows, though it does have the advantage of a location barely two hours from Manhattan to the north and Washington to the south. As a matter of fact, it was an accident, mainly due to my mother having been born and bred in the First (and nearly the smallest) State in the Union. My father joined the Diplomatic Service, which accounts for my having lived in London and Paris and the Republic of Chad, not to mention Lisbon and Bonn and a few less salubrious climes, by the time I was fourteen, at which point I was sent back to the States for four years' incarceration in a Maryland boarding school. I use the term advisedly, since I have never been able to decide whether it bore a closer resemblance to Dotheboys Hall or to Alcatraz. My mother had cousins next door in Delaware, who volunteered to serve in loco parentis, except during long vacations, when I was shipped back to wherever my father happened to be posted.

After boarding school I was briefly dragged to Wilmington, kicking and screaming, to be a debutante before traipsing up to Harvard for several misspent years—it has always been said of me that I inherited my eyelashes from my mother's side of the family, and my brains from my father's. I consented to the coming-out party (Mother) and the choice of college (Daddy's alma mater) only after extracting a promise of two years' financial support at the Sorbonne after I had done some time in Cambridge. They agreed, obviously supposing that I would settle down and forget all about it after my freshman year; but boy, were they wrong! Cambridge is, in its intellectual way, every bit as provincial as Wilmington; so once I'd kept to the letter of the law, off I took like a shot for the City of Light.

One of the things I like best about my parents is that they always keep their promises, even when they have to grit their teeth to do it. Besides, they both adore Paris, even if they were a shade concerned about the prospect of their little girl sinking into the mire of *la vie bohème*; and my mother is an inspired flibbertigibbet, who feels that any child of hers would be far better off cavorting in the cafés of Paris than toiling in the Harvard libraries.

A couple of years spent studying art history at the Sorbonne and painting the odd masterpiece in my garret when I wasn't haunting bistros with Harry, who was writing the Great American Novel in his attic in his spare time, and then I began an apprenticeship under Eugène Savoyard. He died a year later, of too much rotgut; at least, that was what they said. Practically no one now has ever heard of him, though I'm convinced that someday he'll be up there alongside Vermeer and Giorgione. His brushwork is brilliant; and he had the color sense of Matisse, along with the draftsmanship and delicacy of Dürer. I'd be willing to bet a year's salary that eventually the few canvases he didn't destroy will fetch millions at Sotheby's or Christie's. I have three that I managed to rescue before he set fire to them: one of an alley cat, remote and proud, sitting on a windowsill beside a cracked and empty flowerpot. The subject sounds like kitsch, but take my word for it—the painting isn't. It's superb; someday I'll be able to sell it for a king's ransom. Then there's his portrait of me in a sky blue kimono lined in scarlet, painted in Whistler's style. It shows off what an incredible colorist Eugène was; that should fetch a pretty penny too. As for the third—well, never mind. I couldn't bring myself to part with it, even for millions.

After Savoyard's death, Harry talked me into marrying him; and we moved to New York, where he planned to write the Great American Play. Somewhat to his surprise and mine, he did. And then things fell apart; the center did not hold. And I, damn it all, have not yet painted the Great American Picture, or anything close to it. When things between us began to go wrong, I left Manhattan. It had been a hell of a lot of fun, and now it was just hell. One of my many cousins—I have cousins the way dogs have fleas—was a Delaware judge who told me about an opening for a police artist in Wilmington. It meant I had to take police training, but why not? I'd always loved reading whodunits. So I held my nose and jumped off the deep end, and somewhat to my surprise I took to the training like a duck to water.

So here I am at the tender age of thirty-five, living in the sticks, presumably until I get hung (not hanged!) in MOMA— the Museum of Modern Art to the uninitiated. I get along with my associates, especially that young scapegrace Jacko Benson, with whom on the following Monday I was hard at work on the Janet Davies rape case. We had only recently formed a Rape Task Force, although the attacks, now at least eight in number, had begun nearly two years earlier.

"Lists, lists, lists!" I tried to shuffle the papers in front of me together like a giant deck of cards, and only succeeded in making a bigger mess out of them. "If I see one more list, you'll have to ship me off to the nearest loony bin posthaste."

"Faith, me beauty," said Jacko. "And what can be eating you this morning?"

"I happen to have a hangover," I growled. "Not that it's any of your goddamn business."

"Well, whaddaya know? Your one and only ex must be in town." Jacko raised an eyebrow in my direction.

"My, my, aren't we the little Sherlock," I said nastily. "And he isn't my one and only." My head was throbbing to beat the band; nowadays I find that even good Champagne will give me a headache if I overdo it.

"I'm honing my skills," retorted Jacko, with a dignity that ill became him. "Got to keep in practice."

"Well, sorry to burst your bubble, but Harry's not in town." Strictly speaking, that was true. He was on his way back to Virginia; at that moment I reckoned he was just about passing Washington on the Beltway.

Jacko was crestfallen. "I better turn in my badge. I could have sworn the only times you get sloshed are when you're out with your ex."

"Let's get back to work," I said hastily, feeling a modicum of guilt over my success in deceiving him. "Has the FBI analysis from the Jervis rape case come in yet?"

"Nah. I checked with the feds and they say it will be at least another couple of weeks."

"My God! It's already been ten months. When I took Janet Davies's evidence down there, I told them that we need to have all the DNA typing expedited. The attacks have been steadily growing more violent, which usually gets the lab moving."

"That knife was real scary," Jacko agreed. "We need to grab the son of a bitch before he starts to use it."

"We need our own DNA lab in this state, that's what we need."

"Tell that to the good ol' boys down in Dover. They been kicking that one around for years. If some politician's wife got raped and murdered, we'd get a lab fast."

"Don't get any ideas, Jacko," I warned him. "Stick to more orthodox methods. So I guess it's back to the lousy lists. Has Janet sent in all the ones we requested?"

"Yeah, here they are." He ticked them off as he handed them to me. "Organizations she belongs to—that one's short. Guess she doesn't like meetings. Places she shops—supermarkets, gas stations, hair house, dry cleaner, massage parlors—joke, ha-ha—all that jazz. Repairmen and delivery men—plumber, electrician, UPS, FedEx. Mailman. Medical stuff—doctors, dentists, any lab work done in the last couple of years. Jeez, Kate, I'm beginning to see what you mean about lists. If I have to look at many more of them, I'll be your roommate at the funny farm. I hope Harry won't mind."

He gave a lascivious wink with one of his china blue eyes.

He looked so comical—like a lecherous choirboy—that I couldn't help laughing.

"Cut it out, Jacko," I advised him. "The role of seducer ill becomes you. What's next on the agenda? Is that *it*—I hope—for the lists?"

He glanced down at his desk. "Nah. Here's another."

"Oh, God. Spare me."

"Hold your horses. This one's a snap to deal with; I wish it wasn't."

"It looks pretty long," I objected.

"Yeah, but there's nothing new. It's the roster of police departments we notified about the rapist."

"You mean the ones we contacted about the unsolved rape cases?"

"That's it. All two hundred of them. Around the state, in Maryland, in south Jersey and southeastern Pennsylvania. Not a peep out of any of them so far."

"The bastards," I said. "We sent out an SOS months ago."

"C'mon, Kate, be reasonable. You know how shorthanded cops are anymore. How shorthanded we are."

"I know, but we'd better send them a reminder. Now that the creep has started playing with knives."

"*Two hundred* reminders? Aw, Kate."

I was inexorable. "All two hundred. Get going." Then I relented. "I'll take half."

The engaging smile that could coax coins from a miser flashed out. "Jeez, Kate, you're a pal."

So we both set to work.

CHAPTER 5
Mid-September

THE WATCHER IS IN THE GARAGE. He has just come in from a tour on his motorcycle around the fields in back of his house. He likes to ride his cycle over the ruts and furrows of a field, to weave in and out of the trees in a wood; when he does that, he feels more in control—telling it what to do, coaxing it, urging it on—than he does riding it along a metaled road. Now he is polishing it, checking for scratches on the paint after his ride. He loves the motorcycle. It is black and sleek and powerful. Like him in his black clothes, when he is gearing up for an attack. When he is dressed and ready for action he feels invincible, as if he were wearing burnished black metal armor that no weapon could pierce.

At the moment he is dressed in well-worn blue jeans and a denim work shirt, clothes suitable for puttering around machinery. But he is also wearing his black Keds. He tells himself he has them on because they are new and he wants to be sure they are comfortable, to make certain he won't be slowed down by a heel rubbed sore or betrayed by a squeaking rubber sole, but the truth of it is that wearing the sneakers makes him feel powerful. Even though they are not yet broken in to service— though they have not yet heard the harsh breath of fear rasp in the throat of his prey, though they have not yet padded beneath him in silent pursuit—still they share a secret with him. He flexes his toes and thinks, *I will wear them after. Around the house. When I polish the car. At work.* He smiles, pleased at the thought. Whenever he wears them, they will remind him of where they have taken him, what he has done while they were laced on his feet.

The Watcher gives a final swipe at the gleaming surface of the Harley with the rag in his hand, and hangs the cloth on a hook beside the door into the kitchen. As he does so, he inadvertently knocks over an open burlap bag. He swears and catches it as it topples over, but some of the contents tumble out onto the concrete floor. He swears again and kicks it as he goes into the house. Unknown to him, something that has spilled from the bag, a minute dark sphere one millimeter in diameter, is lodged with several similar objects from the fields he has recently ridden over in a tiny pocket at the top of the flat band of rubber joining the sneaker's sole to its canvas upper.

His wife is in the kitchen, preparing dinner.

"Hi, honey," she greets him, turning her cheek toward him for a kiss.

He ignores her, and opens the refrigerator door to look for a cold beer. He finds a bottle and snaps the door shut.

"What the hell's in that bag by the door?" he asks, rummaging in a drawer for a bottle opener. "That's a lousy place to leave it. It tripped me up, nearly broke my neck."

"Oh, honey, I'm so sorry. I thought I had put it away in the gardening cupboard. It's seeds I bought for the garden. You know I went to that talk last week at the Delaware Horticultural Society? He said to plant some of that and then dig it under for mulch." Her husband rarely questions her; when he does, she is so pleased by his interest that she bubbles over with information.

"Yeah?" he replies, staring past her as he takes a swig of his beer. He couldn't care less. Gardening, a new fad his wife has recently taken up, does not interest him.

"He said to use it as a ground cover, it enriches the soil. It's related to turnips and stuff, but it's got a funny name for a plant. It's called rape. Can you imagine? I was embarrassed when I had to ask for it at Southern States." She laughs at the memory. "They said this may be the last year they keep it in stock. They said hardly anyone on Delmarva grows it anymore."

The Watcher's imagination is tickled by some of this information. "It's called rape? Like? . . ."

"That's right. Like what it sounds like."

"You don't say. Rape," he muses. "Just the way it sounds. Well, well, well."

He smiles, for the second time that day.

CHAPTER 6
Late September

LATE SEPTEMBER. Too early for Indian Summer to set in; true summer has not yet been replaced by autumn. The days are warm and humid, the nights damp and cool. Soon the Watcher's season will be ending, unless the winter is unusually warm. He does not like to play his games in the cold, especially when there is snow. When the weather is icy it is not so easy to move around, and the snow makes him too readily visible. He prefers a dark landscape in which to hide—dull and unreflecting, velvety deep shadows untinged with white. Places to bolt if someone should pass by, places to hide until it is time.

The Watcher will miss his games when winter comes. Perhaps there will be a mild spell; sometimes they have an unseasonably balmy December or January. But he can't count on it. And he doesn't like to play his games too close together. They need to ripen. The waiting is a part of the thrill. The longer he waits, the more his blood fizzes in his veins, effervescing like the bubbles in Champagne, making him drunk with anticipation of what he knows is coming. When he is ready to make his move, then the cork will pop. That is how he will know when it is time.

———

NEW CASTLE, A PRETTY, SLEEPY LITTLE TOWN SURROUNDED BY REED-filled marshes, drowses beside the Delaware River in the last breath of summer. The centerpiece of the place, the oblong green, is a kind of park bordered by public buildings constructed in the eighteenth century—courthouse, academy, church, and a somewhat more recent arsenal, erected to house armaments during the War of 1812—all of brick and stucco overlaid with a mellow patina. Surrounding The Green is a cobweb of cobblestone streets and alleyways, where houses with picturesque shutters and fanlights and shining brass door knockers are overgrown by ivy and wisteria and Virginia creeper; at their back are gardens whose board fences spill over with trumpet vine and fragrant honeysuckle. Here and there wrought-iron foot scrapers have been set into the brick sidewalks, and granite blocks for mounting horses stand at the curb. It is a picture-perfect place where even the police department is housed on the perimeter of The Green, in an old building that was once the sheriff's house.

But the Watcher knows that the police station usually shuts up shop at 5:00 P.M. or so. At night it might as well be situated miles away, and right now it is three in the morning with not a police car in sight. He has parked his car some blocks from his intended destination, in a cul-de-sac where no one is awake to notice a stranger at such a late hour. The one he is watching lives in a house at the end of The Strand, the street that runs along the river's edge. She has a dog, a small black-and-tan terrier, but the dog does not worry him. If the dog should prove to be a problem, he has the knife. This time he has brought his own.

He fingers it, deep in his hip pocket. It is a folding knife which he will open, ready for action, as soon as he has entered the house. He is still angry over the interruption last time. But the revelation of the knife almost made up for it. Why hadn't he thought of using a weapon before? With the knife he is completely in control. Powerful, invincible. If only he had realized that the last time. Instead of bolting from the house, he should have faced down that unexpected shouting voice. If only he had not been so startled, he would have startled the Shouter with his knife. Before the Shouter knew what was happening, the knife would have sliced into his chest, blood spurting alongside the releasing blade, hot blood splattering, reeking, smearing his face, the foolish face with its gaping mouth and staring eyes, the face that reminds him of Jerry, his so-called brother, the one time he was tricked into meeting him. That would have paid him out for interrupting the Watcher's work. Sometimes when the Watcher can't sleep, he thinks about that face. If only he had done it instead of running away. Done it and then gone back upstairs with the bloody knife in his hand. He likes to imagine what her face would have looked like then. Maybe he will go back there sometime. Go back with his knife when it has all died down, when she thinks she's safe again. The Watcher would like that. It is something to look forward to.

But tonight he has something else to look forward to. Maybe two, he thinks. There are two of them, two he's been keeping an eye on, this one in New Castle and another one only a couple of miles away. He has never done two in one night, but his blood is fizzing more furiously than ever before. The times between them are growing shorter; it is getting harder to wait, to rein himself in. Maybe this is the night he should do two. It all depends on how long this one takes, on how long he can hold himself in before he uses the knife. Once he begins to use the knife, he knows it will go quickly. Once he starts with the knife, he will not want to stop. With so much time at his disposal, time without interruptions—the entrance of the Shouter on the scene last time was a fluke, he tells himself, a once-in-a-million mishap—he has a feeling that the first one tonight will take a long time. A very long time.

One by one the lights in the windows of the houses have been extinguished until every house in sight is dark. The Watcher crouches in a small alley that connects the back gardens of two rows of houses, one row fronting onto The Strand, the other facing Second Street. Wildflowers are growing in the alley— tiger lilies, and wild carrot, and a great swath of honeysuckle, within whose depths he has concealed himself. Now he slithers out into the open, crawling along the alleyway on hands and knees until he reaches the back fence of her garden. A gate in the fence opens onto the alley. If necessary, he had planned to climb over the fence in order to get in, but she has left the gate unlocked. A good omen, he thinks.

Easing the gate latch up gradually so it disengages without a sound, he enters the narrow garden. He has reconnoitered this territory before. He had planned his foray to take place last night, but on his arrival he had seen lights in two upstairs rooms instead of one, and a car with D.C. plates parked in back of hers on the street. He realized then that she had an overnight visitor. It had made him angry, all that good time wasted. If he had known earlier, he could have done someone else on his list instead. He could still have gone to the one who lives nearby. There was time. But he did not want to go anywhere else. He has been planning this one for a long long time. His list has priorities. This is the one he wants to do now.

After last night's disappointment, the enforced waiting makes him feel like a lighted firecracker ready to explode. He concentrates on banking the fire within him. He has to keep himself under control until he is safely inside the house, until he has her fast, unable to escape, crushed, humble, acknowledging him the victor. Then the blood will be his release. He can scarcely contain himself at the thought of the blood. And the knife. He feels now as if he has always used the knife. He knows what it will feel like, he has gone over it so many times in his dreams. It is as if the Shouter had not kept him from using it on the other one, had not made him leave before he had finished with her. When he thinks about that time, it seems as though he had opened her with the knife, cut into her flesh again and again, the many wounds gaping into mouths dripping blood, spewing blood, vomiting blood, until she was empty of blood. Blood drenching her long hair, redder than her red hair, blood for him to dip his hands in. Bathe in. Touch. Taste. Smell.

During an earlier reconnoiter he examined the lock on the side door. It looks as though it would be easy to pick. And the neighboring house has no windows on that side to overlook him. The side door of the house he plans to enter is sheltered from the street by an arch let into the brickwork of the facade, which provides a covered alleyway leading back to the garden. He does not want to jimmy the front door. Even in the dead of night it is too open to view for his taste; his instinct is to seek cover. But it occurs to him to check the gate at the alley entrance to see if it is locked, to make sure he has more than one means of exit.

The alley gate is not locked. Gently he eases it open; it is well oiled and makes no noise, so far as he can tell. But to his dismay, within the house he hears a dog's frantic barking. He swears angrily under his breath. Somehow that terrier of hers must have heard something, somehow sensed the hot breath of the hunter nearby. From the alley he peers out at the house front, where lights show at the windows, first on the second floor, then in the hall downstairs. The barking stops. A moment or so later the lights are extinguished in reverse order. He will give her half an hour to calm down, he thinks, or maybe an hour. By that time she will be asleep. The dog too. He dwells with pleasure on what he will do to the dog once he gets into the house. Before he does her. So she can watch. He decides to leave the alley gate open, in case he should have to get out that way.

But the dog is in no mood for sleep. Just as the Watcher is about to move back into the garden, the dog begins barking again, a shrill monotonous string of yap-yap-yaps that sounds as though it has no intention of stopping for hours. In the Watcher's pocket his hand clenches reflexively around the knife, the folding knife whose blade he has so lovingly whetted until the edge is as thin and sharp and piercing as a new razor blade. He has to do it tonight, he thinks, if he doesn't do it tonight he'll explode.

Suddenly he has a brilliant idea. A bold stroke. One that carries small risk, since everyone in the other houses on the street is asleep. But he must move quickly, before the dog wakes any of the neighbors. He steps over to the front of the house, where the lights in the windows are blossoming from top to bottom again, and gives the brass door knocker several sharp official raps. The dark fanlight over the front door flares yellow.

"Hush up, Sporran," says a woman's voice. The dog stops its barking. "What is it?" she calls out.

"Police," he says, grinning to himself. "Your car has been in an accident."

There is a pause. Then, "My car?" she says. "No, it hasn't."

"Isn't this your blue Escort parked in front of the house?" he asks her, knowing it is. He has watched her drive up in it a number of times.

Pause again. "Yes," she responds after a moment. "But it hasn't been in an accident."

He grinds his teeth with rage. *Open the door, you stupid bitch,* he demands silently. It is becoming more and more difficult to contain his fury. But amazingly he manages to keep his voice steady.

"Someone ran into it on the street tonight while it was parked. Why don't you go to a window and take a look at it?" *Why the hell did I say that?* he thinks in despair. It will make her want to take a look at me and my badge while she's about it.

But surprisingly it does not.

"Yes. All right," she answers.

He crouches as close beside the door as he can so she won't catch a glimpse of him. A pale glimmer shows briefly in the window nearest the door as she peers obediently out at her car. *Stupid bitch,* he thinks again, this time with approval. The face in the window disappears and a moment later her voice returns to the front door.

"I can't see anything," she says.

Then open the door and come out, he screams at her silently. He waits until he knows he has his voice under control.

"It isn't badly damaged," he tells her, "but I need your registration to make out the report."

"Why do I have to do all this now?" asks the voice irritably. "I'm tired. It's the middle of the night. Can't it wait till morning?"

Because I say so, bitch, he thinks angrily. It had not occurred to him that she might refuse to open up for the police.

"I only need a minute." Miraculously, his voice sounds placating.

"I'm exhausted," the voice retorts rebelliously. "The police station is a block away. I can go there in the morning and do anything that needs to be done then."

He clamps his teeth together with all his might to keep from screaming at her. To keep the fizzing inside. It is not yet time to allow it to escape. That would be disastrous. But it is growing more and more urgent; he does not know how long he can manage to suppress it. He has to get inside the house soon. Very soon. One thing at least is on his side. She isn't suspicious. Yet. He's sure of that. He clenches his fist around the knife in his pocket as a promise to it and to himself that it will not be much longer. Soon. Soon.

"Look, miss," he says, coaxing her, trying to keep his tone of voice reasonable. "It will only take a couple of minutes of your time. Then you can go right back to bed."

He waits, trembling with eagerness, for the click of the key turning in the lock. He is poised on his toes like a dancer, primed to spring forward through the doorway into the hall the instant a crack of light appears down the side of the door to indicate it is opening. He shivers all over like a hound waiting to be unleashed, frantic to be let loose on his quarry.

No click. Just that hated voice.

"No," it says with a finality he is forced to recognize. "I don't want to. I'm dead tired. I'll go to the police station in the morning; I'm not going to deal with anything now. Good night."

He hears footsteps move away from the front door, and a second later the yellow fanlight goes dark.

Behind his eyes everything turns red. The color of rage. His body feels as if it has received an electric shock and absorbed all the energy from it. It feels as if anything he touched would instantly shrivel, blasted by the power stored within him. He feels as if he can do anything: as if he must do something, or erupt.

He does not waste time on the front door. It looks heavy and strong, the kind of door built to repel marauders in the turbulent days when the house was first built. The frenzy roiling in his brain does not prevent him from remembering that the side door looks flimsier. If he doesn't succeed in breaking the lock, he'll break down the door. He has to get to her. Now. He has promised himself.

He runs through the arch down the brick path, his tongue

lolling out of the side of his mouth like the tongue of a loping beast of prey. In his back pocket he carries a stout angled blade with a handle, a paint scraper, bought a few days ago at a hardware store in case of need. He needs it now. He takes it out and jams the blade hard into the narrow crack alongside the lock of the door, heaving with all the strength at his disposal. His anger makes him incredibly strong. The door shifts inward. He can feel the lock begin to give way. As his mind records this fact, a piercing pulsating shriek reverberates within the house. All his will is so concentrated on getting the door to open that he does not at first notice the sound, overwhelming in its intensity; but gradually the crimson fog suffusing his brain dissipates sufficiently for danger to register. Bewildered, he half turns from the door, still clutching the paint scraper, as the noise ululates horribly in his ears.

Christ! he thinks. *That will wake the neighbors! That will bring the cops running if they're hooked up to it. Even if they aren't, she'll have called 911 by now.* He hadn't known she had an alarm. None of the others had one. Why the hell would she bother, quiet little town like this? He feels a vast sense of grievance, a red inchoate rage that threatens to overtake him and shake him by the throat. If only he had her here right now, him and his knife. Thinks she's so goddamned smart. Thinks she's outwitted him. He and his knife will show her who's smart and who isn't. Then his instinct for self-preservation takes over and he runs in the direction of his car, parked blocks away in the dead end. A few moments later he reaches it and gets in, starts it and drives jerkily away. Away from one projected victim and toward another.

CHAPTER 7
Late September

BLOOD. A deluge of blood. Pools of blood stagnant on the bedroom floor. Glazed black tiles of blood that crazed as it dried. Splashes of blood. Dull rust-colored spatters of blood. All shades and conditions of blood. Blood in its diverse but less than infinite variety. In the police force I've become used to the sight of blood. Other people's, that is; the sight of my own is quite a different story. But that apartment was unexpectedly sickening. The vile sickly sweetish scent hit my nostrils in the hall of the building before I got as far as the front door of the apartment. The entrance opened into the living room, which looked normal enough, but there the smell was stronger. Beyond that room there was a short hall—bedroom to the left, bath in the middle, kitchen on the right. A few smears of blood were visible on the paint of the wall between the bedroom and bathroom doorways. The bathroom, seen through the open door, looked as though a veil of diluted watercolor—Venetian red—had been sprayed on the white porcelain basin and bathtub and over the towels tossed on the floor. The white hand towels, that is. There was a dark blue bath towel that didn't show a thing.

The bedroom was like a slaughterhouse; at least, like the ones I envision in my Technicolor nightmares. I've never actually visited a slaughterhouse, an omission for which, after viewing

Lila Harrison's bedroom, I am profoundly grateful. Her body—what was left of it—had already been taken away for autopsy, another omission for which I am grateful, despite my generally phlegmatic reaction to the sight of blood.

The Rape Task Force cuts across jurisdictional lines, so although Lila Harrison's apartment building was technically within the bailiwick of the county police, we were all there in strength. The place had already been immortalized on film by the police photographer; however, since the way I analyze things is by painting them, I had brought along the tools of my trade, a familiar sight to my co-workers at a crime scene. There was, alas, no way for Lila Harrison to give me a description of her attacker, but her bedroom certainly provided me with ample material for a psychological portrait of the killer. That, by the way, would be a fascinating and horrible project—to attempt painting a depiction of what lies in the sewer of his mind.

All that the room in which Lila Harrison had been butchered retained of its former occupant was a sprawled chalk outline on the bloodied carpet. Tim Mundy, one of the police detectives assigned to the task force, emerged from the kitchen as I was taking my sketchbook and traveling case of watercolors out of my bag.

"Sorry you didn't get a look at the body in situ, Kate," he said. "The ME couldn't wait any longer to get started, and we were unable to reach you at home."

"No," I said. "I went out last night."

"Till six in the morning?" he asked, cocking a sardonic eyebrow in my direction.

I did not deign to reply to this jab; instead I concentrated on looking innocent, a thing I do tolerably well when I put my mind to it. It's none of his business, or that of the police department, if I spend a night now and again with my ex-husband. Harry, though impossible to live with, is a lamb; and he returns the compliment. Half the time he's not around, anyway. He can't write a word if there's anything moving within a radius of ten miles, which tended to make life difficult for his wife. So when the muse descends, he drives off to a cabin he owns in the mountains of northern Virginia and scribbles away diligently, with time out only for short naps and long glasses of bourbon, until he can scribble no more. Unlike me with my painting, he is wildly successful (which may also have had something to do with our divorce; I confess to a touch of the green-eyed monster), and keeps a pied-à-terre in New York, as well as one in Wilmington. Although these expenses constitute small change for his bank account, I suspect he might give up the Delaware pad if I weren't around. Which, maddening though he is, I must confess I find distinctly flattering.

Tim gave up his probing, since it was clear I wasn't going to indulge his " 'satiable curtiosity."

"If you don't like the looks of the crime site, you should have seen the body," he remarked, eyeing me for signs of revulsion.

"I'm just as glad to have missed it. Though," I told him with (if I do say it) admirable nonchalance, to deflate his masculine superiority, "the sight of blood doesn't faze me."

"Tell me another," he scoffed. "A little of the juice, maybe, but don't try to kid me that bloodbath in there didn't shake you up."

"Did it upset you? Poor boy. Not me," I announced smugly.

He glared at me, not pleased to be bested by a woman. "Come on, Kate. You're having me on."

"God's truth. The reasons for the presence of blood bother me, but not the blood itself. Unless it's my own."

"Your own?" he said incredulously.

"Sure thing. I can face oceans of blood without turning a hair, unless it belongs to me," I told him. "If I see a drop of my own, I'm done for."

"So what happens?" he inquired, with what I thought was unnecessarily ghoulish avidity.

"I faint," I said shortly. "Don't you? I'd better get on with my sketch."

"Don't use up all your crimson lake," Tim said with a grin, trying for the last word, as usual. A real smart aleck, that boy, and apt to surprise—I shouldn't have supposed he'd ever heard of crimson lake. I couldn't help being impressed. But of course I wasn't going to let him get away with it.

"I always use alizarin for blood," I told him haughtily, and without more ado began my sketch of the bedroom.

LATER ON, BACK AT THE STATION, JACKO BENSON RAN OVER THE INFOR-
mation they had amassed on the case so far for my benefit.

"Mrs. Harrison was supposed to go out for dinner last night with her daughter and son-in-law," he told me. "It was her birthday. Yesterday, I mean. Her seventieth birthday. So they came to pick her up. Her daughter had tried to phone in the morning to wish her happy returns, but she wasn't worried when her mother didn't answer because she was going to have her hair done—in honor of the celebration, they said. She was excited about dinner. They were going whole hog, taking her to the Green Room at the Hotel duPont. Wouldn't mind my kids taking me there when I'm old and gray."

"You'll have to wait a while," I told him. "First get a wife, and then start thinking about it."

"Yeah, well, the daughter had to go to work, where apparently they frown on personal calls, so she figured she'd save the congrats till they picked her mother up. Both she and her husband got home from work at around a quarter to six and did a fast change—"

"Where do they live?" I interrupted.

"In Alapocas. Nice house. They can afford the tab at the Green Room. They got to the old lady's apartment at around six-thirty. That's when they'd told her they'd be by to pick her up. When no one answered the door, the daughter panicked and insisted her husband get the janitor to open the place up. Seems he wanted to call the hotel first in case the mother had misunderstood and taken a taxi there, or a friend had dropped her off, but the daughter wouldn't wait for that." Jacko paused.

"So they got the janitor," I said.

"Yeah. They got the janitor. By that time it was nearly seven. It was lucky he was still in his office. If you call that lucky." His blue eyes were somber as a storm-filled sky. "The daughter's still under sedation at Christiana Hospital. We got all this from her husband, who isn't in much better shape. The ME reckons it happened sometime the previous night. He's working on the autopsy now. There is something else, though, something that might fit in. There was a call in New Castle the same night. It was pretty weird. Some guy posing as a cop tried to talk his way into a house in the middle of the night, and when the woman—she was alone in the house—wouldn't open the door, he tried to break in. Her security alarm went off and scared him away. Rosebud thinks it may be the same guy." Rosebud was our code name for the head of the Rape Task Force, a tall gaunt lieutenant with the unlikely name of Flowerdew.

"Did she get a look at him?"

"No. She said she never thought of it. She wasn't suspicious, she said, just tired, and mad at being waked. That's why she wouldn't open up. She said it was around three-thirty A.M. when he showed. Dumb but lucky, that's what she was." He shrugged. "Weird, ain't it?" he went on. "The one he didn't get in New Castle is thirty-two. I mean, the victims are either youngish, or else real old, like Lila Harrison and that one in Delaware City."

"I guess he doesn't care what age they are," I said.

"I guess. I hear tell"—he lifted a suggestive eyebrow—"that you weren't at home when Rosebud tried to reach you."

"I had a big evening," I answered lightly.

"Sure you did. I hear tell he tried to get hold of you till the not-so-wee hours, but you never answered." He winked at me.

"Is nothing sacred? Can't a girl have a little privacy?"

"Not if she's a cop. Not according to our Rosebud."

THE NEXT MORNING I RAN INTO ARCH LARRABEE IN THE CORRIDOR OUT-side my office.

"Well met, Kate," he said to me. "I've been wanting to have a word with you about our rapist. Have you noticed that the intervals between attacks—that is, if we're right about all of them being by the same man—have been narrowing ominously?"

"It's alarming," I agreed. "Especially now that he's taken to using a knife."

"We desperately need those DNA analyses—for all of them,

but especially for the Delaware City rapes. The lab needs to get a move on. Have a look at this." Arch pulled a crumpled sheet of paper from the pocket of his tweed jacket, unfolded it, and showed it to me. "The first six attacks were roughly three months apart, beginning the November before last, nearly twenty-three months ago."

"Except last winter." I pointed to the paper. "There's a big gap between Rachel Jervis and Nicole Taylor. Early November to late March—over four and a half months."

"My theory about that is that the first winter the rapist was active was a mild one, without much snow. But last winter was unusually brutal; very few comparatively warm days, and lots of snow and ice. It could have kept him from moving around the way he must to keep an eye on his prospective victims. If we're right about the same perpetrator making that second attack on Millie Raeburn in Delaware City," said Arch, "the pace increases. Raeburn's second rape was on May twenty-third, less than two months after Taylor; then Marie Newcomb was raped on July twelfth."

"And then Janet Davies on the night of August seventeenth," I added. "About a month after Newcomb."

"And now Lila Harrison, on September twenty-second. He's stepping up his time, as well as his level of violence. I think he's going to kill from now on. Unless we stop him," Arch said, stuffing the paper back in his pocket,

"We have to stop him!" I said, horrified at the implications so baldly laid out. "My God, he might go back to Janet Davies! He might go back to all those women at some point. And this time it probably wouldn't be just a matter of rape." I didn't know why it seemed even more horrible to contemplate the murder of the women who had already been attacked than that of as-yet-unknown victims, but somehow it did. Perhaps because the women we had met seemed more real than anonymous potential targets; perhaps, I thought, because there ought to be some way to protect them, but our available resources would not permit it.

"No," Arch said soberly. "The next time it almost certainly won't be just a matter of rape."

"HEY, KATE! Listen up! Talk about weird! You ain't gonna believe this!" Jacko tumbled into my office a couple of days later, Sun-kist orange hair flying in all directions, looking as if he spent his life in perpetual motion, like a jumping jack.

"After working here for three years, I'll believe anything. What have you found—a photograph of the rapist in flagrante?"

"No. No photos. But get this. One of the techs came up with some objects he found stuck in the blood on the carpet in Lila Harrison's bedroom."

"Objects? How often do I have to tell you to be precise?" I was exasperated. "Stop jabbering technical jargon at me; you know I can't stand it. What do they look like, for God's sake?"

"Cool your jets, why don't you?" said Jacko, offended. "I was just getting to that. They been tentatively identified as seeds."

"Seeds?" I said, startled. "What kind of seeds? What the hell have we got—a Mad Gardener? 'He thought he saw a Buffalo upon the chimneypiece. He looked again, and found it was his sister's husband's niece. "Unless you leave this house," he said, "I'll send for the police." ' "

"Huh?" Jacko was bewildered. "Whazzat?"

"Your education is sadly lacking," I told him severely. "That's 'The Mad Gardener's Song' by Lewis Carroll; any civilized person would know that. But where could those seeds have come from? Lila Harrison lived in an apartment—not a locale conducive to seeds . . . . Wait a minute. Were there any potted plants in the place? Maybe herbs growing in the kitchen? I don't recollect seeing anything along those lines when I was there."

"Nix. There wasn't nothin' like that. I checked."

"Then her attacker may have dropped them or tracked them in. You're sure they're seeds?"

"C'mon, Kate, you're messing up my story," Jacko said plaintively. "Button up for a sec, can't you?"

"My lips are zipped," I said, suiting the action to the word.

"Okay, here it is. We're pretty sure they're seeds because when the tech—Steve Perry—told us what he thought they were—I mean, they looked like less than nothin'—we sent them over to the Delaware Department of Agriculture for confirmation, and George Layard—he's the seed lab super, so he should know—said Steve was right on the nose. But there are four seeds, all from different plants, he said; and he told us he won't know for sure what plants they are till he grows them."

"He has to grow them to know what they are?" I was indignant. "And he's supposed to be an expert! Crimminy! How long will that take?"

"He said sixty days, minimum. Eighty, max. For a grow test. And he doesn't do it; he's sent the seeds to the U.S. Department of Agriculture."

"Sixty to eighty days?" I said, horrified. "Sweet heaven! We could have a slew of dead women by then. The rapist has begun to kill. And he's stepping up his pace."

"Hey, Kate, don't overdo it," Jacko protested. "Maybe the seeds are no big deal. We don't know for sure they're connected with the rapist. And even if they are, that doesn't mean they're gonna help us catch him. Anyhow, Layard said he has an idea what kind of plants they come from, just that he can't be too specific till he sees the plants."

"Well, what kinds of plants does he think they are?" I demanded.

"He says three of them look like different kinds of meadow grasses, and the fourth one is from something like a cabbage maybe." He paused and cogitated. "Or a turnip, or maybe mustard."

"Some expert. That's a pretty wide field. At any rate, it sounds as if someone has been wandering in a vegetable garden. Does Harrison's daughter garden?"

"Flowers, not vegetables. We checked. And the meadow grasses, if that's what they are, sound like country. So maybe the killer is a farmer."

"Oh, great." I groaned. "What a major help that is. Delmarva is lousy with farmers. Not to mention the bordering states."

"When we find out for sure what the plants are, maybe that will help narrow down the area he could be from," Jacko offered hopefully.

"Sure. And maybe the moon is made of green cheese. Ah,

well, hope springs eternal. Let's keep our fingers crossed. And our toes, while we're at it."

"So you don't think the seeds Steve found are gonna help us catch the rapist?" Jacko was crestfallen.

"Oh, Jacko, what do I know?" I replied. "I hope they'll help as much as you do. God knows every little bit helps, the way building up layers of pigment on a painting makes the subject of the picture intelligible at last. If we're lucky, we'll garner enough detail for our picture to enable us to identify the rapist. I just hope we can do it before he kills another woman: I have a very nasty feeling that he isn't going to wait for another sixty to eighty days."

CHAPTER 8

Mid-October

JANET DAVIES WAS SITTING ON A CHAIR IN MY STUDIO—A NINETEENTH-century copy, not a bad one, of a sixteenth-century armchair, the seat and back covered in faded green cut velvet. Janet was draped in a piece of Fortuny fabric I had picked up years ago at a secondhand shop in Manhattan: rose-tinted cloth printed with fronds of leaves in dull silver. The color of the background brought out the shade of her hair wonderfully well, and the silver highlighted its gleam. I had arranged the cloth around her, pinning it into a sort of sleeveless shift, and caught it at the waist with an old tasseled rope of rusty gold. With her hair loose in tendrils, she looked like a Pre-Raphaelite dream girl—but at least twice as ravishing as Rossetti's women, and with a brain to boot, instead of the mooncalf stare with which they gaze out of the canvas.

I knew I should not have been painting her. I should not have had any unofficial contact with her until the case was closed. I should have had my head examined. But I was dying to get her down on canvas, and she had phoned me that morning with a frantic appeal in her voice that I had not been able to resist.

"Kate?" she had said. "They told me at the Rape Task Force

number that you're off duty today, so I looked up your home number. I hope you don't mind my calling."

"No," I had replied cautiously. "Have you remembered anything else you think we could use in our investigation?"

"N-not exactly." Silence. "I thought you might like to make a start on painting me. If you're not busy. You . . . I . . . you said you'd like to paint my portrait."

I was taken aback. "I'd like to. Very much. But I can't do it in the middle of the investigation."

"I understand," she said hurriedly. "It's just . . . since it's your day off, I thought you might have some free time. But I know how busy you must be."

"I've a couple of hours free this afternoon," I replied. "That wasn't what I meant. Having you pose for me—that's a personal thing. I'm not supposed to get friendly with someone who's involved in an investigation I'm working on."

I heard a sudden intake of breath.

"Oh. I'm sorry. I'm really sorry. That means I shouldn't talk to you." Then a burst of speech with an impetus that made itself felt, even filtered as it was through miles of telephone wire. "But I have to talk to someone! Someone who understands what I'm going through, at least someone who has an inkling. My family is all in England on a visit and I haven't anyone really close around here. Except Tom, and it's about him in a way, so I can't discuss it with him. And I don't want to talk about it on the phone, so I can't talk to any of them. A phone is so impersonal. Would you mind? We don't actually know each other, but I have a feeling about you. I'll die if I don't talk to someone."

There was a suppressed sob, which made up my mind for me. To hell with protocol! She desperately needed someone to talk to, and I liked her.

"Come on over," I had said. "I'd love to paint you."

So there she was, looking like the Lily Maid of Astolat. Even the violet shadows under her eyes were right for the role. I took up my palette and started mixing colors, squeezing tubes to release blobs of oil pigment onto the surface of the wood.

"Talk if you like," I told her. "I'll let you know if it starts to interfere with what I'm doing."

"Thanks. I was terrified of moving and spoiling something for you."

"Make yourself comfortable. You know the general pose I want, so you can go back to it when I've got everything set up, and I'll fine-tune it."

She moved her shoulders and her head to loosen the muscles. I looked at her again, and said, "What a shame Nourmahal isn't here. You'd make a spectacular double portrait; your hair is almost the same color as hers."

"Nourmahal?" Janet asked, startled.

"My dog. She's a saluki. Rather a Pre-Raphaelite type herself, with her burnished red-gold coat—a very proud beauty."

"I've seen Afghans and borzois, but I don't think I've ever seen a saluki."

"They're similar in type, but salukis are shorthaired. They're desert animals, the only breed of dogs with a single-layered coat, to help survive the heat. A saluki is supposed to have been the first domesticated dog; carvings of salukis thousands of years old have been found in Mesopotamia."

"Where is she?" asked Janet. "I'd love to see her."

"You will at some point," I promised. "At the moment she's down in South Carolina, being bred. I took her there last week, and I don't know when this case will let up long enough for me to go back and pick her up; it was really decent of the lieutenant to let me have a couple of days off. I don't want her to come by plane, so either I'll have to drive down again to collect her, or wait until someone from the kennel heads this way for a show. I really miss her; the place seems empty without her."

"Why a saluki?" Janet asked curiously.

By way of response, I inquired, "Have you read anything by Michael Gilbert?"

She shook her head.

"He's a terrific English writer of detective fiction, which I read by way of recreation—like taking a busman's holiday, I suppose," I explained, "who has a Persian deerhound named

Rasselas in some of his best stories. I fell hopelessly in love with Rasselas; and the closest I could come to a Persian deerhound was a saluki. Hence Nourmahal. She's an aristocratic creature, and rather aloof. But every so often a stray wanders in—people are apt to drop off unwanted dogs in the country and leave them to fend for themselves—and she's very civilized about sharing me with an intruder until I can find it a home."

"You mean they just abandon their pets, and leave them to die?" Janet was clearly shocked.

"Puppies are cute, but sometimes when they grow up, they're not so amusing," I said. "And an untrained animal can be destructive, especially a large dog. It's one reason why I don't like pet shops. A reputable kennel will make sure its puppies go to a good home."

"The next time you get a stray, let me know. My house is small, but there's certainly room in it for a dog. I've been missing dogs since I left home; we always had three or four when I was growing up."

"I'll put you on my list," I promised. "You didn't have any trouble finding your way here, did you?"

"No," she said. "Your directions were terrific. I didn't get lost, but I might have if I'd tried to find it on my own. You're really tucked away back here, aren't you? It's a lovely place. I feel as if I were a thousand miles from anywhere."

"It's peaceful," I agreed. "I adore it. It helps keep me sane when too much police work gets me down."

"This doesn't look like a house, if you know what I mean. That's part of its charm."

"It doesn't, does it? Not surprising, since it wasn't a house to begin with. Just after the First World War, when the du Pont family began to make big money, one of them built a ghastly copy of a French château—a real blot on the landscape, according to the photographs I've seen. Over there." I waved the ocher-filled paintbrush in my hand in an easterly direction. "Fortunately it burned down during the fifties. I gather there were suspicions at the time that the heirs had grown tired of paying real estate taxes on the place, and torched it. This building was the stable which, luckily, was far enough away from the big house to survive the fire. Downstairs, before renovations were made, was stabling for the horses, and this studio was the hayloft."

"It's gorgeous," she said, clearly meaning it. "No neighbors?"

"Not within a mile or so."

"Do you have a garden? I wish my house had more than a postage stamp. You have so much land around here. I really envy you."

"Just a small kitchen garden last summer, with tomato plants and some herbs. But there are remnants of stone walls where the château stood, which I've been thinking of turning into a rose garden next spring; my landlord said he wouldn't mind. Old-fashioned roses—they're my favorites.

"Would you mind giving your head a shake to loosen your hair around your face a trifle more?"

Janet tossed her head, and, as she did so, noticed a painting on the opposite wall.

"My God!" she said, clearly *bouleversée*. "Is that a self-portrait?"

I glanced at the painting of a young woman, half goddess, half tart, a blue-and-scarlet kimono, gold embroidered, slung carelessly around her. "I only wish I could paint like that," I said.

"You're obviously the model," said Janet. "What a magnificent robe that is! It looks," she added shrewdly, "as if you're not wearing anything underneath."

I said only, "He was a very good painter."

"I'll say! Who is he?"

"Someone named Eugène Savoyard, whom I knew in Paris when I studied there. He's dead." I took up a stick of charcoal. "Stay just like that for a few minutes, will you? I want to rough in the figure. That's right."

Obediently she held her pose, and was quiet. One of the things I like about Janet is the fact that she knows when it's best not to say anything. For several moments as I worked, there was a companionable silence. After a bit I broke it.

"You wanted to talk to me about something?"

With some hesitation, she replied, "I . . . I don't want to bore

you. I mean, we don't know each other very well. It's just . . .
this sounds silly, but you have a generous mouth, not pinched
the way some people's are. I know I'm not making sense, but
you look as though you would listen and be kind."

I was touched and flattered. "I won't be bored. Say whatever
you want to. You never know, it might lead to something that
will help us even if it doesn't seem to have any connection with
what happened to you."

"As a matter of fact, it has everything to do with what happened to me, but it isn't the kind of thing that would help the
police. It's Tom. . . . Well, Tom has been wonderful about everything. I stayed in his apartment for several nights after . . . it.
And then I thought it was time to move back to my own house.
Sort of on the principle of remounting the horse that's thrown
you. I was afraid that if I didn't go back soon, I might never
return there."

Close to tears, I judged, she bit her lip.

"I'm ready for you to take the pose now," I said, reverting to
business in order to break the tension and give her time to regain
her composure. "Yes. Just like that. Good. You're a quick study
when it comes to posing. Don't misunderstand me for saying
this, Janet, but maybe you need to try a rape support group. Or
a psychiatrist. They did tell you, didn't they, that the Crime
Compensation Board will reimburse your psychiatrist's fees if
you consult one?"

"I don't want to spill my guts to a group of women with
whom the only thing I have in common is the fact that we've
been raped," she said violently. "And I don't need a psychiatrist.
I need a friend."

I felt like a royal stinker. From the little I'd seen of her so
far, I liked Janet immensely; she struck me as the kind of person
I'd like to talk to if I were in her shoes. "What the hell," I said,
capping the tubes and adjusting the easel so the light fell evenly
on the canvas, leaving no shadows. "Talk away. I'm all ears."
As well be hanged, I thought, for a sheep as for a lamb.

Now that she had my unqualified permission, she paused, but
a moment later it all came out in a rush.

"I told you, didn't I, that Tom has been an angel. I mean,

while I stayed at his place—he only has one bedroom, which he gave up to me while he slept on the sofa. He even brought my breakfast on a tray every morning, with a rose in a wineglass. It's a real bachelor's pad—no vases," she explained. "And he's not much of a hand with toast. He kept burning it and pretending he hadn't. But I could tell, because he had to scrape the slices he brought me."

Her turquoise eyes grew briefly tender at the thought, and I hoped I could reproduce that fleeting look with paint. Perfect for the Lily Maid dreaming of her parfit gentil knyght.

"It sounds as though he made quite an effort," I said, feeling that some remark was called for, but not knowing precisely what.

Her mouth formed a seraphic curve and her gaze turned inward. "He's very sweet. Once, before . . . before *this* happened, I mentioned that I love fresh orange juice, so he went out and bought an orange squeezer, and gave me a glass for breakfast every morning."

I waited for further confidences, but none emerged, though clearly the wench had not yet unburdened herself of what she had come expressly to get off her chest. So I prompted her.

"You were saying that you moved back to your house."

"Yes. Tom . . ." She stopped talking and tilted her head with a pensive look, an attitude that would have driven Burne-Jones to distraction over his inability to duplicate the erotic purity of her gaze. After a moment she said haltingly, "I wanted to move back home. I needed to move back. But I was still scared. So Tom moved in with me. I mean, he still has his apartment. It's a temporary arrangement, for as long as I need him. And I like having him there. I don't want him to leave. But I don't want him to feel imposed upon. And he seems content. He keeps reassuring me that he doesn't want to leave yet. Only . . . before this happened, he was trying to get me into bed. And I was definitely interested. But . . ."

"But?" I prompted her. She clearly wanted a nudge.

"He was going at it too hard and too fast. And I was in the middle of a case, and I couldn't afford to be distracted. And I thought he wasn't quite grown-up enough. But now I've seen what a decent, kind man he is under all that bluster, I've discovered that I really care about him. But he's being too angelic. He doesn't make a move to—well, you know—now. Of course," she hurried on, "I wouldn't want him to . . . to . . . Not till I've passed the HIV test. If I do. I've been too frightened to take it yet. But I want him to hold me close. I need to have a man I care about hold me. Just hold me. And I do care about him." Her voice broke and thinned to a near whisper. "I feel as if it's driving me insane. I don't want him to leave."

She looked down at her hands and her voice returned to its normal level.

"If he does, he may never . . . we may never . . . But I don't want him making a pass just because he feels sorry for me. I think the main reason I'm upset," she added unexpectedly, "is, though God knows I don't want to risk exposing him to AIDS, I'd hate to think that's what's holding him back. That he's a coward, even though I couldn't blame him for being one. Especially when I've just learned to . . . to be fond of him. Do you know what I mean?"

"Absolutely," I agreed, mixing a silvery gray on my palette for the pattern of the Fortuny cloth. "I'd feel the same. But it's entirely possible that that's the last thing on his mind. Don't convict him without a trial."

"I won't." Janet achieved a wan smile. "I seem to be having a delayed reaction. I felt fine right after the attack, except for my bruises. But for the last few weeks everything I see or do makes me want to cry."

"Not surprising," I told her. "Par for the course."

"It is?" She sounded hopeful.

"So I understand. You were comparatively lucky; the attack on you was brutal, but it didn't last long, so you may recover a lot faster from the experience than a woman who has gone through hours or days of fear and pain at the hands of a rapist. But even so, there's apt to be a letdown once you lower your defenses a bit. Look, Janet, you've been through a lot and you've handled it remarkably well. Just let things ride for the time being. Take Tom at face value; try not to worry about all the possible ins and outs of his behavior." I thought for a moment, and then said, "I tell you what. If you need a hand to hold when you decide to take the AIDS test, mine's available."

"Would you?" Janet's color deepened. Even the blue-green of her eyes was brighter, and she smiled for the first time since she had arrived. "Kate, if you'll go with me, I think I might be able to face it."

"Think about it," I suggested. "Don't rush yourself, but once you get that over with, you may find your problems with Tom solve themselves. And your twenty-eight days' waiting period is up, so you can take it at any time now." I stretched, and set down my brush. "The light's beginning to fade. What about a cup of tea? One with a dollop of rum? I'll make a special exception and let you have a look at yourself, if you like. I usually keep my pictures hidden from all eyes but mine till they've arrived at the varnishing stage."

After she had gone, I castigated myself for getting so involved with a witness in an ongoing case. It was distressingly unprofessional. But how often do you meet someone whom you feel you've known forever? I could count times like that on one hand, the times when you have an instant rapport with someone: you click, and you both know it. You both know, too, that if you didn't see each other again for the next fifteen or twenty years, you would be as close as though you had last met only the day before.

CHAPTER 9

Late October

IT IS NEARING THE END OF OCTOBER. The rolling country above the city of Wilmington, just south of the Pennsylvania state line, is vivid with autumn color. Scarlet, crimson, and vermillion, lemon, apricot, and pure gold stipple the green of the hillsides. The fall has been wonderful, rivaling the famous autumns of New England. No need to travel north this year.

But the Watcher does not heed the beauty of the countryside, except for the splashes of red on the landscape. These catch his eye; he likes them. They remind him of blood, of the blood he released with his knife, the blood that splattered so satisfyingly over the green walls of the bedroom.

He drifts into a reverie bright with blood. That time seems so close, but it is too far away. He is greedy for more times like that one. It was a revelation, like the first time he picked up a knife. He dwells with pleasure on the sight, the smell, the warm feel of the blood. When he first touched the knife in that row-house kitchen, he had no idea of the vistas it would open before him. He does not want to wait much longer before he uses his knife again. His blood is beginning to fizz, the way it did in the New Castle garden. He will go back to that one, he thinks, the one he missed that night. But not yet. She has been warned, she is on her guard. He will wait until she has had time to forget to be careful, and then he will get her. It is a game, a game he must win. A game he is bound to win; the odds are all on his side. But the one in New Castle is for later. He needs one now. One like the last one. The last one was thrilling. He had never imagined it could be so thrilling. He looks at the gouts of red on the hillside, and a frisson trickles along his spine.

He is a little uneasy at being out here in the daylight. He feels as though he must stick out like a sore thumb, since there are no other people to use as camouflage, the way he usually does. But, he reminds himself, that means there is no one to see him. And even if her neighbors should pass by and notice him, what would they do about it? He is just a man who has stopped his motorcycle on a dirt road to enjoy the spectacular view. Besides, neighbors must be few and far between up here. He has not seen any other houses for a matter of miles, except the burnt-out shell he noticed, not far from her house. He made a careful note of its location; it will be a good place to conceal his cycle.

The Watcher is pleased with himself. It wasn't easy to find her house; her mailing address is just a P.O. box number. He had to follow her to find out where she lives. In a way he enjoyed doing it. It made him feel extremely clever. But he was also annoyed that he had to take the time to follow her when it didn't suit him. In the long run—not so long now—she'll pay for his inconvenience. He'll make sure of that.

After he had first spotted her he was angry, furiously angry, to find out she was a police officer. It frightened him. It nearly threw him off the scent. He almost dropped her from his list. But it is a point of pride with him never to eliminate a prospect. And when he began to think about it, the fact excited him. They're stupid, the cops. They couldn't catch him even if he got her. That would be really satisfying, to get a cop. In a way it would be his crowning achievement. He would be thumbing his nose at them, letting everyone see how dumb they are. Watching the news on TV will be quite a show after he's done her, he thinks, gratified by the prospect.

The Watcher cannot tell whether this house has a security system like the house in New Castle, but even if it has, it is so deep in the country that there will be time, a lot of time, before anyone responding to the alarm can get there to see what's wrong. If there is an alarm, he will take her to the burnt-out house where he is not likely to be interrupted until he has finished with her. This is the first time the Watcher has seen the house up close, so he takes a good look around to plan his campaign of entry. He decides that the back door leading into the kitchen is ideal for his purpose. It is made of small panes of glass surrounded by a wood frame, so if the lock proves too difficult for him to jimmy, he can break the glass and wood out of the door frame and climb through. It's a funny-looking house, he thinks—built of stone, with a big hipped roof and small windows, except for a large one set at the second-floor level that looks as though it is the height of the room it illuminates. He will take her into that room. He thinks with pleasurable anticipation about the scarlet shimmer of the full moon, glimpsed through blood-smeared glass.

The Watcher is pleased by the construction of the back door. This one is going to be dead easy. And now he's been blooded. Now, after the last one, he knows what he had been looking for the whole time, and how to get it. So much better even than he had imagined beforehand it would be. The effervescence begins again, making him giddy and a little drunk. He can hardly wait. Then he thinks, why should he wait? He can come back tonight. He doesn't have to wait; his timetable is his to plan, his to execute. He can do whatever he wants, whenever he chooses. This place is so secluded that he can pick any time that suits him. He is sure that she lives alone: he has made a number of short trips past here by automobile and motorcycle at various times of the day and evening in the last week or so, and each time he has seen only her car parked in the driveway. Furthermore, on the list her name is down as Ms. So she will be there tonight, waiting. Waiting for him to do whatever he wants to do.

Yes, the Watcher decides as he mounts his motorcycle, he will come back tonight. He doesn't think he will be able to stand to wait a day longer.

CHAPTER 10
Late October

As I pushed open the heavy glass door that led to the Salon Primavera, I caught sight of a familiar face.

"Janet!" I exclaimed, pleased to see her looking so well. Two weeks earlier she had gritted her teeth and taken her HIV test, which she had passed with flying colors: the knowledge clearly agreed with her. She looked in possession of herself again, as though she owned the world. Her hair was gleaming, artfully wind tossed, and very becoming, a testament to the skills possessed by the high priests of Wilmington's premier beauty salon. In a suit tailored from bronze Irish tweed and a pair of knee-high butterscotch suede boots, she was an acknowledged knockout.

"Kate." Janet's smile was vibrant with well-being. "That scarlet coat makes me feel warm just to look at it! How's the portrait coming along? Do you need me for another sitting?"

"Not yet, alas. The days are beginning to shorten, and the hell of it is that at the moment I haven't any free daylight time in the studio—we're working overtime on the rapist. But I'll be in touch. Which reminds me. I was about to phone you to ask if you'd mind coming in to go over that list you gave us."

"Sure thing. When do you want me? I could manage it 'most anytime this week. It won't take long, will it?"

"Only half an hour or so. Tomorrow?"

"Tomorrow will do nicely. Would noon suit you? I can pick up a sandwich on my way back to work."

"We can eat our sandwiches together, if you like. There's a good deli near my office."

"I'd like that."

"Your hair looks terrific," I told her admiringly. "Did Alessandro cut it?"

"Hardly. I'll have to be a full partner before I can afford that kind of outlay. But Piero's good, too."

"Small world. I'm on my way to an appointment with Piero. Tell me—I've often wondered. You don't suppose, do you, that he's really a dyed-in-the-wool Florentine?"

She gave an eloquent shrug. "You've got me. He sure doesn't look or sound it. And judging by Alessandro's accent, I'd say Flatbush was more likely to be his home base than Rome. But rumor has it that nobody gets hired to work at Primavera who doesn't swear he first saw the light of day in la bella Italia. It's more *eleganza*."

I laughed. *Eleganza* was the adjective most favored by Alessandro, who was much in evidence at Primavera, overseeing the running of his demesne.

"You're looking marvelous," I told her. "And it's not just your hair. Are things going well?"

"Yes," answered Janet, with a laugh of sheer delight. "Now that I've found out that I'm not going to come down with a dread disease, I've realized that the attack doesn't matter any more. It doesn't mean a thing to me. I feel so fortunate that poor woman last month wasn't me." She shuddered. "But even when I heard what had happened to her, I wasn't afraid. I was sad, and desperately sorry for her, but I wasn't afraid. When I realized that, I couldn't believe it. All my fear had evaporated." She snapped her long slender fingers. "Poof! Just like that. I can't thank you enough for going to the laboratory with me. Getting the test over with was just what I needed."

"I was very glad to do it. That's fantastic news." I was pleased, but somewhat surprised, by the rapidity of Janet's recovery; many women took much longer to emerge from their shock and terror. I didn't want to throw cold water on her enthusiasm, but it was important to warn her. "I don't want to sound morbid," I said, "but it might be a good idea if you were to exercise some caution for a while. It's rare for a rapist to return to a previous victim, but it has been known to happen; and we think this one may have. He's erratic, and becoming more so. Do be careful until we get him."

The inner light illuminating Janet's face dimmed briefly, as if a shade had been lowered and then raised.

"Thanks for the warning. I will," she said. Her smile beamed forth again, strong as a floodlight. "I've been wanting to tell you," she added. "Tom's great. Everything's great now. I never expected to be so happy. Even before the attack. And afterward . . . I thought I'd be miserable for years. But here I am, less than three months later, unbelievably happy."

I hated to put a damper on such obvious joy, but I had to be sure that Janet understood my warning.

"I can't tell you how delighted I am to hear that," I said warmly. "But you need to remember the rapist isn't sane. I don't think you ought to feel paranoid about it. Just remember he's dangerous. Very dangerous." I returned with relief to a far more agreeable subject. "I'm so glad things with Tom have worked out."

"He's a darling. He has far more depth to him than I ever imagined he had, before—before the attack. This will sound strange, but I think, if I hadn't been attacked, I might never have seen that side of him. The rape made both of us grow up fast. So although I hate what happened to me, in the long run it may have changed my life for the better, not the worse." She hesitated, then continued in a rush. "I'm going to marry him." That incredible smile broke through again. "He doesn't know it yet. I mean, he's asked me, but I've told him I'm not ready to talk about it. When I marry him, I want him to be sure it's not just to have a protector handy. I'm sure, but I want him to be, too. So I hope you catch the son of a bitch soon. I don't want to wait too long for my orange blossoms."

"I'll do my best," I promised. "I'm so pleased to hear your news. It's the first time I've heard of a rape case producing a love match. See you tomorrow. We'll celebrate over Cokes and tuna salad."

"Ciao—my one word of Italian, in case Alessandro is within earshot."

She flirted a hand at me and went off in the direction of Market Street. I entered the willow green *faux-marbre* antechamber of Primavera, where I saw the great Alessandro conferring with his lissome receptionist, no doubt chosen for her uncanny resemblance to one of Botticelli's nymphs. He had never cut my hair either—the cost of one trim would have kept me in paint and canvas for several months—but you couldn't miss Alessandro. He wore beautifully cut Italian suits of silk tinted the same tender leaf green that adorned the walls of his salon. I envied him his tailor. Judging by his suits alone, the place must have been a gold mine.

He glanced incuriously at me as I approached the (pale green, but of course) marble counter, and moved off. He was a good-looking man with regular features and dark hair that was long, covering his ears, waved and beautifully shaped—in-house, not a doubt of it. A large woman upholstered in a purple suede suit—Stacia Lackworth, married to du Pont money, fancied herself a patroness of the arts in the Medici style; I'd met her here and there at parties over the years—swept up to him and bussed him enthusiastically on the cheek, disarranging his pretty curls and exposing his left ear. I saw then why he made it a point to cover them. They were not pretty. In point of fact, few ears are shell-like, the ideal of aural beauty; but his were lobeless, which made them, to me at any rate, peculiarly unattractive. I suppose it's just my artistic sensibility. At least, I reflected, his defect spared us the sight of a masculine earring; judging by those suits, exquisite but slightly outré, I wouldn't have put it past him to sport an emerald stud.

Alessandro looked less than pleased at being enveloped in Stacia's comprehensive embrace, but he submitted and returned her greeting politely enough. At length she released him and sailed out without a word to me—not surprising, she generally reserved her notice for those with at least a couple of million in the cashbox, a fact which, along with the suits, gave me a pretty fair idea of Alessandro's income. Stacia's freshly arranged hair was more in the manner of Boucher than Botticelli, a style which made her look even taller than her height of nearly six feet.

Alessandro went off to oversee his kingdom, and I headed for Piero's cubicle to get my locks shorn. Appearances made it unlikely that Piero, a willowy young black man with a drawl straight out of the Deep South, was a genuine twenty-four-carat Florentine; clearly Alessandro was not one to let nationality stand in the way of talent. It was hard not to notice that Piero's ears, unlike his boss's, had lobes, since one ear was hung with a piratical gold hoop.

Piero was a fast worker, so when my hair had been cut and dried I made my way downtown to Reynolds', an old-fashioned ice-cream parlor that is one of Harry's pet hangouts in Wilmington. He swears they make the best BLTs on the East Coast—his favorite lunch, washed down with a chocolate egg cream. One of the many things I like about Harry is the way he can lunch one day on extra-dry martinis and sushi, the next on BLTs and egg creams, and seem perfectly natural eating either. In fact, there's so much I like about Harry that sometimes I wonder why I bothered to get a divorce. Then there are the other times when I wonder why the hell I ever married him in the first place.

Right now, however, I seemed to be in the first phase: mad about the boy. I hadn't seen him for nearly a month, and so I'd begun to miss him like the devil. I'd forgotten all his irritating qualities and could recall only his more endearing ones, of which I must confess he possesses quite a number. At least, that was the way it seemed to me at the moment.

We sat in one of the booths at Reynolds', gazing soppily into each other's eyes like a couple of teenagers as we ate our lunch (egg salad on a kaiser roll for me, with a full-fledged vanilla ice-cream soda. I don't fool around with egg creams. I only drink the real thing).

"Has anyone ever told you that you have a Nefertiti nose?" Harry asked me. "The one on that ravishing bust in the Berlin museum."

"As a matter of fact, yes. You have. Hundreds, if not thousands, of times," I replied.

"And wingèd eyebrows," he went on, unheeding. "Like birds. They could lift you up and fly away with you. Dinner tonight at La Chaumière?" he asked, switching subjects without skipping a beat. His ability to move seamlessly from the sublime to the nearly ridiculous has always amused me.

"That would be divine," I said. La Chaumière has without a doubt the best food in town, as good as nearly any restaurant in Manhattan. I sometimes wonder why the genius in the kitchen wastes his time down here in the sticks, but I'm not complaining, particularly after a serving of his smoked salmon quenelles with lobster sauce, which come as close to perfection as anything on this earth. As for his desserts, they're as good as my own, which is saying a lot. Savoyard, who taught me to cook, had an ungovernable passion for *les desserts,* among other things.

"Your place afterwards, or mine?" The hopeful expression on Harry's face made him look like a small boy, despite the fact that he is forty years old and stands six feet three inches in his stocking feet.

I found him exceedingly hard to resist; still, I didn't want to seem too easy.

"This case we're working on right now is taking a lot out of me," I replied evasively. "I really ought to make it an early night."

He looked so crestfallen that I had to catch myself to keep from laughing.

"I'm going back to Virginia tomorrow," he said plaintively. "There's a scene simmering in my brain which I have to write down before it gets away from me. I'd hoped we could have—a little time together before I leave."

"We'll have dinner together," I said innocently, purposely misunderstanding.

"That isn't what I mean, and you know it," he told me crossly, his lower lip protruding ominously. He looked exactly as he must have at the age of six when he was told he couldn't have another cookie.

This time I couldn't help laughing. He was absurd, and I adored him. Besides, I'd had every intention of giving in; I'd just wanted to give him a healthy scare. He's too sure of himself sometimes, and too sure of me, despite the divorce.

"My place," I said. "That way I'll have everything I need to get ready for work, so I can sleep later."

"Sleep?" Harry asked with an expressive lift of an eyebrow.

"Whatever. Suit you?"

"Anything that suits you suits me," he declared passionately, his chatoyant hazel eyes intent on mine. His age, I concluded, had risen to eighteen or so. Judging by my somewhat limited experience, playwrights are even more emotionally volatile than poets. It makes me wonder if I have the temperament to be a painter. Perhaps that's why my pictures haven't been discovered yet by the National Gallery or MOMA; perhaps I'm too phlegmatic to be truly creative. In the table of the elements, Harry is fire and air while I am earth and water—heavy and cold. I comforted myself by thinking that if one can't live without air, neither can one exist, on this planet at least, without water.

"Sometimes," I said, idly toying with the hand that was not holding half of his BLT, "I feel like your mother."

This time he cocked his eyebrow so high that it met the lick of hair falling across his forehead.

"What a horrible thought!" he said, shocked. "I'm no Oedipus. That's the last thing I'd want you to feel like. Especially tonight."

"Don't worry. I expect it will have worn off by that time." I blew him a kiss across the table.

"You certainly don't look like anybody's mother," Harry remarked, examining me inch by inch, until I began to blush, despite myself. I never blush. "You look like a dissolute young gypsy painted by Caravaggio. A gypsy with something ribald on her mind. I do hope I'm reading you aright." He winked.

"Enough of this badinage," I told him briskly. "If we're going to make a night of it, darling, I'd better get back to the grindstone pronto. The task force is hard at work on the serial rapist, and as it is, I've had a long lunch hour. I feel guilty taking a night off, but I do need a break. I've been going flat-out for a couple of weeks. You know, sandwich at the desk and that sort of thing."

"Any luck so far?"

"Not yet. We're getting worried. I told you, didn't I, that he killed his latest victim?" I swallowed hard, remembering Lila Harrison's apartment. "The method he chose was—excessive. And what has us really going full tilt is that the psychiatrists we've consulted say now he's begun, he's almost certain to keep on killing."

Harry's eyes grew dark with what, because I know him so well, I recognized as anger.

"No. You hadn't told me any of that," he said slowly. "You're sure it's the same man?"

"No doubt about it. Thank God for DNA profiles; they'll help convict him when we catch him. But up to now it's been taking close to twelve months for the analyses to come back from the FBI lab over in Maryland, so we haven't had proof positive. We have to send the samples there because Delaware doesn't have a laboratory that can handle DNA testing. It's a highly specialized procedure."

"How long would it take to run the samples through if you had your own laboratory?" he asked.

"A couple of weeks."

"That's outrageous!" he exclaimed, furious.

"You're telling me. But at least the FBI lab is expediting our evidence, now that we've had a homicide in the series. So the semen found in Mrs. Harrison's case was rushed through, and we got the report yesterday. We were fairly sure it was the same man, because he had used a knife for the first time during his previous attack, but it's good to have confirmation."

"When was the previous attack?" Harry asked. "A year ago?"

"No; in August. Six weeks earlier than Mrs. Harrison."

"Then how," he demanded, using that rapier brain, the possession of which is one reason why I love him despite myself, "do you know that the first knife attack is part of the series if you haven't got the DNA analysis for it yet?"

"Clever you," I said admiringly, patting his hand. "Now I know why they let you into Harvard all those years ahead of me. The answer is, we didn't, though we were pretty sure because of some other similarities to the previous attacks. Now we do, though, because the lab rushed the evidence from the August attack, too, and we got both reports at the same time."

Harry had a troubled look. It's an expression that rarely crosses his face. "You be careful."

I was somewhat taken aback. "Yes. Of course. I'm not in any danger. Don't be silly, Harry."

His look did not lighten. "I wish you weren't a policeman. Or policewoman, or whatever you want to call yourself. Let's get married," he added abruptly.

"Again? It didn't work last time." But I was briefly tempted. I always am when he brings the subject up, which is every now and then. "Why do you think it would now?"

"I love you."

Even though I already knew he did, it fairly took my breath away to hear him say it. It has never been a thing he has found easy to do.

"And I love you," I said lightly, in an attempt to leaven my own admission. "But we can't live together. It just doesn't work. You know that."

"I love you," he repeated stubbornly. "I want to keep you safe. This job of yours is too dangerous. Either marry me, or stop being such a damned fool and accept some alimony. God knows I can afford it. I'll give you enough so you can paint all day long without a care in the world. And go foxhunting. Horses galore," he added cunningly.

I rose from the table. Phlegmatic no longer, I was in a towering rage; fortunately I had finished my sandwich. Trying to tempt me with hunting was the last straw; the prospect was too perilously tempting.

"No! Absolutely not! I've told you before. I won't take your money. Don't try to bribe me again with hunting. And don't you dare trivialize my painting. It may not be much, but it means everything to me. Just be—because I haven't made millions like you doesn't—doesn't mean . . ."

It was horribly embarrassing. I was very near to tears. Above everything, I wanted to get away from him before I started to blubber. I stole a quick glance at Harry. His face had lost all its color.

"Kate. Darling, I didn't mean . . ."

"Oh, yes, you did." To my horror I heard myself sniffle. "Tonight?" I said. "Six-thirty? My place?"

"Yes. Yes, of course."

"See you then." I waved a forgiving hand at him and ran out of Reynolds' because I could feel tears beginning to force themselves through my lashes. Even though I had far more important things on my mind, I suddenly thought, *Damn him! Typical of Harry. The bastard didn't so much as notice my hair!*

CHAPTER 11

Late October

THE DINNER AT LA CHAUMIÈRE WAS SUPERB. I was having a heavenly time and so, I could tell, was Harry. I had made a vow to myself to forget what had happened at lunch; I knew he hadn't meant to put my back up. He had only been trying to be helpful; and it was a very generous offer. It wasn't his fault that I have a thing about money—his money. I suppose it's just the green-eyed monster surfacing. So I made a real effort to enjoy myself at dinner; not that it was difficult, heaven knows. There's no one in the world I'd rather be with than Harry when the mood is right. I was wearing a new silver dress; Harry likes me to put on the dog when he takes me out on the town. He's the possessor of a fastidious painterly eye; sometimes I wonder why he chose writing for a trade instead of painting. And then I start to wonder, as I did that evening, whether he'd be better at it than I am. And so it goes, and so it went—envy once again rearing its ugly head. I firmly tamped down all unworthy thoughts and gave myself up to unbridled revelry.

I was glad I had worn the dress when Harry said it matched my eyes. "Sometimes they shimmer like moonstones, but tonight they're shiny as quicksilver."

"How would you know? You didn't notice my hair at lunch, when I'd just had it done in your honor at hideous expense."

"I noticed," he said. "Very nice. But I didn't think you wanted me to mention it."

He was right, of course.

"Besides," he added, taking my hand and looking deep into my eyes, "hair is merely the icing on the cake, like a ribbon or a bracelet. It doesn't mean anything. But these lovely lamps, these windows of the soul—they do. That's why I notice them."

My heart moved within me. I said flippantly, "Guillaume de Salluste, not Shakespeare. I may play with paint, but I'm not a total illiterate," and drank deep from my wine glass to cover my confusion.

At Harry's request Gérard, mine host at La Chaumière, had laid in a case of the best vintage year available of Moët et Chandon, my favorite tipple, though I don't exactly turn up my nose at Veuve Clicquot. In fact, I'll drink anything that passes for Champagne, so long as it's reasonably potable; with my income, what's in my own cellar is strictly domestic. It's sweet of Harry to indulge me in my pet extravagance. Thoughtful and generous, and also (dare I say it?) a shade self-serving, as he knows that with enough real Champagne coursing down my gullet, I find it hard to say no. Not that I would, mind you, but I suppose he thinks of it as an insurance policy.

As a matter of fact, it may have been a canny move on his part that evening, because when we pulled up at the house in his weatherbeaten pickup truck (no Yuppie affectation, that—he needs it to get to the Virginia cabin when it snows), I was seized by a sudden fit of conscience.

"Duty calls," I told him. "Oh, what pain it is to part! But you'll be back in a couple of weeks; and, Harry darling, I really ought to get booted and spurred and hotfoot it out of here tomorrow at the crack of dawn, if not sooner, to *revenir à mes moutons*."

He eyed me coldly.

"What a disgusting mix of metaphors," he informed me. "Thank God you took up painting instead of writing."

I was sufficiently highflown on the Moët to take umbrage at this slur.

"Right," I said briskly. "That's it. Not so much as a nightcap for you, my lad. Take your coat and hat and go. Thanks for a lovely dinner and all that."

THE TENSION HAS BEEN BUILDING IN THE WATCHER ALL DAY, UNTIL NOW he feels like a puff adder swollen with venom, which he must release or he will burst. Even while he was at work, he could not stop thinking about his mother and what he would like to do to her. His mother, safe down in Florida, so many miles away. He was thinking about how it would be if she lived all alone out in this isolated place the way Kate Marbury does. He could not stop remembering how she had left him when he was a kid. How she left his father. His father never got over it. He never got over it. He was only six, but he can remember the terrible things she said when she took off with that fat-cat lawyer she worked for.

"You little creep!" she had shouted at him. "You're not supposed to be here! It's all your fault. That abortion didn't work, so I got married to Dumbo here. What a chump I was, wasting my best years on you and your stupid father. I wish you'd never been born! Well, thank God it isn't too late. I got a chance now, and I'm taking it."

Not entirely comprehending, he had run weeping to her, and she had cuffed him, sending him sprawling to the floor, his lower lip bruised and bleeding. He'll never forget that, never forgive.

So now that she's an old woman, she's trying to make up, trying to worm her way back into his good graces. Now that he's made good, she wants her little boy back. She's really been bugging him lately. Ever since Jenny died in that car crash two years ago and Jerry moved to Hong Kong, she won't leave him alone. But she's too late. He doesn't need her anymore.

He remembers the way his father cried, remembers the way his father held something she had left behind—a scarf smelling of jasmine and lilies and hyacinths—against his cheek and wept. Massive, gut-wrenching sobs that frightened the small boy who watched. He had never seen his father cry before.

Now he is preparing himself for the night that lies ahead.

Getting ready has become a ritual, with its own rules and gestures. When he is reconnoitering his victims, he wears an assortment of outfits, disguises of various kinds, so he won't be spotted; but when the time to act arrives, he always wears the same clothing. Reverently he takes out the black T-shirt, the black jeans and sneakers, the gloves, the knife. Reverently he unfolds the garments and puts on each item with great care, handling them as though they were priestly vestments. The dried splashes of Lila Harrison's blood are scarcely visible against the black clothes, but he touches each place in turn, remembering. Then he takes up the butcher's steel and slowly, ritualistically, with measured strokes, begins to whet the knife on it, although it is already so sharp that it will pierce whatever it touches. He is preparing for the sacrifice. When he has finished, he smiles beatifically, holding it before him in both hands. This is his religion.

"I NEED A GOOD NIGHT'S SLEEP, HARRY," I SAID, BUTTRESSING MY argument.

"I'll bet you do, after the amount of Moët you put down during dinner. Except I seem to recall you're one of the fortunate few who don't get hangovers."

"How dare you impugn my sobriety?" I was righteously indignant. "I'm not the least bit tight, just a little . . . elevated. You get out of the car this minute. Out! I said. At once!"

To my vast irritation Harry threw back his head and gave a shout of laughter.

"What's so funny?" I asked, just barely managing to restrain an impulse to hit him.

"You are. I can't get out of the car. Or rather, I could but if I do, you'll be stuck with me all night after all." Seeing my look of incomprehension, he enlarged on the subject. "It's my car, nitwit, not yours."

"Stop laughing. You sound like a bloody hyena," I retorted crossly, but I couldn't help seeing the humor of it, and a moment later I began to laugh, too. Soon we were clinging to each other, helpless with laughter. By a major exercise of self-control, I managed to stop before he did. "Come on," I said, getting out of the truck. "I suppose you might as well stay—Nour's away being bred, so I need something to warm my bed for me."

"Darling Kate!" Harry leaped from his side of the truck and moved around to take me in his arms, then galloped up the front steps, saying over his shoulder, "You won't regret it. I'll bring you breakfast in bed tomorrow morning. I'll cook pancakes. I'll fry bacon. I'll—"

"Oh, shut up and come here." We kissed in the light of the hunter's moon, a long swoony kiss that took my breath away. Kissing Harry is like that, as if we had just met, as if we had just unexpectedly found each other across a crowded room.

He picked me up.

"The key," he murmured in my ear. I handed it to him. Without another word he unlocked the door and carried me up to bed.

THE WATCHER IS ANGRY. Very angry. He drove his cycle to the burnt-out house and parked it behind one of the vine-covered stone walls, so there would be no chance of any passerby spotting it. It might seem an unnecessary precaution, since there are no neighbors within a matter of miles, but the Watcher is meticulous. He takes no chances. He has the feeling that if he does everything right—even when he is so impatient that he is ready to explode—if he performs the ritual properly, it will all happen precisely as he wants it to. So he stowed the cycle away in the shell of the house where no one could see it, and smoothed down his clothing, and pulled on his gloves, and checked the knife, snug in his trousers pocket. But despite all that, it wasn't any good. He must have done something wrong. Because there are two cars parked in the driveway of the house, her green Jetta and a battered gray pickup truck with Virginia plates.

It's almost 3:00 A.M., and the lights in her house are all extinguished. Someone must be staying the night. Unless . . . unless she has borrowed the truck for some reason, to move furniture maybe. But it has an out-of-state license plate. He does not dare take a chance on it. If she has an overnight visitor and he breaks into the house, he will have alerted her; and then he will have to wait, wait too long, before the next time. He does not want to wait at all, but it is better to wait for a night or so than to have to move her down to the bottom of his list. Like the one in New Castle. He does not want another failure, even a temporary one; the fermentation is working, working, in his blood but he tamps it down, telling himself to be patient. He must be especially careful not to give warning to a policewoman. The payoff will be worth the wait. It won't be long, he promises himself. Only a day or so. Soon. Very soon.

I WOKE, YAWNING, TO THE SMELL OF COFFEE. "What time is it?" I asked. It seemed awfully dark outside; the bedside lamp cast a yellow pool of light on the dark polished floor.

"Early," said Harry, pouring coffee from a thermos jug into my favorite mug. He added sugar and heavy cream, not milk (how well he knows me!), until the liquid was a pale rich buff, then spiked it with a dollop of Grand Marnier and handed me the result. "Here's your all-in-one breakfast. Orange juice, coffee, et cetera. All that's missing is an egg."

"Why now?" I inquired suspiciously. "It's too early for coffee. Especially coffee loaded with Grand Marnier."

"Would you prefer B and B? Sorry, you're all out. Your liquor cabinet needs restocking," he told me briskly. "Never mind, next visit to Wilmington I'll see to it. It's never too early for coffee. Besides, I want to be certain you're awake."

I stared at him over the rim of the mug. "Why?" I was still foggy with sleep. I don't really wake up till the sun creeps over the horizon.

"Drink deep," he ordered. "Because I want to be sure you know what you're doing. I want you fully conscious when we make love."

"Oh." Obediently I drank my coffee, which was just as I like it, Grand Marnier and all. When the mug was empty I set it down on the bedside table and opened my arms to him.

Later, as I was dressing to go to work, Harry observed, watching me, "You have the longest legs of any dame I've ever seen."

"The better to ride horses with," I responded, smoothing a stocking over one of the articles in question.

"Among other things. . . . Speaking of other species, though Nourmahal is a charming companion, her absence from the premises is not altogether undesirable. She takes up a lot of room on the bed."

"Don't be unfair," I protested. "She only gets up when she's invited."

"Umph," he responded noncommittally. ". . . I suppose I could drive down to Virginny tomorrow," he said lazily. "The scene won't dry up and fly away in one little old day."

I was sorely tempted. But I needed to concentrate on the serial rapist, and Harry is all too distracting. Already I was feeling slightly guilty about the previous night.

"No, darling, you go off and write your play. Time is tight for me at the moment; this rapist is really scary. We need to get him soon. If we're lucky, by the time you come back we'll have nabbed the little brute."

His eye caught mine in the mirror that hung over the dressing table.

"Sure?" he asked.

"Sure," I responded, with more determination than I felt. "You know you ought to get that scene down on paper before it fades. And you can't write here. It's not solitary enough; you've tried it and failed. You don't want to trade the Pulitzer for another night of depravity."

"You wanna bet?" Then he gave a gusty sigh. "I reckon you're right. But there are times when I'm with you that I don't give a damn about the odd honor. By the bye," he went on casually (I always suspect his casual tone), "speaking of being with you—*Paradise Enow* is going to be produced by the Royal Shakespeare."

"Oh?" I responded, mentally gritting my teeth. I ought to be able to get over being envious of Harry's spectacular success. I mean, it isn't as though he were a painter, for God's sake; and I have no bent for writing. But telling myself that doesn't get rid of the feeling. Envy, I have learned all too well, is not rational.

"I'll be crossing the pond for the opening," Harry went on. "It's planned for early April. I thought you might like to come."

"April in London can be hell," I responded sourly. I was not in the mood for odious comparisons—his talent and mine, his career and mine. I didn't fancy being the little woman on the Great Playwright's arm.

"It can be the cruellest month," he agreed. "Or it can be the best part of the English summer. We won't know which till it happens. Do come," he wheedled, adding, "We'll stay at the Connaught; the weather there is always balmy," as a further inducement.

In my current frame of mind, it was a mistake. I adore the Connaught, but since I can't afford the tariff there nowadays, he was rubbing salt into my wounds. Not intentionally, of course, but . . .

"Sorry," I said lightly—as lightly as I could, considering that I was seething underneath. "No can do."

"Why not, sweetie pie?" Harry cajoled. "Rearrange things. It shouldn't be hard to do. April is months away."

"I have a rapist to catch, in case you haven't noticed," I replied with asperity. "A trifle more important, I should have thought, than a mere opening night."

He ignored my second sentence. "You're sure to have nabbed him by then; you just said so. Anyway, you're not the only member of the rape squad. Someone could cover for you for a few days. Someone did," he reminded me, "when you drove Nour down to Charleston earlier this month."

That remark gave me the excuse I had been wanting; I flared up with a royal display of pyrotechnics. "In case you have forgotten," I said wrathfully, "I just happen to be the only police artist on the rape squad. I happen, furthermore, to be the best damn police artist on the East Coast. And suppose we *haven't* caught the rapist by then? There's no guarantee we will have. Suppose he attacks, and kills, while I'm in London? How do you think I'd feel? Not to mention the minor consideration that my being away might impede the investigation. Of course, all this pales in significance beside a First Night." I spat out the last two words with a vicious snap.

At this point Harry unwisely tried using common sense to calm me down; he ought to know me well enough to have realized this was the wrong approach. "Kate, I know you're good at your job. But no one is indispensable. Even you could be spared for a couple of days if you haven't caught the bastard by then."

I could feel my face grow scarlet with rage. "How right you are," I snarled. "No one is indispensable—except the World's Greatest Playwright, that is. The rest of us are just easily replaceable peons. In which case, you can easily replace *me* at the Connaught with some slick little dolly bird from the flock of theater groupies that will be following your every exalted move."

I had finally got to him. He stared at me with fury in his eyes. "Maybe I will, at that."

"Do. Go ahead. Vapid little airheads are just your type. Why don't you pick up a dozen or so when you go to England? And you can go to hell, too, while you're about it." I picked up his trousers and threw them at him. "I never want to see you again, you son of a bitch!"

"I would return your key this very instant," said Harry, ice in his voice, "except for the fact that, richly as you deserve to come back and find that a bunch of burglars has left the house an empty shell, you would no doubt accuse me of the theft. So since I shall have to lock the door before I leave, I shall keep the key and mail it back as soon as I can find a post office where I can get rid of it."

"Fine. I have a spare I can use. But be sure you do. If I don't get it back in five days, I'll have the lock changed. And send you the bill. How fortunate that Nourmahal is off at the breeder's," I added nastily. "Otherwise I should have to take her to work with me to make sure you didn't kick her on your way out."

And on that note I stalked out of the room, down the stairs, and out the front door to my car.

CHAPTER 12

Late October

As I passed Buck Gallagher's office that morning, I noticed that Mrs. Raeburn had come in and they were going over her contact lists, adding any stores and services which she might unintentionally have omitted when she initially drew it up. I knew she was in her seventies, but she seemed to have aged since the last time I had seen her. Not surprising, poor woman. Hard enough to have to go through that experience once. But twice! She must wake in the night, I thought, wondering if he's going to come back a third time.

Buck can be a bit rough in his manner, but I was pleased to see how gently he was handling her. As if she were his own mother. After Lila Harrison's murder, Rosebud had ordered the investigation stepped up—not that we had exactly been dragging our feet, but her killing had given our hunt for the rapist absolute top priority.

Buck wasn't the only one hard at work on that aspect of the investigation. Tim Mundy, I saw as I went by his cubicle, was discussing lists with Nicole Taylor, a pretty young brunette; and I could hear Arch on the phone arranging a meeting with another of the recent victims, Marie Newcomb.

I did my own bit along those lines that afternoon, when Janet and I settled down in my office with Cokes and sandwiches and began to go over the lists she had made up for us shortly after her attack; by concentrating hard, most of the time I managed not to think about my quarrel with Harry. The lists comprised our attempt to locate a link connecting all the women who had been attacked by the rapist; a link which, we hoped, would prove to be the weak link in the chain of anonymity surrounding him. At some stage he had had a contact with all his victims which might help to identify him, if only we could pinpoint it. So we asked the women to write down the names of shops they had patronized, repairmen they had used in the past few years, any deliveries to their houses, medical services (doctors' offices, laboratories, etc.). We reminded them to list the everyday services it's easy to forget, such as gas stations, supermarkets, garbage pickup, liquor stores—even post offices. As everyone who reads a paper or watches television knows, post offices are not immune from the presence of psychopaths.

We sat munching our sandwiches and poring over photocopies of Janet's list. Mine was annotated, correlating names handed in by the other women who had been attacked by the rapist. Except, of course, for Lila Harrison. Her daughter had drawn up a list for us as best she could, but so far it hadn't been much help. Wilmington is comparatively small, so it wasn't surprising that there were a number of places the lists had in common, stores where all the women had shopped, even though they lived in different areas.

"No suspicious telephone calls?" I asked Janet idly. We'd had all the women keep a log of any incoming calls that seemed questionable, but so far nothing useful had turned up.

"I nearly forgot!" she exclaimed, rummaging in the handbag she had parked beside her chair. After a moment's search she produced a microtape in its crystalline case.

"What's that?" I asked her, my interest heightened.

"It's a tape from my telephone-answering machine," she replied. "I had a very strange call while I was out yesterday evening. It probably has nothing to do with the attack on me, but since you asked me to keep a record of any unusual phone calls, I thought I'd give it to you. It was a man's voice. I forgot to ask Tom to make a tape for the machine before he went away on a business trip—he won't be back for several days—so it's still my voice answering the phone. The man leaving the message gives a strange kind of laugh and says something like, 'Hey, I like that voice. Real sexy, you know what I mean? I wouldn't mind hearing it again.' And then . . . I can't remember the rest of it, except he ended with something like 'Be seeing you.' Anyway, here it is." She handed it to me. "I know it's unlikely, but I thought there was an outside chance that it might be the man who raped me. I don't remember ever having had a call like that before. And if it is the rapist, I hope the voice will help you catch him. I'd be over the moon if I could help to nail the son of a bitch." There was a determined glint in her eyes when she said this.

"Did you recognize the voice?" I asked her, as I placed the tape in an evidence bag and made a note of its source.

"I don't think so . . . but I can't be sure. I don't remember anything distinctive about the voice of the man who attacked me. Did the others he raped notice anything unusual?"

"Their descriptions were all pretty much the same as yours," I said. "Medium voice, neutral diction, no distinguishing accent or other feature. But if the caller is the rapist and they were to hear his voice again, someone might recognize it; and even a slight trait, the kind you wouldn't be apt to notice consciously while you were being brutalized, might help us. It's definitely worth a try."

We returned to our lists. As Janet scanned her copy, she asked, "Do mail and phone contacts count? To another city, I mean. I ordered some bowstrings from The Fletcher in Manhattan in . . . I think it was in early May, and I forgot to write it down. But surely New York is too far away?"

"There's not a chance the rapist commutes from that distance," I replied. Curiosity overcame me. "Are you an archer?" I asked her. "That's rather an exotic sport nowadays."

"It's even more exotic if you shoot with an Asiatic bow," said Janet.

"An Asiatic bow? Never heard of one. What is it?"

"It's shorter and lighter than an English longbow, or the kind the Indians used. It's more maneuverable than those, and you can fire it more rapidly. It was specially adapted for shooting on horseback. That's what I used to do when I was a kid."

"You shot on horseback? Good God, what did you shoot at?"

"Nothing alive, I promise you," Janet said, laughing. "It was target shooting. We galloped past and tried to hit as many as we could. It was a lot of fun." She smiled reminiscently.

"Where did you perform?" I was fascinated. "At horse shows? Pony Club? Are there competitions in equine archery?"

"We did it pretty much on our own—the local Pony Club, I mean. I was living out in Montana, and we used to pretend we were playing Indian. Come to think of it, I don't know why there was a Pony Club out there; probably because the wife of the local large-animal vet was an Englishwoman. She ran it. It was my mother's great-uncle who taught us to use the bow; he'd been a champion archer at Princeton. He came out for a visit one year and stayed the entire summer. I think his family was glad to get rid of him for a while—even at his advanced age he was a bit of a rogue—but my mother liked him. He was a terrific cook, and she said that as far as she was concerned, he could stay forever. She was none too fond of the kitchen, and he used to shoo her out of it and take over. Anyway, he taught me and my brothers and all our little pals how to shoot, and how to fletch an arrow: that's feathering the end to balance it, so it will shoot true. He even made bows for us. I still have the one he made me. It's beautiful, made of wood and the horns of an antelope someone had shot—with a gun. Uncle Bos wouldn't let us shoot anything living, but he said if someone else had, you might as well make use of it. Otherwise, he said, its death was a total obscenity, with no meaning or purpose."

"I gather you still shoot," I said, intrigued, "since you've been buying supplies."

"I like to, when I get the chance. I adore target shooting. I haven't shot on horseback for years, though. Some friends living over in Maryland have let me set up a couple of targets on their farm, and when I go to see them I take my bow along. I try to stay in practice; I feel it's the least I can do, considering what Uncle Bos did for me. Anyway, it would be a shame to let that bow go to waste. It's a real work of art."

"You're welcome to shoot at my place if you like," I told her. "We could set up a target out by the original house, the one that burned down. It would be safe there; there's not a soul around except me for miles."

"Do you know," she said, her eyes lighting up, "I'd really like that. Then I could get enough practice to keep my hand in."

I thought of the dull evening that stretched ahead, now that Harry had gone, of the vain regrets that would revolve unceasingly in my mind if I were alone that evening, of the thoughts that would drive me melancholy-mad if I were left a prey to them. "Why don't you come out for a scratch supper tonight, and take a look at the lie of the land?" I offered. "Bring your bow if you don't mind; I'm dying to see it. I have to work late—till seven-thirty or eight. But I could make us an omelet."

"I'd love to," she said.

"Great! It'll be dark when you come out, but we could walk over there with flashlights—I have a big torch—for a quick look."

"Why don't I pick up a snazzy pizza from that place in Greenville on my way out and bring it along? Then you won't have to do any cooking."

It sounded like heaven. "That would be terrific, if you're sure you don't mind. I have wine. And fruit for dessert." I'd bought some incredible pears for Harry—his favorites—which, with one thing and another, we'd never got around to eating. They were dead ripe. And I had some Gourmandise—that kirsch-flavored cheese layered with young walnuts. Or, I thought, if I felt energetic, I could whip up a bain-marie of zabaglione.

"See you around eight-thirty, then? What about artichoke hearts, rosemary, fresh tomatoes, fontina? On the pizza."

"Yes, to both questions," I answered.

Janet scooped up her sandwich paper and soda can, deposited them in my wastebasket, and waved a farewell as she left my office. I thought with gratitude of the companionable evening ahead substituted for one echoing with emptiness, an evening suddenly to be anticipated, not dreaded. Moreover, the tape sounded promising. It wouldn't do to count on anything in this case, but we desperately needed a break of some kind. Maybe,

I thought hopefully, this would turn out to be it. As far as I knew, the rapist had never phoned any of his victims before. But then, until he attacked Janet, he'd never used a knife. There's a first time for everything. Hope flickered. I breathed on it gently, to keep it alight. With that kind of criminal, you never knew. He was clearly unbalanced; he might do anything at any time. The rules of logic, I thought to myself, didn't apply to him.

CHAPTER 13

Late October

As soon as it is nearly dark the Watcher rides his motorcycle out to the burnt-out house. Lucky, he thinks, that the time change has just taken effect so dusk falls an hour earlier; he is eager to begin. On the way there he checks out her place; there are no cars, not even her green Jetta, parked next to the house. He is glad the pickup truck with the Virginia plates is gone, but the fact that her car is not there yet makes him uneasy. Maybe she's staying in town for dinner. Maybe she's gone to a movie. Maybe... He gives a grunt of anger. He is wound up tight. He does not want to wait very long. The longer he has to wait, the harder it will be to keep himself reined in, to keep his fizzing blood corked up in his veins.

As he heads away from the stone wall behind which he has hidden his motorcycle—black like the clothes he wears, its license plate smeared with mud so the number is unidentifiable— a strong wind stirs the dry leaves that still cling to the branches of the trees overhead, clashing them against each other. They sound like the whirring of cicadas. He takes care to tread lightly, but he can hear a faint whish-whish from the fallen leaves beneath his feet as he moves cautiously along the ground, using his penlight sparingly to find his way among the trees with their broad trunks and susurrating branches. The wind is piercingly chill, but despite the fact that he wears no jacket, only his thin knitted black turtleneck shirt, he is not cold. His blood seethes with the thought of what he has come to do; he needs no clothing to keep him warm.

The Watcher reaches the edge of the clearing that surrounds her house. It is dark now, but he takes no chances on being seen. The moon, nearly full, shows itself fitfully among the clouds chasing across its face, high in a sky of marbled black and silver. It is stunningly beautiful, but he does not waste time admiring it. Beauty holds no interest for him. He makes good use of the occasional moonlight, waiting to advance each step until the shreds of clouds are blown away from the moon so he need not turn on his flashlight. His heart pounds with powerful thuds like a heavy mallet that strikes the ground, shaking it. After what seems a long time to him, he sees a faint gleam of headlights along the road, and draws on his rubber gloves with shaking hands in anticipation of her arrival.

But it proves to be a false alarm. The far-off lights follow the road, describing an arc, and disappear. The Watcher swears monotonously in a muffled voice. He has been made to wait too long. When he gets hold of her, he will make her pay for his wait. But, he reminds himself, he must not go too fast. He will have to rape her before he starts to use the knife. Because once he uses the knife . . . The tolling of his heart thrums faster, faster, until he feels as if it is about to leap out of his chest.

In an attempt to mitigate his excitement, he mulls over the details of his plan. Should he break into the house now? It would be easy enough to open a window, even if they are all locked, and wait inside for her. No, he tells himself painstakingly, as if he has not already gone over all this in his mind many times before, if she has a burglar alarm that reports to a central station (he has been warned by the one in New Castle), it will go off too soon for him to do what he wants to do. If he breaks in early and there is an alarm, he will have to leave and wait for another time. But he won't wait for another time; he won't. He would burst if he had to wait. He wants to do it now. Besides, he has to stay outside in case someone comes home with her. He has to be certain she is alone. But if she isn't alone, he will be forced to wait, wait, *wait*. The hateful word drums in his skull, thudding with the regularity of his heartbeat until he is ready to lift up his head and howl like a lycanthrope at the shrouded moon sailing above.

Another set of headlights mounts the crest of the hill. The sight of them calms him. Instinctively he knows this car is the right one, this is the one he has been waiting for. It is her car. Even though he cannot see what it looks like, there is no doubt in his mind. He checks to make sure the knife is in his pocket, then takes it out and lovingly tests the blade with a feather touch so he will not cut his gloves. Even without pressure, however, he can feel the deadly sharpness of the edge he has so carefully honed. As the car slows and the headlights swerve onto the lane leading up to the house, his body is relaxed, at ease, but balanced ready to spring, ready to do whatever he may require of it. He has a quick moment of panic when the lights stop. He fears the car belongs to someone else after all, has taken a wrong turning, until he remembers that her mailbox is at the end of the lane next to the road. She is picking up her mail. Reluctantly he replaces the knife in his pocket and steps behind a massive beech tree for concealment.

I GLANCED AT THE CLOCK ON THE DASHBOARD OF MY CAR. A little before eight o'clock. Good, I thought, that would give me time to straighten the place up a shade before Janet's arrival. When Harry makes coffee, he leaves a shocking squalor in his wake which it never occurs to him to clear up afterward. Clutter is something he simply doesn't notice—the things he uses stay wherever they happen to fall. I blocked from my mind the bitter knowledge that this was the last time I would be cleaning up after him.

I entered the house and went upstairs for a moment to hang up my coat, then to the kitchen to take a look. When I turned on the lights I saw that, as I'd suspected, it was a ghastly mess. "Damn Harry!" I said. "Damn him, damn him, damn him!" Close to tears, I straightened up as quickly as I could. When the place looked reasonable once more, I noticed that the trash pail was full to overflowing. So I emptied it into a large plastic bag, the kind with drawstrings, and unlocked the back door in order to toss it into the waiting garbage can outside.

To my astonishment, the door seems to fly open of its own volition. It hits me. I stagger back. Something hits my face. It's a man, dressed in black, a black man with a light complexion, at least that's what I think he is because I have a bare instant to assimilate a picture of what I see. At the back of my mind's eye I retain the image of a face set in a grimace, a mask of hatred surmounted by some kind of Afro. Then his arm crooks around my neck in a stranglehold. I try to stay calm, try to remember my police training, how to break a hold like that, my gun, where is my gun?—upstairs, where it's no use—my God I've got to get out of the house, get into the car, where are the keys? In my pocket? On the hall table? Oh God where? Stay cool, I think, if I can get away maybe he'll snatch my handbag and go, if I get in the car even without the keys I can lock the doors, use my car phone with the auxiliary battery to call for help, hold him off till help comes, but oh God suppose he finds the keys? He'll unlock the doors and get at me.

I break loose, run toward the front door, he catches up to me, hits me in the face, I stagger, something running into eyes—blood?—so I can't see in front of me but I keep running, he hits me again, I keep running he hits me foggy everything is foggy hits me again doesn't hurt so much feel doorknob in my hand turn knob hits me can't run any more can't stand feel my knees give way feel myself falling but doesn't hurt can't feel much can't feel much at all.

He jerks me toward him. I look at my hand the one he is pulling on it's scarlet. Scarlet? I think crazily, or rose madder? Vermillion? And I realize it's blood my blood and suddenly I feel dizzy dizzier than I had a second earlier my head swims and I clutch desperately at my disappearing consciousness thinking not now please God I can't pass out now!

THE WATCHER IS PERPLEXED. The bitch has fainted. He has not cut her yet, but she has passed out. He carefully calibrated the blows he gave her to stop her flight; he is certain they were not hard enough to knock her out. He does not know what to do. There is no point in raping her now, while she is unconscious; if he does, she won't realize what's happening to her. He doesn't want to wait too long, because one of the blows he gave her has cut her eye and another has split her lip and she is bleeding, and the sight of the blood inflames him, inciting him to use the knife so there will be more blood, blood everywhere, bright blood, bright red blood.

But he manages to restrain himself, though with difficulty. He wants to execute the plan as he has mapped it out. He wants to see how much he can frighten her: he wants to watch the understanding of what he can do to her, what he will do to her, dawn in her eyes. Making her understand is a large part of the thrill of what he is going to do. The pursuit of his chosen victim—beating her until she is forced to give in, until she falls, defeated—always quickens his blood. But it is only a preliminary. Just as the rape, which used to be the main event in his attacks, has dwindled to another preliminary, now that he has the knife. Both, however, are necessary to make his victims realize how powerful he is. It is the fear in their eyes that gives him pleasure, the terror of what he may do to them. Sometimes he thinks that what they expect him to do is infinitely worse than anything he can do. It is that thought which drives him when he plies the knife.

She is still unconscious. Or is she only pretending, in an attempt to fool him? He decides he will have to revive her so he can carry out his plan. He goes to the kitchen for some cold water to throw over her. There is an ice-water dispenser on the refrigerator door, and he holds a bowl he finds on the counter against the dispensing switch to fill it. That should wake the bitch up fast, he thinks viciously.

HEAD SWIMMY BUT AT LEAST I'M *HERE* AGAIN, AWAKE. Then I remember why I passed out, what happened, and I yearn to return to the soothing depths of unconsciousness. Hear movement, slit an eye, lids sticky but can see. Black-clothed back disappears down hall.

On way to kitchen? Maybe a burglar, maybe leaving with swag, I think hopefully. But sinking feeling in pit of stomach tells me no, he looks and acts terrifyingly like the rapist we've been tracking, Janet's attacker, almost certainly Lila Harrison's killer.

Oh my God, I think, Janet! She'll be here soon. Hope flares, also fear for her along with fear for me. All too likely to kill again. Janet will walk in all unknowing, he'll kill us both. My eyesight maddeningly fuzzy but good enough to see black shape go into kitchen. I try to rise, movements wobbly and far too slow. Still horribly groggy from blows to head. Probably concussed. Shaky but halfway to standing by holding on to leg of hall table when he reappears with something, can't tell what, in his hand. Oh God. Sees me, curses, runs toward me, throws something cold, wet, in my face. I gasp, let go table leg, fall back.

"Fucking bitch," he says, standing over me. He takes hold of skirt, pulls up. Skirt is narrow, I can hear it rip. "Take off your tights," he says to me.

Here we go, I think dully, I knew it was coming. I don't feel fear or horror or disgust, just numb. Partly I guess blows have anesthetized brain partly what of brain still works is consumed with thought of knife and what comes after how to get away before it happens how to save myself, myself and Janet. Janet. If I can get outside as she drives up, get into car somehow, we drive away. Only chance left for me because just then he spots car keys on hall table and pockets them.

"Hurry up," he says, and hits me again, a casual backhand.

I bite back a whimper, didn't expect it to hurt anymore but it did although it feels in a funny way as if it were happening to someone else. So does the rape. I know it's happening but I don't feel anything except a distant revulsion as if I were remembering a long-ago incident that no longer affected me. At any rate I'm not paying attention to what's happening to my body because my whole will is concentrated on listening for the sound of Janet's car and wondering how to get out how to get away from him long enough to reach her car and warn her. My only chance. Her only chance. Will I be able to do it? Oh God please.

Is that the hum of an engine? Too soon too soon he's still busy raping me. No it's going away down the road not turning in. If only he'll go to another room at the right time so I can get out of the house before he realizes. If I'm strong enough if I'm not too woozy can't think about that got to pull myself together he's saying something. What? What? Everything sounds so far away.

THE WATCHER HAS FINISHED RAPING HER. It was strangely unsatisfactory. He must have hit her too hard that last time, he thinks. She doesn't seem to pay attention to what he is doing to her. She doesn't seem to realize that he is hurting her, humiliating her, and that there is worse, far worse, to come. He zips up his jeans and puts his hand in his pocket for the knife. Wait till she sees the knife. That will show her. Everything else was merely a prelude to the knife.

His hand scrabbles frantically in his pocket. It is empty. The knife, his knife, is no longer there. His mind scrabbles frantically around inside his brain like a spider trying to escape from a glass jar. Where is it? What has he done with it? He tries to remember when he last touched it, where he took it out of his pocket to gloat over it. Outside. In the dark. He glances down at the woman. Her eyes are closed. She looks ill. He won't have to worry about her trying to get away from him now. Anyway, he has her car keys. She can't escape, not in the short time it will take him to find the knife. He stirs her with a contemptuous foot and turns away.

HEAR FOOTSTEPS, HIS FOOTSTEPS, MOVING TOWARD BACK OF HOUSE. Peer out of eyes, carefully, so if he should be looking at me he won't see I'm awake. It's all right, his back is to me, he's headed toward kitchen. He turns to go through door. I notice inconsequently that his Afro is askew, a little lopsided. It has a slightly surreal look and I wonder if it is merely a trick of the light and my bruised eyes, or if he is wearing a wig. Silly thing to think about at a time like this, but time is working in strange ways—

sometimes, like now, standing still in its tracks, at others racing past like using the fast forward button on a video. Very queer, I reflect languidly.

A moment later—or is it an age?—I hear back door open. At same instant, it seems to me—am I only imagining it? Oh God please not—a faint faint the faintest burr of what just possibly might be the distant engine of a car. Janet's car? I pray he won't hear I flex knees stretch out hands toward banisters of staircase. Must hurry only chance taking too long he'll be back soon back any minute now back any second got to save myself save Janet. Slow so hideously slow pulling myself up by infinitesimal degrees weight resting on knees now halfway there Kate keep going keep going don't think about him what he's doing when he'll return pull pull harder faster harder. Feel so weak feel like being thoroughly and comprehensively sick no time for that now on my feet but very wobbly afraid to let go banisters might fall. Must let go humming sound louder if he hears it he'll come back. Let go banisters let go loosen hand open fingers let go let go!

THE WATCHER CURSES VOLUBLY AS HE SEARCHES IN THE FALLEN LEAVES for his weapon, his treasure. The knife, he must have the knife! He needs the knife. Briefly the thought flickers in his mind that there are knives in the kitchen. Like the first time, the revelation. But he does not want to use another knife, he thinks petulantly. He wants his own knife. His knife knows what to do. How to do it. His knife is sharp, his knife is clever, his knife is beautiful. No other knife will do the job. Not the way he wants the job done. His heart thumps in his chest, throbbing like the engine of his motorcycle, thrumming so loudly that he does not hear the motor of the approaching car. He is facing away from the house toward the woods, feverishly scratching at the piles of dry leaves, raking them over with his penlight, so he does not see the glow of the headlights; in any case their beams are hidden from him by the bulk of the house. Suddenly he spots a silver glint in the sea of dead brown leaves, and his hand dives down to retrieve it.

SLOW TOO SLOW SOMETHING STINGS MY SWOLLEN EYES MUST BE TEARS of rage, at myself for being so damnably so dangerously slow. But I've managed to get unaided from staircase to wall, where I inch along in the direction of the front door. Will I ever get there, I wonder, despairing, will I get there in time mustn't think about that surely he's come back now. Then I think with sudden hope, maybe he's gone, left for good. But I know he hasn't gone I know deep down he hasn't finished with me he's coming back don't know why he went out but no doubt in my mind he's coming back. Car noise very strong now must be Janet my only chance he must have heard must be in back of me ready to strike ready to use knife one he used on Lila Harrison can't think about that move *move!*

THE WATCHER IS ELATED. He has found it, it is in his hand! He flicks it open and gazes lovingly at the long slender glittering blade. Holding it in front of him like a talisman, he makes his way to the back door of the house, his eyes fixed on the knife. When he turns into the hall from the kitchen, it is a moment or so before he can wrest his eyes away from it to look at the woman lying on the floor. He is so thoroughly immersed in his inner world that it is another moment before he can adapt to the realization that the front door is ajar and she is no longer in the hall. He races to the door and runs outside, not stopping in his course to open it, but pushing it aside with his body. His eyes, which had adjusted from the comparative darkness of his search for the knife to the brightness of the house, now must readjust to the dark. But an instant after his pupils dilate to capture the fugitive light, he is blinded by a sudden stabbing flood of brilliance, as if a bank of searchlights have been trained onto the entrance of the house. Instinctively he shields his eyes with his free hand.

JANET GUIDES HER TOYOTA ALONG THE LANE TO KATE'S HOUSE. It is the first time she has driven there in the dark and she is not sufficiently familiar with the way to know all the potential pitfalls it presents, so she eases the car around the turns and over the bumps in the rough dirt road. She stops near the front door beside Kate's Jetta, switches off the ignition and headlights, then gathers up her things from the passenger's seat and gets out. At that moment a narrow oblong of light shows itself at the entrance—Kate, she supposes, who, having heard her car drive up, is hospitably opening the door for her. But Janet's eyes are dazzled by the sudden brightness and she does not immediately see Kate, who has made her uncertain path through the doorway and is clinging to the frame, fearful that if she lets go she will fall, unable to rise.

"Janet," she croaks, "Janet." She cannot see, but she is certain Janet is there. Someone is there, someone who can help her. But she must move quickly. She must explain fast, or they will both be finally, irretrievably, lost.

"Kate?" Now Janet does see her, and gasps. Her friend's hair is tousled like freshly forked straw, her face is an unrecognizable smear of blood. Her shirt hangs open, her skirt is ripped up the front, she is shoeless. She wambles forward as if she may fall at any second. She looks, Janet thinks with a flash of clarity, much the way I must have looked when Tom saved me.

She starts forward with the impulse to help, but instinctively Kate, though she cannot see her, knows she is coming and cries out, "No! Still here! Stay in the car. I'll . . . I'll come to you."

To Janet's horror the front door of the house flies fully open and a dark figure, a nightmarish figure, a figure out of her own nightmares, emerges. She is amazed by the swiftness of her movements and her thoughts. During her rape her brain had been dulled by sleep and fear and apprehension; then her mind and body had moved slowly, as they do in nightmares. She had been living a nightmare. But now, rapidly though her brain seems to comprehend what is happening, her hands and legs have assimilated it all and taken action on their own before she has a chance to direct them.

She discovers that she has already switched on the ignition

and the headlights. The figure stands silhouetted in their chrome yellow beams, a hand raised in an attempt to protect his eyes from the glare. She finds that without thinking at all she has dropped her handbag and the pizza box, and in a practiced flow of movement braced the bow she carries by stepping between the loosened bow and the bowstring with her right foot, the bow's belly facing forward, its handle behind her right knee, one bow tip against her left shin, the other in her right hand, which is nocking the string. Again without thinking and in a flash, she steps out of the semicircle thus described, slides her right hand down to grasp the bow handle and reaches for an arrow in her quiver, which she must have slung on her back before bracing the bow, though she has no recollection of doing so, for it is there as her hand expected.

Quicker than thought she nocks the arrow and draws the bow, the arrownock touching her chin. Now that she has comparative leisure for observation she sees that the dark figure, so perilously close to Kate, holds a thin shining object in his right hand. She sights along the length of the arrow and looses it; it skims between them, seeming to graze his head. Janet swears and nocks a second arrow. He had dropped his hand from his face and she had aimed for his eye, but at the last second her traitorous arm shifted; it is not an easy thing for a civilized being to kill in cold blood. The dark figure hesitates; the second arrow singing past his ear, on purpose this time, sends him back through the doorway in a panic, back (though she does not yet know it) through the house, out the kitchen door, through the woods to the burnt-out house and his motorcycle.

She runs toward Kate, oblivious to her pleading to keep back.

"He's gone into the house," Janet pants. "I'll get you to my car. Don't worry, he's nowhere in sight. We'll get in the car and drive away."

Pity floods over her as she guides Kate to the car and settles her into the back seat; it is as though she were comforting her doppelgänger. Kate seems dazed, only half-conscious; Janet locks the car doors, then drives out to the road while she calls 911 on her car phone. She wants to get Kate to a hospital as quickly as possible; she also wants to put as much space between them and the rapist as she can. As they head down the road toward the Kennett Pike a motorcycle roars past, nearly sideswiping them. For an instant Janet wonders if it is Kate's attacker and briefly contemplates following him, but the cyclist is driving so fast that pursuit would be suicidal. A second later he disappears from sight.

CHAPTER 14

Late October

HE IS PANTING AS HE REACHES DOWN IN THE RECESS UNDER THE MAT AND pulls out the key. It is always left there at the back door of the shop so that the first person arriving in the morning will be able to open up, since the janitor, who does for all the businesses in the building, each with a separate rear entrance and cellar, as well as an individual front entrance, is not always available to let them in. Because the owner of the business keeps the cash in his office safe, there is little for thieves to steal—shampoo, conditioner, inexpensive individual hair dryers, towels, hair brushes. It is not the kind of business that particularly attracts burglars; the jeweler at the far end of the building, on the other hand, is a very different story.

He wheels his motorcycle into the cellar—nothing to surprise in that, for he often rides it to work, as do several of the other hairstylists who have cycles—and uses the faucet in the big sink to wet down one of the dirty towels waiting in a large canvas bag to be picked up in the morning by the linen service. With this he wipes off the mud obscuring the license plate. Then, employing his penlight with caution so no passerby will spot a suspicious light in the shop and possibly ask the police to check, he makes his way up to the main floor, where he enters one of the hair-washing cubicles in the rear of the shop. There he gives himself a thorough wash, drying himself with one of the fresh towels awaiting the clientele in the morning. There is not much blood, he thinks, dissatisfied; only a few spatters from the cuts on the woman's face, where he hit her. The other time, the first real time, the time that has proved the pattern—the ideal—for all future times, there was a lot of blood.

That first time he had hated washing the blood off his skin so soon afterward. He would have liked to leave it on long after it had dried, but he knew that to do so would be dangerous. Tonight he had brought a change of clothing in his saddlebag and a plastic bag to hold his wet bloody clothes, but he had not needed them because the other one interrupted him at his work. So there was blood still visible on him when he reached his bolt-hole. But not enough.

The thought of the blood makes him tremble. Too bad he cleaned up, he thinks. He could have gone out again. He wants to go out again. It's safe enough; even if the police know now about the attack tonight, they can't patrol the whole northern part of New Castle County, not the way they would need to do to catch him. So he need not have washed off the blood. He is miles away from the place where he raped the woman, and even if they have found out about her by now, they won't expect him to go out again. It is probably safer for him to go out now than it would be if he had not already committed a rape tonight, he argues with himself, so long as he stays away from the general area where he was earlier. That will be easy. There are plenty of places right here in town.

A name, a face, spring to mind. One from his list. She lives near here, in Westover Hills. No need to take the motorcycle. He can walk. She is recently divorced, without children. He overheard her talking to a friend when she came in to have her hair done. Perfect. So he checked her out. He's been by her house a couple of times, and he was thinking that he ought to do her soon. Because her friend was urging her to put a security system in the house, and she said she was looking into it. He doesn't want any more trouble like the one in New Castle. Maybe, he thinks, it's just as well he was interrupted tonight. Now he'll have time for Westover Hills. And he can always go back again for Kate Marbury, after the furor has died down. Something to look forward to. In his way he is an optimist.

He does not need to look up the address. He has already committed it to memory: 18 Suffolk Road.

Even though the night air is cold, his clothes are dry enough to go out in. Not much blood fell on them from Kate's wounds, and what there is does not show. That is one of the reasons why he wears black clothing.

It is still relatively early in the evening, so he waits for several hours in the warmth and dark of the basement. He sits there with his eyes open, dreaming. Dreaming of what he is about to do, dreaming of the blood. When he judges it is time, he lets himself out of the building and puts the key back in its accustomed place under the mat, feeling in his pocket as he does so to make certain of the knife, although he had checked it only a moment or two before. Mother, he thinks, fondling the blade. Mother.

Now the hour—1:00 A.M.—is so far advanced that only an occasional vehicle traverses the major streets of Wilmington, and in the upscale neighborhoods like Westover Hills, virtually no traffic is moving. Here and there a light still glimmers among the trees, but most of the houses have gone dark. Nevertheless the Watcher takes care, melding into the shadows, invisible unless one were on the lookout for a movement of some kind. But there is no one to see. He approaches number 18 Suffolk Road from the rear of the house; the garage is shrouded by hedges, making it easy for him to slip, still undercover, as far as the back door. There is a dead bolt on the kitchen door, which prevents him from prizing it open with the screwdriver he has brought along for the purpose; but he is pleased to note that the upper half of the door, like the one at Kate Marbury's house, like so many kitchen doors, is made of glass panes set in thin mullions, easily knocked out. He has also brought a glass cutter with him, which he uses to slice a hole in one of the bottom panes. He is prepared to break out a space large enough to permit him to enter, but when he reaches in to check the lock, he finds that the key has been left in it. He smiles to himself— not a pleasant smile—turns the key, and enters the house.

"JESUS! ANOTHER ONE," SAID JACKO BENSON. His freckles were preternaturally vivid against his fair skin as he stared in at the unspeakable object lying in the indescribable room. The technicians went phlegmatically about their business as if the sight were an ordinary one; but even to them it was far from ordinary. "It's got to be the same guy. It's got to be."

"It must have happened last night. After Kate." Flowerdew's face was grim. "He was interrupted with Kate. Thank God. If he hadn't been, Kate . . ." He paused, silently looking in at the carnage. Then he said, biting off the words, "She would have ended up like this. The bastard."

"Yeah. Remember the time he didn't get in down in New Castle? He went somewhere else then, too." Jacko stopped, remembering the scene in Lila Harrison's apartment.

"He's stepping up. Two a night. And the killing. It's scary. Real scary," said Tim Mundy.

Flowerdew nodded agreement. "But it makes a crazy kind of sense, crazy being the operative word. And if anyone is nuts, this son of a bitch is. Both nights he was unsuccessful the first time. . . ."

"Whaddaya mean, unsuccessful?" Jacko asked, so indignant that he forgot he was speaking to a superior. "You saw Kate. He raped her. And he beat her up bad." He hit his thigh with his fist in a gesture of frustration.

"Unsuccessful, my boy," Flowerdew told him, "because he didn't have time to kill her. Janet Davies intervened with her little bow and arrow like a goddess from the machine." Flowerdew, a graduate of a liberal arts college, sometimes displayed his erudition to his colleagues. "If it hadn't been for her, Kate would have looked like this by the time we found her." He gestured at the body sprawled on the floor.

"Where was her gun?" asked Jacko in an agony. "Why the hell didn't she have her gun when she needed it? Silly bitch." But the term was not meant as an insult. He could not bear to think of what Kate had gone through, all for the lack of a gun.

"Don't be an idiot, Jacko," Flowerdew told him, not unkindly.

"Believe it or not, I have an idea of what you're feeling right now; and as a matter of fact, I'm in pretty much the same frame of mind. But it's no use backtracking and trying to figure out what Kate might have done to keep from being raped. It won't help us get our hands on the perp. You heard the way she said it happened. Do you make a habit of carrying your service revolver when you put out the trash? Besides, it would have had to be cocked and ready, to do her any good. Hell, if she'd had any idea the bastard was waiting for her out there, she wouldn't have opened the door in the first place."

"I always thought bows and arrows were kind of like pop-guns, you know? Playing at cowboys and Indians," said Jacko. "But if Janet Davies hadn't had one along with her . . . I guess you're right about Kate's gun."

Queasily he eyed the pathetic huddle on the floor, limned in shades of black and crimson, the rich somber tinctures of death. It looked more like a prop from a horror movie than anything found in real life, and Jacko was not yet as hardened as he liked to think.

"How is she?" he asked, his voice hoarse. He cleared his throat. "I mean, right now."

Flowerdew shrugged his sloping shoulders. "The doc says she's not talking much except yes, no, thank you. He says she can walk, but she just lies there most of the time. He says it takes time. Sometimes a lot of time."

Jacko burst out, "It stinks when any woman is raped. But when it's one of us . . ."

"Yeah, well, that's the way it is. We got to get him soon. You remember that woman down in Delaware City who was raped about five months ago? The one who was attacked eighteen months earlier and thought she recognized her assailant, thought it might be the same guy?"

Jacko nodded.

"Turns out she was right on target. The DNA lab expedited the rape evidence for us after the Harrison murder, and the results on that one just came in. They also match up with the results for Lila Harrison and Janet Davies. That means this creep goes back again. He's a repeater. So maybe Kate isn't out of the woods. Or Janet Davies. Or the New Castle woman whose alarm scared him off before he did Harrison."

"We need Kate," said Tim Mundy. "Is she ready to do a sketch yet? She's a whiz with those things, and now that she's seen the creep, we may have reached a turning point in the case."

Flowerdew shook his head. "The doc says not to push her, it takes time. The trouble is, time is what we haven't got. We need to have her working on it now. But he's right. We got to cut her some slack. If we don't, he says it could take her longer to get over the rape. Maybe a lot longer."

As Flowerdew said this, Jacko's ingenuous young face turned scarlet from the pressure of the thoughts he was trying to repress.

"But, Lieutenant," he blurted out before he was able to stop himself, "suppose she never gets over it?"

CHAPTER 15

Late October

WHITE LIGHT PRESSING ON MY CLOSED EYELIDS. Heavy against them. Leaden. White lead, weighing them down. I feel groggy. Unaccustomed lassitude pinning me to bed. Don't feel like moving. Can't move, too much effort. Remember eyes were open a few moments ago. Or was it hours ago? Or years? Time playing its nasty little tricks again. I know my eyes were open because I remember the faces. Beautiful faces, bending over me. I remember thinking in wonder, Am I dead? Is this really a hospital? The nurses are all so beautiful. Even the doctors. Gorgeous young plastic surgeon, stitching up my face. Kind blue eyes, cerulean blue. Empyrean blue. May have been a dream. But I haven't been sleeping. I've been awake all the time. My mind's fuzzy; they gave me a shot, to ease the pain, I suppose, but it didn't put me out. I remember everything. All the low voices, the examinations, the discussions, the treatment.

Now I feel myself rolling, rolling. I must be going to another room. Funny feeling, moving with no effort of my own. Traveling blind. I try to open my eyes, but they refuse. Willfully they remain fast shut. It's a long long way. Still rolling. Roll roll roll your boat gently down the stream.... No. Not right. I feel a little drunk, must be the shot. Or the shock. Someone once told me adrenaline acts on the system like gin. What's the rest of the song? Merrily, merrily . . . life is but a dream. That's not right, either. When he came boiling in the kitchen door at me, I remember thinking to myself, This isn't real. It's a bad dream. It must be. If only it all were a dream. Wake up in the morning, give a shudder at the nightmare I had, thank God it was only a dream after all, brush my teeth, go to work. Teeth . . . oh, God, did he knock out my teeth? No. I can feel them with my tongue. They all seem to be there. No jagged stumps. Jaw broken? No. I can move it. Things could be worse. But my eyes . . . oh, dear God, please make my eyes well. Don't let him have damaged my eyes.

We've stopped. No diminution of light, but I feel myself being lifted, for all the world as if I were incapable of lifting myself, which at the moment I expect I am. Lifted and deposited on what I suppose is another bed, a more permanent one. I'm not sleepy but I feel drained, as if I were in a state of suspended animation. Is this the way people in comas feel? Able to hear, able to experience sensations, but unable to see or respond?

A nurse. Speaking. Takes my hand and puts something cold in it. Ice pack, she says. Keep swelling down. For eyes. To help eyes heal.

Yes, I murmur, I understand.

TWENTY-FOUR HOURS OF DIPPING CLOTH INTO WATER TO CHILL IT, THEN laying it over eyes. Nurses come in and out.

Anything you want? they ask me. Very kind.

Yes. Please. A morning-after pill. I won't get pregnant. I'm damned if I'm going through an abortion if I can help it. I don't want to take any chances.

You've already had one. Shortly after you came in, she tells me. You needn't worry about that.

That attended to, I think of something else to worry about. I grit my teeth to give myself courage, and ask, My eyes?

They should be fine. Swollen for a while, but the ice water will help.

Thank God, I say under my breath. I hear departing footsteps.

Later. Another voice. Can I get you anything?

Nothing, thanks. Oh, maybe more ice for eyes.

Something to drink? You must keep hydrated. The more you drink, the sooner the intravenous drip can come out.

Hate IV. —Yes, please.

Coke? Ginger ale? Apple juice?

I don't give a damn what I choke down in the way of liquids, but I don't want to hurt the feelings of kind beautiful nurse. —Ginger ale, please.

Later. Voices. First Janet's, then Rosebud's. I'm too tired to open my eyes, too tired to talk. Later, I think. My mind focuses on the word, as if it will percolate into their brains by a kind of osmosis if only I can think it hard enough. Thinking it is easier than speaking it. I recall telling Rosebud about the attack, everything I could remember, in the emergency room. So why make the effort to talk to him again? No point, no need. And I'm so tired.

Later still. The nurse again. —Your lunch is here.

Not hungry. Couldn't eat if I tried. The thought of food makes me ill. —No lunch, thanks.

You must eat to keep up your strength, she tells me.

But I haven't the strength to lift a fork.

FORTY-EIGHT HOURS LATER. I'm still holding an ice pack to my eyes with as much concentration as if I were painting a picture. If there were such things as astral bodies, I think, I could float to the foot of the bed and look at myself lying there with my eyes covered by the ice pack. I wonder if astral bodies are capable of wielding a paintbrush. If so, I could paint *Self-Portrait of Raped Woman*, making use of foreshortening the way Mantegna does in his portrayal of the dead Christ. Striking effect. Who knows? It might make MOMA and my reputation.

Still no desire to eat. I haven't slept, I just lie passively on the bed. I find I can make my wobbling way to the bathroom when required. I open my eyes only for that and the beautiful plastic surgeon when he came to see me—I wanted to see if he was as drop-dead handsome as fancy had painted—pretty close, actu-

ally, but then I'm still taking painkillers, so perhaps I'm hallu-
cinating. I spend the rest of my time continuing to bathe my
eyes with ice water, my blind hand endlessly moving back and
forth from the dish to my eyes, from eyes to dish, like an au-
tomaton.

FIFTY-EIGHT HOURS, MORE OR LESS. A nurse came in an hour or so
ago to take away the ice-water dish.

It's been almost two and a half days, she says. You needn't
bathe your eyes any longer.

Thank God for that. I was beginning to think I was risking
the prospect of optical frostbite. I lie here with my eyes still
closed. What to do with myself, now that eye tending is no
longer required? Just lie here and do nothing. I lie still in the
bed like one of those marble effigies they used to carve on noble
tombs, hands folded on my breast, feet neatly together. I only
lack a marble greyhound curled under them. The thought of
Nourmahal comes to mind. Thank God she was at the breeder's.
He might have killed her. She's strong and brave, but he must
have had a knife. The knife he used last time.

Suddenly my eyes fly open and I say, "To hell with this! I'm
tired of it!" I slide off the bed, rootle in the closet, find the
clothes someone must have brought for me (the rape squad has
the ones I was wearing when I came in), and put them on. I've
come back to life.

CHAPTER 16

Late October

FLOWERDEW'S CADAVEROUS FIGURE LOOMED IN THE DOORWAY OF MY hospital room. He carried a bowl of surprisingly lovely flowers, huge nodding apricot roses with thick curving matte-surfaced petals and enormous lilies, pure white, their flaring anthers a deep velvety crimson.

"Why, Rosebud! What a nosegay," I greeted him, surprising myself. His nickname, so far as we knew, was a deep dark secret; we had never dared to use it in his presence.

But he accepted the sobriquet with such nonchalance that it made me suspect he had known about it all along.

"They happened to take my fancy," he told me, "and I thought you might want to immortalize them. Do you ever paint portraits of flowers, like Georgia O'Keeffe?"

"So far I haven't gone in much for vegetation. Those, however, are quite an inspiration."

He placed the flowers on the windowsill carefully, like everything else he does; and since I was occupying the only chair in the room, he settled himself on the edge of the bed like a giant bird of prey.

"You're looking pretty good, considering," he observed.

I laughed, but not for long. Laughing hurt my mouth.

"Your standards of pulchritude aren't very high, Lieutenant."

"Have you taken a look at yourself yet?"

"Why bother? It would just upset me. Besides, until recently, I couldn't; I've only just stopped bathing my eyes every two seconds with ice water. I figure the longer I wait, the bigger the improvement."

"The doc told me there won't be permanent scars."

"No," I agreed. "I was lucky."

"Very lucky. You haven't heard what else happened that night."

"Nobody would tell me anything," I said crossly. To be honest, though, I hadn't asked. Until a couple of hours earlier I hadn't been interested in anything, but now I felt aggrieved at being left out of the loop.

Over his glasses Rosebud gave me what the Victorians used to call a speaking look, but wisely held his peace.

"You making some notes?" he asked, changing the subject to the pad and pencil in my lap, which I had wheedled out of one of the nurses.

"No," I replied airily. "Just doodling." Then I relented. "If you must know, I've been trying to sketch the rapist's face. But it's maddening. When I try to picture it in my mind's eye it seems incredibly vivid, like a Polaroid camera shot, but I can't seem to get it down on paper. What I've done just isn't quite right." I showed him the sketches. "It makes me wonder how the police portraits I do ever come out; I mean, I'm supposed to have a trained eye. If I can't remember what my assailant looked like, how can I expect anyone else to remember theirs?"

Frustrated, I tossed the pad and pencil at the bed. I missed. Rosebud chivalrously bent down and picked them up.

"Don't be too hard on yourself," he cautioned me. "You've just been through a hell of a lot, in case you don't realize it. Don't push yourself."

I glared at him, unnervingly close to tears. "Does that mean I'm off the Rape Task Force?" I demanded.

"Not unless you want to be, Kate." He noticed the almost imperceptible easing of my tension—even for a cop, Rosebud is an incredibly observant man—and added, "I don't want you to go too fast, that's all. The doc says it could be bad for you."

In my relief I could have kissed him, but I restrained myself. It would have been horribly unprofessional; moreover, he'd have had a fit. "Now that I've gotten over the funk I was in," I declared, "I want to get back to work. It would be the best medicine for me. I'm raring to go. I feel like such a fool over the way I behaved, lying around in bed feeling sorry for myself like a maiden with the vapors. I'm so ashamed."

"Look, Kate, take it easy for a while."

"I don't want to take it easy! I did that for three days, and I thought I was going crazy. I want to help catch the little stinker."

He eyed me, undecided.

"You know and I know that right now you're our ace in the hole. And we need to catch this guy as fast as we can." He paused for a moment, then continued. "After he left your place, he went somewhere else."

I caught my breath. "He did? You're certain it was the same one? What happened?"

"He went down to Westover Hills. A house this time, not an apartment. But otherwise it was the same as Lila Harrison. Worse, if possible. So you see, we need to move fast."

"Oh, God," I said. "That poor woman. Dead."

"And tortured before she died. Besides the rape. It lasted a while." His face was gray with remembering.

"How terrible." I was desperately sorry for the unknown woman, joined in a peculiar sort of bond with me, but at the same time in a shamefaced kind of way I couldn't help feeling glad that I was alive and in one piece, more or less.

"Something else."

"What else?"

"He's a repeater. You remember Millie Raeburn, the woman in Delaware City? The one who was raped a second time by an intruder a year and a half after the first attack? She thought it might have been the same man."

I felt myself stiffen. "I remember."

"We got the DNA results back. It turns out she was right. Same guy both times. And the same guy that did Harrison."

"Christ," I said. Why the hell did he have to be a repeater?

The thought of having him return to my house made my skin crawl.

"So," Rosebud told me gratuitously, "you need to be careful."

"Of course I'll be careful," I said impatiently. "I'm all grown up now, in case you hadn't noticed. Plus I'm a cop."

"Neither saved you last time," he pointed out gently.

"For God's sake," I burst out, "don't you think I've been going over and over it all in my mind, wondering how I could have been so criminally stupid? Wondering why I didn't have my gun at hand, why I didn't take any precautions before I opened the back door? But I've opened that door thousands of times. I never dreamed—"

To my horror, I had to stop and bite my lower lip to keep from crying. My emotional state clearly still had its ups and downs; and I couldn't let Rosebud see me cry.

But he must have sensed something, since he bent over me and clumsily patted my shoulder. The contact was oddly comforting.

"We all have times like that," he said. "Sometimes even worse, when something you've left undone means that somebody else got hurt. Especially when it happens to be another cop. Look, Kate, you're alive. We've all been saying our rosaries, or praying to whatever god we want to believe has charge of things, because you're alive. Especially after seeing that shambles in Westover Hills." He veered onto a related subject. "You need to have someone stay with you for a while. Till we catch the creep."

As he said "we," he gave me an inclusive look which permeated me with a pleasant glow.

"That's okay. I phoned Janet Davies an hour ago. She's offered me a place to stay for several days. Tom McIlvaine, the friend who scared off the rapist, will be there, too. So that's all right and tight."

"For several days?" He eyed me dubiously. "What about afterwards? I told you, the creep's a repeater."

"I've also spoken with my landlord. He's going to put in a security system right away, and I'll stay with Janet till it's installed. He said he's been thinking about one for the place for the past year or so. He was very apologetic about having put it off, but I explained it wouldn't have made any difference about the attack on me."

"A security system's a good idea, Kate, but it's not good enough. Not now. Not if he should return. Even if we get the security company to flag the location so they notify us immediately when it goes off, it'll take us fifteen, twenty minutes to respond. By that time . . ."

He didn't finish. He didn't need to.

"Look," I told him, "for the time being I'm going to carry my revolver with me when I'm alone in the house. I'm having a giant bolt put on the bedroom door. As soon as I hear the alarm, at whatever time of the day or night, I'll be ready. What the hell am I supposed to do, Lieutenant, visit all my friends round-robin until we catch the son of a bitch? It could be months, even years. Or would you prefer me to move into some soulless hive of a high-rise apartment house in Wilmington? No, thanks. I'm not letting him disrupt my life like that. It would mean he had won. But he hasn't. He *hasn't*. I won't let him."

Rosebud was silent for a moment. Then he asked tentatively, "What about your ex-husband?"

"No!" My voice sounded startlingly loud to me, reverberating in the pale yellow-painted box of a room. "I can manage on my own. I'm not getting Harry involved in this."

"What if Harry wants to get involved?"

I froze in sudden fear. "Damn you, Lieutenant. You haven't? . . ."

"I haven't. But I tried," he admitted. "I couldn't reach him. He hasn't got a telephone, not even an unlisted line. I tried all the towns in northern Virginia, but no luck. I contacted the post offices, too, but they wouldn't give out any information." He was disgusted. "Not even for a police investigation."

"My God. You didn't tell them? . . ."

"No. I was tempted to hint we suspected him of committing some undisclosed crime. Then they would have had to cough up his whereabouts. But I didn't." He gave his lugubrious grin. "I was afraid you'd be furious."

"You were right. I don't want Harry bothered!" I saw no

point in telling Rosebud that Harry and I were through. It was nobody's damn business. "I can take care of myself. He has better things to do at the moment. He has a play to write. And," I added bitterly, "an opening in London to attend."

The look Rosebud gave me was disarmingly mild. "Shouldn't Harry be allowed to make his own decisions?" he asked.

I stared at him as icily as possible, considering my swollen eyes.

"I want, Lieutenant Flowerdew," I said, enunciating each word with wounding precision, "to cope with this situation myself. Solo. As I have already pointed out, I am both adult and a policewoman."

The look I turned on him must have been even fiercer than I'd realized, for to my astonishment he quailed, and said meekly, "All right, Kate."

I had won. For the moment.

CHAPTER 17

Early November

THE WATCHER PULLS HIS CAR INTO THE DRIVEWAY, PARKS IT BEHIND HIS wife's station wagon, and lets himself into the house. "Helen?" he calls.

"I'm in the kitchen," she replies. "Oh, what a shame!" She comes out to the hall and gives him a welcoming peck. "You just missed your mother's phone call. She said she was going out, but if you call back right now you could still catch her." Her tone is tentative.

"In a pig's eye I'm gonna call that bitch," he says, his voice rough. His mother is a very sore point with him.

"Oh, honey," she says helplessly. "She's your *mother*."

She cannot understand why he dislikes his mother so; she loves her mother. It distresses her that he acknowledges no family, now that his father is dead. He acts as if his mother and half-brother don't exist. Helen feels guilty that she has such a superabundant family, when he has no one. She wishes he would respond to his mother's overtures the way a son should, especially after his half-sister's death; poor thing, Helen thinks, she needs contact with both her remaining children.

"My mother. Big deal. When did she ever act like a mother?"

He hates talking about his mother. He hates her so much that he is afraid he might inadvertently give himself away.

"I'll be out in the garage," he says. "The Harley could do with a polish."

Without waiting for a reply, he goes upstairs to the bedroom, changes from his work clothes into jeans and a sweatshirt, and goes out to the garage. But instead of starting work on his motorcycle, he picks up a hammer, takes a plank of wood that stands in a corner, and begins to hammer nails into it with sharp, vicious blows. His purpose is unclear; one end of the plank is already studded with nails that have been driven into the wood in no discernible pattern. As each hammer blow falls, piercing the wood, he gives a thick growling mutter deep in his throat, followed by a groan of satisfaction.

"Bitch. Bitch. Bitch. Bitch." It is a monotonous litany, during which it almost seems as if he is driving the nails, one by one, into his mother's flesh.

CHAPTER 18

Early November

IT WAS SATURDAY. Janet Davies was taking advantage of free time and an unusually warm day in early November to paint her front door. The grimy white paint was past being improved by washing, and she had decided she wanted something bright and cheerful, instead of the bland absence of color displayed by the other front doors in the row of houses along Broom Street. So first thing in the morning she had gone over to Shinn's and bought some blue-green paint that matched her eyes. Now she put down her paintbrush and stepped back to appraise the effect of the first coat. It was pleasing, she thought, against the soft pink of the bricks. Kate would approve. One of the reasons she had decided to get on with the painting right away was because Kate was coming to dinner, and Janet wanted her professional opinion of the color. The previous night had been the first Kate had spent in her own house since her rape; the security system installation finished, she had insisted on going home.

One of Janet's neighbors in the houses along the row, an older woman, stopped to see what she was up to and eyed the door, her forehead creased in a frown; it was plain that the color did not please her.

"That's awfully bright, isn't it?" she asked, the question clearly rhetorical.

"I like it," said Janet innocently. "Don't you? It's like those gorgeous front doors in Dublin. You know, the ones on the poster. Or London, where they go in for primary colors."

The woman gave a sniff. *We're not living in Dublin or London,* her sour expression intimated; *and the standards in Wilmington, thank heavens, are very different from those places!*

Janet picked up her brush and dipped it into the paint can, then laid down a corrective stroke over a place where she had failed to cover the original white.

The woman had not moved. "Aren't you afraid," she asked curiously, "of making yourself conspicuous?"

For several moments Janet failed to understand what her neighbor was talking about; when at length she did, the realization filled her with a deep delight. She had forgotten the rape! In only three months, it had gone clean out of her mind.

"Do you mean the attack?" she inquired. "That's ancient history." She was so happy she was hard put to it to keep from laughter.

The woman was taken aback by her response. "I thought," she said, "all the publicity. . . " Her words trailed off uncertainly. But then her tone sharpened. "I mean, everybody *knew,*" she said waspishly. "And a bright-colored door like that, well, it reminds people."

Janet stared at her incredulously. Has the woman any idea, she wondered, how incredibly bitchy she sounds? The bizarre workings of her neighbor's mind intrigued her.

"When you have red hair, you get used to being conspicuous," she returned, her Persian turquoise eyes wide and guileless. "I'm afraid there's not much I can do about it. I could dye it, I suppose."

The woman flushed. She had the faintest of suspicions she was being made fun of. She was offended; she had only meant to be helpful.

"Oh, I wouldn't do that if I were you," she answered meaninglessly, for lack of anything better to say. "Well, good-bye."

She walked off in the direction of Delaware Avenue, but could not resist glancing back over her shoulder now and then at Janet, who had resumed her painting and did not notice.

"WHAT A ROTTEN WOMAN!" I EXCLAIMED INDIGNANTLY.

Janet giggled. "I think she's hilariously funny. What does she expect me to do—paint my front door dove gray? I bet she thinks I ought to robe myself in black, like old women in Italy."

"Down to your heels, with long sleeves and a neckline that covers the collarbone."

"Suitable penance, no doubt, for having caught the wandering eye of a rapist."

"The uniform of a soiled dove."

"You're certainly not wearing one!" said Janet. I was in a coral turtleneck sweater and claret suede trousers. "I wouldn't expect those colors to be wonderful together, but they are; it must be your painterly eye that can juxtapose unexpected colors like those and make them work."

"Thanks," I replied, pleased by this tribute to my calling.

She nibbled on a salted almond and offered me the bowl. "Have some of these. They're heaven. How are you feeling?" she asked with concern.

I reflected as I munched on an almond.

"Comme ci, comme ça. Not too badly, I guess, all things considered. Sore here and there, and I still look like something the cat dragged in. And last night I screamed until the woods rang. Then I felt better. I have a feeling I may do that now and then for a while. What terrifies me, of course, is taking the HIV test. The thought of it frankly scares the hell out of me. But you know all about that." At least, I thought, I wouldn't have to tell Harry about the rape; that was one good thing about our breakup.

"It scared me, too. Remember? I broke out in a cold sweat just thinking about it. But don't worry; you're going to pass with flying colors, the way I did."

I took a pull at my wine. "I'll try not to think about it till the time comes. Do you remember my telling you about the rose garden I'm going to plant next spring? I've started planning it; it keeps my mind off unpleasant subjects. I'd ordered catalogues from all the rose nurseries I'd ever heard of, and I was dipping into them this morning. I threw away a Tiffany catalogue that came in the mail today: who needs jewels when she can have a Reine des Violettes? Or a Louise Odier, or a Zéphirine Drouhin? I'm getting hooked on old roses—they're far and away more beautiful than anything Fabergé ever made, and they smell sublime to boot! And then there are cabbage roses, like Bibi Maizoon. I'll die if I don't have Bibi Maizoon in my garden! She's lusciously blowzy and unbelievably voluptuous, like a Suez belly dancer slightly past her peak. . . . Sorry to go on so," I added apologetically, "but you can see how they take my mind off things I'd rather not think about."

"You make me wish I had room for roses like that," said Janet. "If you need help when you start planting, don't forget me. I miss having a decent-sized garden to play in."

"I'll count on you next spring," I promised. "And don't you forget, I like your aquamarine door; if that woman complains again, you can use me as a reference. Tell her I have sterling credentials; tell her I studied with one of Picasso's pals. You know, you may worry about my being isolated, but there's one thing to be said about living in the country. At least I can paint my front door any damn color I like, without fear of the neighbors insulting me. My nearest neighbor is two miles away as the crow flies, and couldn't tell you what color it is if his life depended on it."

Janet laughed. "I can see there's something to be said for rural solitude," she admitted cheerfully, "though I'm a city girl myself."

CHAPTER 19

Mid-November

THE PHONE RINGS. I answer it. It's the call I've been longing for. The call I've been dreading.

"Kate. Kate, I can't bear this . . . this disagreement of ours any longer. Look, I know I wasn't the best of husbands. And I don't ever mean to downplay your job or your painting. You're terrific at both." His voice is hesitant. "But can't we at least be friends? That's all I ask."

How damnably persuasive that well-loved, sometimes hated, voice is. Why, oh, why, I ask myself, has he managed to catch me at such a weak moment? I force myself to remember the times in Manhattan when Harry's first play was an unexpected smash, the women crawling all over him, the way he enjoyed every moment, the son of a bitch! How can I ever trust him again? I need to defend myself against him. But though I try to whip myself up into a self-protective rage, I'm too bruised, too emotionally sore, to pull it off. I only want Harry, dear Harry, to hold me and tell me everything will be all right.

My silence has been a long one. Too long.

"Kate?" His voice trembles. "Please."

I have never heard him sound like that before. "Yes. Yes, all right. We can be friends," I say. I am afraid to say too much. "How is the play?" A relatively safe subject.

"It's finished. Not just the scene, the whole thing. And it's good. Bloody good."

When he talks about the play, his voice is strong, confident, happy—all the things I'm not. I should be corroded with envy. But oh, my God, it's good to hear his voice. I've been so intent on coping that I haven't allowed myself to miss him.

"I'm so glad," I say. "I knew it would be."

There is a pause. Then he says, "I'm here. In Wilmington, I mean. I hope you don't mind. It isn't because I was sure you'd see me. It's because I thought I would have to dog your footsteps to get a hearing. I can't give up seeing you, Kate." Then, "Just seeing you is all I mean, honest. If that's what you want. May I take you to dinner this evening? I won't ask to spend the night. I promise."

I realize how much I want him to stay, just for comfort; and think in panic, I'll have to tell him. I hadn't thought about it because of our fight. But if he does stay, he'll have to know why . . . why . . . And I haven't taken the AIDS test yet; it's too early. So I can't not tell him. Somehow I'd imagined that he'd never need to know. Besides, I'm a big girl; I can handle this myself. It's strictly my affair. Mine, and that of the police. But I do want so badly to see him.

"That will be super," I say brightly. Too brightly.

"Kate, is something wrong? Something aside from us, I mean? You don't sound like yourself. If something's bothering you, I want to know what it is. I'm your husband, damn it!" Harry is back to normal.

When I speak, to my great relief my voice sounds completely natural; I've had enough time to get it under control.

"Ex-husband, don't forget," I tell him tartly. "Though still first in my heart. For the moment," I add ominously, our private joke.

Harry laughs. I have fooled him.

"At least till after dinner, I hope," he says.

"I think," I answer him, my voice judicious, "though I make no promises, that I can safely say yes to that."

"Splendid. Glad to hear it. Pick you up at seven—will that suit? Dinner at La Chaumière? Or Sal's?"

"Neither," I reply without thinking. I'm not yet ready to display my battered face in public. Suddenly I realize that at the very least I will have to explain that to Harry. "I'm in the mood for a simple supper at home."

"Sure? Thanks to you, I'm in a jubilee mood. I'd love to show you off at the fanciest boîte this burg has to offer."

Wait till you get a good look at me, I think.

"Sure as I'll ever be."

"I must confess it sounds indecently tempting. A fire leaping in the grate and the curtains drawn—the world shut out. We can do the town, such as it is, tomorrow night." Harry is faintly scornful of Wilmington's amenities. "See you at seven. With bells on!"

THE FIRE IS CRACKLING AWAY BY 6:45; I AM INTENT ON PROVING TO myself how capable I am. Though I have decided to let Harry bring in more wood after he gets here, as it is dark, and with my arms full of logs I would be a sitting duck for an attacker; no way to use a gun then. Discretion is the better part of valor.

Harry is ten minutes early. In addition to the security system, my landlord has installed floodlights that automatically turn on at dusk in front and back of the house, so I see his battered pickup truck—the shabbiness of reverse snob appeal, I think fondly—pull into the courtyard near the front door. As he gets out of the truck I open the door and, without thinking, find myself literally falling into his arms. He enfolds me in them. It feels wonderful, like coming home after a long and harrowing journey.

"What a welcome," he says, pleased and surprised by my unexpected demonstrativeness. "Oh, Kate, how I've missed you! Can't we make a pact not to quarrel ever again? It *hurts* so."

"Let's try. It hurt me too," I say, looking up at him.

Looking up is a mistake. I should have kept my face buried in his tweed jacket that smells so comfortingly of peat and woodsmoke and of Harry, dear Harry.

He takes hold of my chin with a surprisingly gentle hand.

"What happened to you?" he asks wonderingly.

"Nothing," I reply, an inane remark.

He inspects my face for what seems at least a year.

"You call this nothing? For God's sake, Kate, who did this? Damn that job of yours!"

"Don't be so silly, darling." The look on his face frightens me, but I manage a shaky laugh. "There's no job in the world less dangerous than drawing faces."

"That's not everything you do. Not by a long shot. Don't pretend it is, Kate. What *happened*?"

It doesn't occur to me to tell him it's none of his business. "It—it had nothing to do with work," I protest. Briefly I contemplate telling him my bruises are the result of an automobile accident, but I decide to bite the bullet and tell the truth. Sooner or later I shall have to. It might as well be now.

"Do you expect me to believe that?" he demands.

"It's the truth, Harry. Oh, Harry, hold me. Please hold me. Tight."

He wraps one long arm around me—only one, as I have taken his left hand and I hold it next to my cheek while I tell him what happened.

"I'm all right now," I finish. "Really I am."

"Jesus. And I wasn't here." It is a cry of agony. "I would have stayed if we hadn't had that argument. It was all because of that play opening in London, that damned idiotic unimportant play."

"Harry, darling, if you'd stayed on that night, nothing would have happened. Then. He would have put off the attack to another time when I was alone."

"If we were still married . . ."

"If my aunt had wheels, she'd be a trolley car," I said. "What's done is done, darling. We're not married."

"He wouldn't have targeted you if you were married." His face is ten years older than it had been ten minutes earlier.

"Who knows whether he would or not? We still don't know how or where he picks his victims. The second woman he raped was married. She was attacked while her husband was away on a business trip to South America for the DuPont Company. None of that matters. But I want you to know that I would have told you, even if you hadn't noticed my face. I mean . . .

there's a new AIDS test I can take, a good one. It's a one-shot deal, and close to a hundred percent accurate. But it doesn't work until at least twenty-eight days have elapsed, so there's no point in my taking it for another two weeks." To my consternation I feel tears running down my cheeks. "I don't want to take it," I wail, despite myself.

Without another word Harry picks me up and carries me into the sitting room. He sits in front of the fire in a big squashy chair that envelops us both in a bear hug.

"Poor little lamb," he says tenderly, settling back in the chair and carrying me with him. "Don't you fret. You'll be all right. I'll take care of you. I'll take care of everything."

Usually I am jealous of my independence and my competence, not to mention my five feet eight inches, but he makes me feel strangely comforted. I'm tired of being brave, I'm tired of coping. I curl up in his lap like a kitten. He is gentleness itself with me, but when I look up at his face, his eyes are bleak.

CHAPTER 20

Mid-November

IT WAS A COUPLE OF DAYS AFTER HARRY'S ARRIVAL. I had just settled myself comfortably on his lap, my head tucked into the convenient hollow between his neck and his shoulder, when the telephone rang.

"Damn!" I said. "It never fails." I picked up the receiver. "Hello? Margot! Hello.—It has? She is? Splendid news, the best! How is she?—Good. Give her a pat for me, will you? I don't know when I can get down to pick her up. Is anyone coming up my way soon?—Oh. Will it be all right if she stays with you for a while, then? It could be till after her whelping, I'm afraid. The case I told you about is pretty tense; I don't know when I'll get time off.—Terrific! It's all set, then. By the way, if one turns out to be a bitch, I'm going to name her Bibi Maizoon.—Quite a name to live up to, isn't it? Talk to you soon. 'Bye.

"That was Margot Stinchcombe," I said unnecessarily to Harry.

"I could tell. Good news about Nourmahal?"

"Pups. Expected very near to Christmas. What a present! I wish I could pick her up. I miss her."

"I'll do it," Harry offered. "Let me bring Nour back for you. She'll be protection."

I was deeply touched. Generally Harry looks upon Nour as an amiable nuisance; and the idea of puppies had not enthralled him.

"No, love. Thank you. But I think in the circumstances it's probably better for her to stay at the kennel. I have no idea what my schedule will be for the next couple of months. And I don't need protection. I intend to be very careful from now on."

"You're not going to stay on the rape squad, are you?" he asked. "They won't make you do that?"

I was annoyed. "They won't *make* me do anything," I informed him coldly. "I want to stay on the squad. I want to get him."

One look at my thundercloud of a face was enough to silence Harry on the subject, for the present at least. Fortunately for all and sundry, the telephone rang again. I answered it.

"Hello. Oh, David. How do?—Right here. Just a sec." I handed it to Harry. "Your agent," I told him unnecessarily.

Harry held me close while he talked, as if to reassure me that I still had the best part of his attention.

"David. What news? I assume there is some, or you wouldn't have called.—Bill Carradine? That's great. I've always liked working with him.—He wants to schedule some auditions starting tomorrow and he wants me there? On the West Coast? Forget it. No can do. I'm here for the foreseeable future."

Agitated squawking emanated from the receiver.

"I said nix. I have other fish to fry. Manhattan for the day, yes. L.A.—the deal's off."

'Stop!' I hissed at him. "You get out there on the first plane, babe, or I'll never speak a word to you again. I kid you not."

He must have realized I meant it because he said, "David? Call you back in a second or so," and rang off.

Before he could utter, I said, "You're going, honey chile. Don't argue, it's a waste of breath. You're going."

"I'm not leaving you. Not till they catch this guy."

His mouth hardened into a thin straight line.

"Oh, yes, you are, because I'm going to toss you out on your elegant ear. This is my house."

"Then I'll hang around outside to make sure you're okay."

"Then *I'll* haul you in for trespass. And stalking."

The absurdity of this exchange made us both start laughing uncontrollably. When I was able to stop, I said, "Look, my love, you have to go. Really. I would have sent you away soon, even if David hadn't called about auditions. I need to be alone for a bit. I need to prove myself to myself."

Harry tilted my chin so he could look deep into my eyes.

"But will you be all right? Promise me to be careful. And will you call me back again?"

"I'll be careful. I don't intend to get hurt like that a second time. Ever. And yes, I'll call you back. You know that without my telling you."

"Soon?" Harry persisted, still holding my eyes with his own.

"Very soon. I'll miss you like hell. But you have to go away for a while; there's no help for it. So fly out to L.A. to meet Bill Carradine. Get the auditions over with, and then come back to me."

"Will do," he promised, trailing a gentle finger along the curve of my cheek. My bones began to melt. Lucky, I thought to myself, that he didn't choose that moment to renew the argument: without a doubt he would have won.

I HAD DASHED BACK FROM RUNNING SEVERAL LUNCHTIME ERRANDS JUST in time to make a meeting of the Rape Task Force, during which Jacko Benson, Buck Gallagher, Tim Mundy, Arch Larrabee, Lieutenant Flowerdew, and I were going over the lists which the women attacked by the serial rapist had given us. I had finished drawing up mine, and we were comparing it with the others. The one for Wendy Monroe, the woman who was killed the night I was attacked, had, like Lila Harrison's list, been compiled for us by her friends and family. Jacko and Tim had phoned the women involved in attacks and asked them to update their lists again, after the two most recent assaults. It was the first time we had all worked together since I had been raped, and the men were treating me as if I were made of some incredibly fragile substance that might crack without warning, a fact which I found both touching and mildly irritating.

"What about the tape Janet Davies brought in the other day?" I asked Rosebud. "I was hoping it might provide a lead of some kind. I wasn't surprised that neither of us recognized the voice on the tape as the rapist's, because we were both under a lot of stress and we couldn't recall anything especially distinctive about his voice, but I thought it might help some other way. Any luck?"

"No dice," he replied. "We ran down all the calls made to her phone that day, and the anonymous caller turned out to be a wise guy who had dialed a wrong number. We checked him out, but he had an alibi for the night she was attacked."

While we were all discussing the case, I was doodling idly on my pad. I had drawn the face of the serial rapist as I remembered it when he burst into my kitchen so often that it had become second nature. Half the time I didn't even realize I was doing it. And that was good, because the reason I kept sketching it was in hopes that some feature I had not so far recollected would leap out of my unconscious, the way it sometimes has for a witness of a crime with whom I've been working.

But no matter how often, how automatically, I scribbled the face of my assailant on the pad, it always looked the same. And yet...I glanced down at the latest rendition...and yet, it wasn't quite right. Something was missing. I knew there was something lacking, but what? Light brown skin, dark kinky hair combed out into an Afro, face with a slightly squared jaw. Nothing unusual there, many men have a face that shape. Eyes wide, staring because of the sudden light. Hard to tell if they were anything out of the ordinary. Nose—nothing out of the way, nothing to spot him by. Not thin, not wide, nostrils flared but not to excess; a nose you sometimes see on a white face, sometimes on a black face, and think nothing about either way. Not especially handsome, not ugly, just a nose. Unexceptional, I thought despairingly, even to me, whose business it is to notice these things and discern minute differences in them.

I tore off the sheet of paper and crumpled it up, and a moment later found I'd begun again on another sketch which was in no material way different from any of the others I had made. As we talked I drew face after face, every one the same, until the floor around my feet was littered with screwed-up scraps of paper. Suddenly I noticed something—not on a sketch, something on one of the lists. Lila Harrison's list.

"Lila Harrison had her hair done at Primavera," I exclaimed, pointing with my forefinger to a line on the list.

"Yeah, that's right," said Arch. "Seems she charged it on her Visa card, and it didn't show up on the bill till now. That's why her family didn't let us know about it earlier."

"Do they know if she'd been there before?"

"They can't remember. They said she hadn't charged it on her card before, at least not in the past year or so, or they would have noticed when they went over her papers. But of course she could have paid cash."

"Janet and I both go to Primavera," I said thoughtfully. "And I seem to remember that several of the other women have, too. What about Wendy Monroe?"

Buck scanned the list that pertained to her. "No. Don't see it. There's no mention of a hairdresser in her case."

"Talk to her family and find out," I told him. "We'd better check all the lists to see if Primavera's on any of them. . . . Hey! Haven't we done that before?"

"Old age getting to you?" asked Jacko, with a wicked gleam in his eye. "Tsk, tsk, Kate, losing it already? We did that months ago."

Silently I thanked God that Jacko had stopped treating me like eggshell porcelain, apt to shatter at a touch; and brusquely told him, "Kindly show some respect for your elders, boyo."

"Yes, ma'am." He saluted me smartly; then, dropping the pose, said, "Several of the women reported having their hair done at Primavera, but it was less than half the victims, so we dropped it off the suspicious list."

"Primavera's out of the running, then." I sighed. "Damn and blast! For a moment I thought I had hold of something. Because there is something. Something in my mind about Primavera, now that the name has come up, and I'm damned if I can remember what it is."

Back we went to our lists.

"What about shoe repair?" Tim Mundy suggested. "A lot of

these women used Schubert's on Ninth Street in Wilmington. So did Lila Harrison and Wendy Monroe. I know we checked Schubert's out early on, with no concrete results, but it might be worth taking another look."

Rosebud said slowly, "That's not a bad idea. In fact, we'd better check all the names on these lists again, using Kate's updated sketch. Jacko can begin work on it after the meeting."

Jacko groaned. "Give me a break, Lieutenant! I've talked to most of the list three, four times already. Can't you send somebody else? What about Buck?" Glancing at Buck Gallagher's bulk, he added wickedly, "A little exercise wouldn't hurt him."

"It's your baby, Jacko," said Rosebud imperturbably. "You have such a winning personality that I'm sure they'll be delighted to see you again. I know it feels like you're raking over dead coals, but it's practically all we've got to go on. Still no prints, the creep's no dummy. Any perp who isn't a cretin wears gloves nowadays. Going by what Janet Davies told us the evening Kate was attacked, it's possible he rides a motorcycle, but we can't be sure. The weather had been dry for a week or so beforehand and we couldn't find any tire prints near the house. So that's the lot."

"Hey, wait a minute." This from Buck. "We got the DNA analysis."

"How often do I have to tell you? The DNA analysis is great, once we have a suspect in hand," Rosebud said. "When we get hold of the guy, we're golden. But until we do, his DNA is less than no use. If we had a DNA data bank for comparison, and if a sample of his DNA was already on deposit, then we'd be headed down the home stretch. But the trouble is, that's not the case. So at the moment we might just as well be back in the bad old days before DNA was discovered. Which means that right now the best we can do is what we've always done in a pinch. Dogged perseverance will do the trick. If we get lucky, that is."

"What about the seed angle?" I inquired. "Any found at my place, or at Wendy Monroe's? I won't even ask if we've heard from the USDA yet about the seeds from Lila Harrison's apartment."

"How wise," answered Rosebud. "Since we haven't. And no, the techs haven't turned up anything more along those lines. They found a couple of objects that they thought might be seeds, but George Layard looked at them and said ixnay. So who knows? The seeds may be a red herring that will just throw us off the scent.

"Okay, meeting over. Off you go to the salt mines, Jacko, my lad."

Jacko pulled a face that made him look like a kewpie doll, but kept his mouth shut.

"To hear is to obey," I said. "Come on, Jacko. The sooner we get going, the sooner we'll get the agony over with." I picked up my copy of the master list and headed for the door.

"Hold it a moment, Kate. Before you go, I need to have a word with you," said Rosebud.

"Okay. Fine," I responded, but I was a trifle uneasy. He was looking altogether too grave to suit me. "See you in a trice, Jacko."

We walked together from the conference room to Rosebud's office, where he settled himself at his desk and motioned me to a chair opposite.

"What's the idea of going with Jacko?" he asked.

The question startled me, but I answered him readily enough.

"We made the rounds together before, and I figure that on this go-round I might see something or someone that will jog my memory."

"That's fine, but I have to tell you you're going as a civilian."

"A civilian? What the hell do you mean?" I was angry and bewildered.

"I mean you're off this case. It's okay for you to hear some of the evidence, and you can go with Jacko to see if you happen to recognize someone in any of those places, but that's it. You're not going as a policewoman. You'll have the same input with the case any other rape victim would have. We'll have to borrow another artist when we need sketches, but that's unlikely to be a problem unless his next victim is lucky like you, and he's interrupted." His voice was grim.

After the first sentence, I scarcely noticed what he said.

"Off the case? Come on, Lieutenant, this case is important to me, and I'm valuable to the investigation. Why would you pull me off it? You promised me . . ."

To my fury I heard my voice tremble.

"You know why, Kate," he told me patiently. "When we catch the son of a bitch, we don't want some smart-ass defense lawyer right out of law school saying the evidence was tainted. I wasn't lying to you in the hospital when I told you you could stay on; I wouldn't do that. But I've just discussed it with the AG, and he says it's too risky to keep you on. I'm sorry. I would have told you before the meeting, but you were out when I got back, so I didn't have a chance."

"But I wouldn't . . ."

"I know you wouldn't, but that has nothing to do with what I'm talking about. When we catch him, you want the conviction to stick, don't you?"

I nodded reluctantly. "But you need me, Lieutenant. You know you need me to catch him."

"I didn't say we weren't going to use all the information you can give us. Some of it is sure to help us get him. That sketch of yours is a gem. I only mean that officially you're off the case."

"But I want to be the one to catch him. Come on, Lieutenant!" I wailed. "Don't do this to me. It isn't fair."

Even as I spoke, I was appalled at myself. I sounded and felt about seven years old. I knew he was right, but I didn't give a damn. I wanted to be the one to catch the little creep, no matter what.

Rosebud gave me a long, level, compassionate look—the kind an understanding father might give his naughty child—and I was silent.

"I know it's hard for you, Kate," he said, "but once we catch him, we have to make sure he remains caught. You see that, don't you?"

I nodded my head sullenly. "Okay, sir," I said. "I'll be a good little girl." And at the time I really meant it.

CHAPTER 21

Late November

THOUGH IT IS NOT YET THANKSGIVING WEEK, MANY OF THE STORES HAVE already been decorated for Christmas; each year it seems as if the season gets an earlier start. The Watcher finds himself both excited and disturbed by the color red that predominates in the windows and advertisements. Scarlet ribbons, bright red bells, crimson-clad Santas—they all remind him of the blood. Berries on holly wreaths look like the droplets of blood that fell from his knife blade; flaring scarlet bows are the splashes of blood landing on bedclothes, walls, floor.

For several days the weather has been clear and sharp and bitterly cold, unexpectedly so for this time of year in Delaware. The stalking season is over. But this year he is reluctant for it to end. Previously the winter was a restful time, a time to plan, a time to add to his list of prospects, a quiescent period; and until now he has been content for it to be that way. But now he does not want to wait until spring. So long. Too long. Months and months away. Far, far away. Like Mother. He cannot wait that long. He won't wait. Besides, this winter he won't be cold. When he thinks about all the warm, warm blood, released from their veins in a pungent shower just for him, he can feel his own blood coursing hot through his body.

Not even winter yet. Not even Thanksgiving. He thinks for

a moment. Thanksgiving. He remembers something he has overheard. The perfect one! He won't have to wait long. And it should be a snap. Usually he doesn't like things too easy, but how can he turn down something really good when it comes his way? Like this one.

Betsy Abbott cast a practiced eye around the barn. All the stalls were mucked out, and their occupants well brushed. Horses fed, clean water, full hay nets. There was little left to do before she drove to meet Nick for dinner down in Delaware but get herself ready for her date.

As she left the stable yard and headed toward the small cottage which constituted part of her salary, she caught sight of Mrs. Penfield getting into her car, and waved to her.

"You're sure you'll be all right here by yourself, Betsy?" her employer asked, a hand on the door handle of the Mercedes.

God, Betsy thought with mild annoyance, as if she hadn't already reassured the Penfields fifty times! That was the trouble with working for your parents' friends. They felt responsible for you. Besides, what would happen if she told Mrs. Penfield no, she wouldn't be all right? Their plans were already made; there was nothing they could do about it at this late date. Of course she was going to be all right! Betsy smiled, thinking about Nick Rector. She hadn't seen him since October, when he had come home for the weekend from the University of Virginia.

It was Nick's first year in college, after graduating from the Episcopal High School in Alexandria. His father had succeeded in keeping his nose firmly fastened to the academic grindstone by threatening to cut off his allowance if he didn't stay down there and work hard for the six weeks remaining before Thanksgiving; and since Betsy's agreement with the Penfields did not allow her many weekends off, they had not seen each other since his last weekend home. He was driving up to Pennsylvania from Charlottesville that afternoon, and they had made a date to meet for dinner in Centreville down in Delaware, the best place nearby to get a meal. The servants in the Penfields' house all had the long holiday weekend off, so no one would know if Nick came back with her for the night. If he did, she thought with a shiver of anticipation, it would be the first time. The first time for her with Nick, the first time for her ever. It gave her a funny feeling, a feeling of being really grown-up for the first time in her life. Her own job, her own place, her own man, she told herself.

"I'll be just fine, thanks," she said, giving Mrs. Penfield a big smile.

"I do feel badly, Betsy, about your spending the Thanksgiving weekend all by yourself."

"It's going to be wonderful," Betsy reassured her. "I'll have Thanksgiving dinner with the Rectors, and you said I could hunt Ratty tomorrow. I'm really excited about it."

Ratcatcher was Mrs. Penfield's big bay gelding, a dream over fences; Betsy was looking forward to hunting him. Maybe, she thought with sudden caution, a night with Nick would have to wait. She would need to be up bright and early to groom her mount and hack over to the meet of Mr. Stewart's Cheshire Hounds, more than half an hour away.

It had not been easy for Betsy to talk her parents into allowing her a year off before starting college so she could work with horses; it was only the fact that no college they considered socially acceptable would take their daughter that had persuaded them, combined with a job offer by friends who lived in southern Pennsylvania horse country and kept a stable of hunters. The Penfields had good horses and easy manners; and so far, except for her distance from Nick, Betsy was greatly enjoying her new life. She had attended the Foxcroft School near Middleburg, Virginia, where life was both horsy and Spartan, and horses were her first love. But Nick Rector was her second; and this autumn, worried about the girls he was bound to meet at college, she had been regretting her indifferent scholarship, which had meant that she could not join him in Charlottesville. His frequent and passionate telephone calls to the Penfields' cottage had reassured her, however, and she could not wait for their forthcoming meeting.

As Mrs. Penfield drove away, Betsy went into the barn to lock the dogs in an empty stall and check that everything was set before taking a shower and dressing for her date: Dusk had begun to fall, and she wanted time to make sure that she looked casual but terrific for Nick. It would take less than fifteen minutes to finish up her stable work, and half an hour to drive to Buckley's Tavern, so she could allow herself almost an hour to bathe and dress. She was planning to wear jeans, but she hadn't yet decided what to do with her hair, and she had some new eye glitter, very glam, that she wanted to play around with; plus some weird but interesting nail stuff she was sure Nick would go for. When she saw him for the first time in six weeks, Betsy definitely did not want to look as if she'd just come in from mucking out stalls.

THE WATCHER HAS USED HIS MOTORCYCLE AGAIN. He likes to ride it, and using it makes everything so flexible. He can hide it easily and take it along country lanes that a car would have difficulty in negotiating. The cold weather does not bother him. The heat in his blood keeps him warm, so warm that it is a relief to feel the cool air against his body. A cycle is, he thinks, the perfect vehicle for what he wants to do.

He had thought of waiting till later in the holiday weekend— Friday, say, because it would be tricky to catch her in on Thanksgiving Day. He does not know what her plans are; she will either go out for dinner or have friends in, he supposes. Besides, it would be difficult for him to get away on Thanksgiving. But waiting has become more and more unendurable. His blood is up. He is on fire. It is more dangerous to attack in the daytime when his victim is awake, but more exciting, too. He enjoys the risk now; as he becomes more expert in his hunting, it takes more risk to make the game thrilling.

And this one is young. He is finding that he prefers them young. The older women he has attacked are like his mother as she is now, but he has chosen the young ones because they remind him of what she used to be like. Good-looking and capable and confident. Too confident, too sure of herself. That's why she was able to leave him, him and his father. That's why the young ones live alone. Because they're too sure of themselves.

It's really their fault that they get raped. If they didn't live alone, if they were with their families, if they were married, dependent on someone, then they would be safe. That girl he's headed for now—if she didn't live alone in that cottage, if she had someone there with her, she would be protected. Like that female cop, the one he'll go back to later. Women shouldn't be cops. Women shouldn't have jobs. Women should stay at home, have babies, take care of their kids, like his mother should have taken care of him. His wife has a job, but they don't have any kids; and if he told her to quit, she'd drop it in a minute. She does what he tells her.

He likes to pick the confident ones, teach them they're not as strong as they think, teach them he's the one who's strong.

The darkness is gathering in a somber cloud over the little knoll in the woods near the Penfields' place that he has chosen as a vantage point, but he is able to see Mrs. Penfield's Mercedes station wagon turn onto the road and head east toward Philadelphia. The cops will never figure this one out, he thinks, grinning to himself. He spotted the girl in Helen's store; he could sniff her out a mile away. But it was last week at work, while Mrs. Penfield was in getting herself dolled up for a dinner party, that he overheard her tell a friend they would all be away for four days, even the servants. All except the girl. It was meant, he thinks. It has all fallen into place for him. The knife takes care of its own. Lovingly he pats the pocket in which it reposes. The knife is giving him all night long, plenty of time to do whatever he wants to do.

In the distance he sees the lights in her cottage. He has reconnoitered the place before, so he knows the layout. At first it had seemed almost hopeless, because there are always so many people around the place. But that hadn't stopped him. He had kept her in mind anyway. He had known his time would come. The knife wouldn't let him down.

When he gets to the cottage, he stops beside one of the windows and flattens himself against the wall before he looks in, so no one inside will be likely to see him. He does not want her to have time to telephone for help, even though they are so far out in the sticks that help would arrive too late to do her any good. The window looks into the bedroom. He just catches a glimpse of his quarry as she disappears though a doorway—the entrance to the bathroom, he realizes, from his knowledge of the building's layout, acquired from a previous nocturnal visit. One of the dogs, a bluetick hound, had spotted him then. But to his surprise and relief, instead of barking an alarm it had padded over and nudged his hand to be patted. On a later tour of surveillance, he learned that at night the dogs are closed up in an empty stall in the barn. So he is not afraid Betsy will be warned by them.

He heads toward the door of the cottage.

SOMETHING'S NOT RIGHT. I don't know what it is. I just feel there's something wrong. And that isn't like me. I may be a painter, but I'm notoriously lacking in imagination. Maybe that's why my pictures don't sell. But Eugène told me I had the right kind of imagination, that I was *féroce,* that I was going to be good someday because I had the necessary fire.

"A real painter has a fierce imagination. He is not neurasthenic. He is not timid or, God save us, *dainty,*" he used to say, in a scathing dismissal of the work that hung in two-thirds of the Paris galleries. "He does not dream of fairies and moonbeams. Emotionally and stylistically, Katy, you are one of the elect."

So it bothers me that I'm feeling...nervous? Antsy? As though a goose is walking over my grave. That's what it feels like. Premonitory. To my surprise I feel the hairs rising on the back of my neck. This is stupid, I tell myself. I'm just upset because Rosebud took me off the case, the bastard. I'm feeling blue because Harry is still in L.A. and it's the day before Thanksgiving, and even though I'm invited to gobble turkey with Janet and Tom tomorrow, there's always an empty feel about the beginning of a holiday when you're alone. That's all it is. But I check the doors and the downstairs windows anyway as the light outside grows dull and fades out of the sky, and before I make myself a drink I set the security system, a thing I don't usually do until I go up to bed.

It doesn't help. The feeling doesn't go away, even after the drink, even after I turn up the heat and put on another sweater.

SOFTLY HE TRIES THE DOORKNOB. The door of the cottage is un-locked. Glee bubbles up inside the Watcher, threatening to spill over in sound, but he is able to tamp it down. In a little while it won't matter how much noise he makes, but right now it is too soon. Reverently he touches the knife, his talisman, at rest in his pocket. The knife has promised him. The knife will make sure everything works the way it should. The knife. His knife. He cannot resist taking it out to look at it. It opens with a barely audible *snick*.

Silently he moves into the bedroom from the sitting room. She has left the bathroom door ajar, and he can hear the water from the showerhead splash on the bottom of the tub. That is good, he thinks. It should cover any noise he may make. As he passes by the bureau he notices a spray bottle of Ravie perfume, with its distinctive scarlet-and-gold label. He is drawn toward it irresistibly. It evokes a scene between his parents when he was small, his father holding the red-and-gold bottle.

"Give it back, Tonio!" his mother screams, lunging at his father, her scarlet-nailed fingers clutching at the scarlet flask.

"Where did you get this from? Whore!" shouts his father, his voice deepened by a passion of anger. "Your lover, he give it to you. Didn't he? Didn't he? No way you could afford it yourself, not on your salary. A whole ounce of this perfume. I read the papers, I see the advertisements, I know what it costs. Whore!" Spittle flies from his mouth as he screams at her.

"Just give it back to me! It's none of your business where it came from. You poor cheap little wop barber. You can't afford to get it for me. You can't even afford Evening in Paris from the local dime store."

He cowers in the doorway. His parents do not notice his presence. His father dodges one reaching red-tipped claw, but the other succeeds in raking his cheek. It leaves four red tracks on the skin, as though her nails are bleeding.

Enraged, his father lifts the bottle high above his head and smashes it on the linoleum floor. His mother gives a shriek of pure animal fury at the sight of her spilled perfume. A moment later a heavy cloud of cloying scent envelops and chokes him. The smell of lilies and jasmine and hyacinths suffocates him. He faints.

Finished with remembering, the Watcher stops in front of the bureau and picks up the bottle. The flask is smooth and rounded, heavy and warm and seductive in his hand. With one eye on the bathroom door, he sniffs greedily at the atomizer top. The heavy perfume floods his senses, floods his eyes with a crimson fog. He presses down on the top and inhales, keeps pressing and spraying until the room reeks of hyacinths and lilies and jasmine. But within his perfumed haze he hears the water flow in the bathroom stop, and instantly he sets down the bottle and pads on his sneakered feet over to the tall wardrobe that stands beside the bathroom door. He opens one of its doors wide and steps into it, pulling the door partly closed for concealment.

A moment later Betsy, wrapped in a towel, passes through the doorway into the room. Startled, she halts and snuffs at the air like a woodland creature, puzzled at the strength of the perfume smell. She shrugs and goes over to the wardrobe.

As she pulls the door open, he leaps out at her, a nightmare made manifest. Surprise takes her by the throat, and at first she can make no sound. Then she is able to scream, and her screams echo around the room, shrilling out into the bitter air, but it is only the dogs and the horses in the nearby barn who hear her. She struggles fiercely and manages to break away from her assailant. She is young and active, and she nearly makes it out of the cottage. But he catches up with her at the front door. He is angry, very angry, and the red miasma evoked by the heavy cloud of scent still wreathes his brain. The Watcher had thought he would have all night to do what he has come to do. But it doesn't take long. It doesn't take long at all.

CHAPTER 22

Late November

TWO DAYS AFTER THANKSGIVING JACKO AND I WERE BACK IN MY OFFICE, going over the crumbs elicited from the people he had just interviewed for the umpteenth time. As Rosebud had decreed, I had obediently stayed in the background during our visits.

"Nothing," I declared morosely. I was depressed. "We haven't got a damn thing more than we had before we went out."

"You didn't see nobody that looked like the guy who attacked you?" asked Jacko. His cowlick stood on end from the innumerable times he had run his hand through his hair in frustration at our lack of progress.

"Not so far as I can remember. We need help with this. We need some kind of lead—nothing to do with these stupid lists—a lead that will fit in with what we already have. Speaking of which, any word yet from the seedgrowers?"

"Nyet."

"Slowpokes," I growled.

"Blame the seeds, not the USDA. Remember," Jacko counseled, "me dear ould grandmither's saying about what happens when you watch a pot."

"Your dear old grandmother's mustache," I snarled. "There's something connected with this case that's roiling around in my brain, something I can't quite recollect, and it's driving me round the bend! I know it's lurking somewhere within my skull, but I just can't manage to winkle it out."

I took my head between the palms of my hands and shook it, with no appreciable result.

Jacko picked up a couple of those repetitive little sketches I had been drawing ad nauseam. By that time I could have done them in my sleep. Maybe I had, for all I knew. He held one close to my eyes.

"Take a good look at it, Kate," he ordered me. "C'mon, c'mon. Concentrate."

I concentrated. Squarish face, nose with broad flaring nostrils, staring inimical eyes, hair in a moderate Afro.

"It's no damn good," I wailed. "He doesn't look like anyone else I've ever seen. Let's go over the lists again."

We went over the lists again.

"Only half the women remember getting their hair done at Primavera at some point," I said. "But Primavera—that word does something to me when I see it, when I hear it. I know in my gut that there's a connection of some kind. There has to be, to make me feel that way."

"Maybe you need to stop thinking so hard about this case," said Jacko. "I mean, it's probably at the point where if you think about anything long enough, it seems like it's got some connection with the rapist. Besides, it's not good for you to overdo it. The doc said—"

"Oh, for God's sake!" I was angry now. "Stop throwing that psychological claptrap at me, about which, I might add, you know next to nothing. I'm sick and tired of you and Tim and Arch and Rosebud and the doctors all thinking you know better than I do how I feel, how I'm reacting. I'm feeling fine. I couldn't feel better. I just want to catch the son of a bitch."

Jacko eyed me nervously and for the moment—no fool, that boy—wisely kept his trap shut to give me time to calm down. He had been fiddling with one of my discarded sketches; and now, to while away the time, he picked up a pencil and began doodling on it, whistling tunelessly. First a goatee worthy of Satan himself appeared, then a pair of curling mustachios—the kind worn by the stage villain in a Victorian melodrama—then a pair of pointed satyr's ears peeping out from behind the bushy curls.

My heart stopped. My brain began to spin in double time, like a roulette wheel that has just been set going by the croupier, and stopped on a forgotten detail.

"Jesus!" I said.

I felt as though the world had halted in its tracks. Memory had suddenly and unexpectedly assumed a brilliant clarity, a miniaturist's perfection of detail. Is this what happens when you die? I wondered. Things you had forgotten, things you didn't remember ever having seen or thought, flashing into mind?

"What's with you, Kate? You seen a ghost or something? You look weird."

"I know," I said.

For a moment neither of us spoke.

Then I said again, "I *know*. What I mean is, I'm almost sure I know who the rapist is."

"You're kiddin' me!"

"You're the one who jogged my memory, Jacko, you and that silly little sketch of yours."

"Now I know you're kiddin' me. It's your sketch."

"But the embellishments are yours. His ears."

"Those are the rapist's ears?" said Jacko, bewildered. "But those are, like, animal ears. Besides, you said they were covered up by his Afro. So did the other victims. None of the sketches had ears. Nobody saw his ears."

"I did," I said. "I did, but I forgot. Until now. His hair must be a wig, because I saw it shift on his head. And when it shifted, I saw one of his ears. I remember now. It was lobeless. That's an uncommon feature. That must be why he makes a point of covering them."

"Hey, that's great!" Jacko exclaimed. "That's going to be a real help. Try a sketch of him with ears like that, why don't you?"

I had already begun on one, and as I roughed out the shape of the rapist's ears with rapid strokes I explained, "That isn't all. I think I know his identity."

Jacko sat staring at the new sketch with his mouth open.

"How come?" he asked me finally.

"I think it's Alessandro. The man who owns Primavera. That way it all fits in."

Stunned silence. Then he said, "Come off it, Kate. I saw him the first time we checked out the lists. He isn't black."

"He doesn't have to be. With all the cosmetic makeovers he's done, he has the wherewithal lying all over the place." Now I was working on another sketch. "If he wore pads in his cheeks—take them out—pads in his nostrils to flatten and broaden them—get rid of them—false bushy eyebrows that Janet described as looking like caterpillars—Afro wig—something to darken his skin—see?" I waved the finished drawing under Jacko's nose. "That one looks a lot like Alessandro, *n'est-ce-pas*?"

"You can't be sure." But his voice was uncertain.

"Oh, dear God," I said suddenly, my voice desolate. "I am sure. But I don't see what the hell we can do about it. There's no way this identification is going to get us a sample of his blood to test for DNA."

We worked on the lists in silence for a while until I said angrily, "This is making me nuts!" I felt like tearing out my hair and distributing it around my office in copious handfuls. "I know it's Alessandro. I *know* it is. It has to be. I feel it in my bones."

"Whatever you say, Kate." Jacko was being infuriatingly polite.

"Stop humoring me, damn it! I can tell what you're thinking. 'Poor dumb broad, she has a bee in her bonnet, but she mustn't be upset at any cost. The doctor said it might retard her recovery.' If you don't agree with me, just say so. I can get my teeth into that."

"Okay. You asked for it, so don't complain." Thank God Jacko was back to being his normal abrasive self. "You're too personally involved in this case to trust your bones. Your so-called intuition has been screwed up by what you went through. It would be different if all the women who were raped had gone to this guy's hair house, but they didn't. So it isn't Alessandro. There must be at least one black guy in this burg with lobeless ears."

"Wait a sec," I interrupted. "Let's take a look at some of the other places on the lists. Maybe one of them will dovetail."

"Whaddaya mean?" Jacko was puzzled.

"I mean maybe somehow the creep Alessandro—I *know* he's the creep—made contact with some of the women another way."

Jacko cogitated visibly for a moment. "Like maybe he owns a wig shop out at one of the malls?" he ventured.

"Yes. Something like that. And you've done it again, Jacko, my pet! There's a maggot at the back of my brain trying to get out. . . . Oh, blast! My mind has turned to mush. Give me the master list."

I scanned it. "Liquor stores, supermarkets, drugstores. Lord and Taylor—nothing there, too big—wait! I think I've got it! DelecTable!" I began to flip rapidly through the pages. "I bet that's it. Let me check."

"What the hell is DelecTable? Oh, that fancy deli out in Greenville where some of them have shopped. What's so special about it?"

"I just remembered. I'm pretty sure while I was getting my hair done one time, I overheard someone at Primavera mention that Alessandro's wife owns DelecTable. What a nitwit I am not to have remembered that before!"

"You're nuts," said Jacko, looking at the sheets of paper. "It says here that Alessandro's last name is Volturo, and the owner of DelecTable—where the hell is it?—wait, I got it—is Helen Carruthers."

"So what? She must have kept her maiden name for business. Come on, Jacko! Give me a hand."

Grumbling loudly, Jacko helped me update the list of the women who said they had shopped at DelecTable, and we compared it with the Primavera list.

"They overlap!" I said after we had examined them.

"Big deal," Jacko replied. "Don't get yourself all worked up over it. Remember? We already compared lists of all the places the women had gone, and there was a lot of overlap."

"But don't you see? Every woman who's been attacked so far has either been at Primavera or DelecTable, or both."

"That happened with the Blue Streak Gallery and—what's

that florist called?—Bloomsberry. There was a victim overlap with the Kitchen Sink and L Boutique, too. And I know there were a couple of others."

Jacko could be depressingly dense, I thought.

"Let me explain it to you in words of one syllable," I said, rather unfairly since he didn't yet know all the facts. "Alessandro could very easily have spotted potential victims at DelecTable through his wife. I've shopped at DelecTable. They keep a book, which they make a point of asking you to sign with your address so they can send out notices of tastings and special sales. If he picked someone out there, he didn't have to follow her home, or even look her up in the telephone directory. All he needed was access to that book, which he's certain to have." Except for me, I thought, but I wasn't about to remind Jacko of that. Since my mailing address is a post office box, the rapist would have had to follow me. "Look, Jacko, it isn't surprising that no one picked up on the match. Even if we had realized Alessandro and Helen Carruthers were married, we probably wouldn't have attached any special importance to the Primavera-DelecTable connection, because we thought the rapist was black. But now. . . And maybe the seeds will tie in, when we find out what kind they are. I'm pretty sure I've seen growing kits for exotic herbs and vegetables there. You know the kind—five seeds and a soil-filled pot for fifteen dollars."

Jacko sat frowning for a moment. Then he grinned at me and said, "Okay, Kate, you've got me convinced. But I still don't think we have enough to convince a judge. There's not much we can do about it unless this guy makes a move."

"Agreed," I said. "But if he's our creep he's going to make a move, and soon. Don't forget he's been stepping up the pace. I think something is driving him. I think the attacks are going to keep coming closer and closer together now."

"Jesus H. Christ!" Jacko said. "That's a real scary scenario."

"You're damned right it is. I'm going to talk to Rosebud about it. I think we need to keep a constant watch on him from now on, and I need you to back me up."

There was a silence. Then, "Okay, babes," Jacko said with a sigh. "If you say so."

"You're a good kid," I told him. "Don't worry, I'll do all the talking. You can be strong and silent in the background."

I knocked on the door to Rosebud's office, and when he called out, "Come in," we marched inside. Jacko's a game lad, but there was a hangdog look about him.

"We think we've got hold of something, Lieutenant," I told Rosebud, and gave him the gist of the argument. "So," I finished, "it's imperative we put a tail on Alessandro right now. That way, when he makes his next move, we can pick him up before he gets a chance to kill again."

Nothing happened. He just sat there, looking at us. Not a word.

"Well?" I demanded impatiently.

"And what," he asked, "has young Galahad to say to all this?"

"Huh?" said Jacko.

"You, Jacko. What do you think of Kate's theory?"

"I think . . . I think it has merit, sir," Jacko said loyally, backing me up.

"Yes. It has merit. It's a possibility, Kate. But only a possibility. You're certain about the ears?"

"Absolutely, Lieutenant."

"But the problem, Kate, is that you didn't remember them right away. It could be argued that you remembered them very much after the fact. And they're the only solid proof there is for your theory."

I stood very straight and bit my lip to keep from . . . to keep calm.

"Does that mean you don't believe me, Lieutenant?" I asked him. To my utter rage I heard my voice shake.

He said, his voice disarmingly gentle, "Kate, my dear, I believe that you believe that's what you saw. You've bounced back amazingly from what happened to you, but you've got to remember that you've been through a great deal, perhaps more than you realize."

"I see," I said coldly.

"I hope you do. I hope you understand what I am trying so clumsily to say. You're a wonder, Kate, you're a bloody marvel, but the experience is bound to have had some effect on you.

And, as usual, we're shorthanded. We simply don't have the time or the manpower to tail someone unless we're sure he's our rapist."

"Yes. I see why you pulled me off the case. That business about tainted evidence was just an excuse. Your real reason is because you don't trust me."

"For Christ's sake, Kate!"

I fled his office and took refuge in the ladies' room until I got hold of myself. I was damned if I was going to let them see me cry.

SEVERAL HOURS LATER I WAS PASSING LIEUTENANT FLOWERDEW'S OFFICE, and since the door was ajar, I heard a phrase that stopped me in my tracks.

"Sure sounds like our creep." The voice was Buck Gallagher's.

I pressed myself against the wall and listened; luckily no one was in sight. I suppose I should have been ashamed, but I rationalized my action by telling myself that we would catch the little bastard a lot faster if I knew everything that was going on. Besides, I was determined to be in on the investigation some way, no matter what Rosebud said. I had a right to be involved.

"I think so, too. The trouble is, the police up in Pennsylvania are playing it close to the chest. I wouldn't have heard about the case if a *News Journal* reporter who lives up there hadn't gotten wind of it and called me for information."

"What's with the Chester County cops?" Buck wanted to know.

"It's a big deal for them, and I guess they want to keep the glory for themselves. You know, society crime wave like the John du Pont thing, or those two preppie kids up in New York. There'll be a lot of publicity once the story gets out. The reason they gave me for not sharing information was they were afraid of leaks. In a pig's eye." I could tell from Rosebud's voice that he was furious. "They just want to hog the spotlight for themselves when they catch the perp. *If* they catch him. As far as I'm concerned, they can have all the credit they want. I just want him locked up. I've seen too much of what he can do."

"So the Chester County cops wouldn't tell you anything?"

"No. The little I learned I got from the reporter, Hank Grimes—you know him, tall lanky guy with blond hair. It happened the day before Thanksgiving. Her boyfriend was the one who found her, and he went into shock. Drove to the nearest neighbors and broke down on their doorstep. They couldn't understand what had happened from him, so they went over to the scene before they called the police. They told Hank Grimes's landlady what they had seen and she told him. You know how it goes. But from what Hank heard, I'd swear it was our creep. Just a little earlier in the evening than the attack on Kate had been, apparently. The kid was supposed to meet her boyfriend for dinner and didn't show up. And what he did to her . . . it sounds like Lila Harrison and Wendy Monroe. It made me sick to hear about it. I had to take Kate off the case, but you know, after her attack I'm not so sure now about my own objectivity."

I heard the scuffling noises of chairs being pushed back, and decided that discretion dictated a swift retreat to my office. Back at my desk I thought long and hard about what I had overheard. The day before Thanksgiving! The day I had experienced that strange feeling of nervousness. It had been Wednesday evening. I was sure of it; and equally sure I had never felt that way before. I was a pragmatist, but it made me wonder if it had been a premonitory feeling, a feeling the creep was up to his old tricks again. One thing was certain: I couldn't tell Rosebud about it. He'd think I was nuts, as well he might.

But leaving all that aside, I was certain Alessandro was the creep. The more I thought about those ears of his, the surer I was about him. And I was very angry at Rosebud. He had no right to keep me off the case. He should have taken my theory seriously, instead of brushing it off as he had. He should have put a tail on Alessandro. I was fed up with working on what amounted to petty cash—convenience-store holdups, car thefts, minor burglaries—when my case, the jackpot, wasn't being handled the way it ought.

After brooding for a while about the iniquities of life and more particularly those of Rosebud, I got an idea. I was going to stalk Alessandro, the way he had stalked his victims, the way he had stalked me. Harry was in L.A. There was no one to know what I did with my time after-hours and at night, the times when the rapist struck. I was going to prove that Alessandro was the rapist.

CHAPTER 23
December

SOLO SURVEILLANCE TENDS TO BE A STINT OF SELF-PSYCHIATRY—AN introspective interlude which is none too agreeable, but revealing. There you are, alone with yourself in the watches of the night. You can't read, it's too dark. Besides, you have to keep your eye on the house you're watching. You can't listen to the car radio, someone might hear. So what is there left to do? Think. And the harder you try not to think about some things, the more apt your perverse mind is to turn them over and over and over.

I learned a lot about myself on those nights while I was watching Alessandro's house—more, unfortunately, than I learned about him. I found myself thinking about Harry and Eugène far oftener than I would have liked; the most unlikely things would remind me of one or the other. For instance, when I glimpsed the winter night sky through the tree branches from my car window, I was reminded of what Eugène had written about my hair, which is short and black and unruly: "... her cloudy hair, a twilight net in which to catch the stars." Not much as literature, but what do you expect? He was a painter, not a poet. Anyway, it sounds better in French.

What sort of life would I be living now, I wondered, if Eugène hadn't died? Damn the black dog that had ridden his back, damn what had been my all-too-callow youth, double damn my shillyshallying. I tried not to think about it, tried not to think that possibly, if it hadn't been for me, that vital creature might still be alive and painting, the Picasso of his age in fame, though not in talent. Eugène was the better painter.

Then my thoughts would switch to Harry. I adored Harry, but I still didn't trust him. Would the time ever come when I could? Oh, hell, I didn't know and I didn't want to think about it. Any of it. In self-defense I began to think about my work instead. I enjoy police work: not just the sketching but the detection, even the slog work by means of which a solution is built up piece by minute piece, like fitting a jigsaw puzzle together. But did I want to keep on doing it forever? If my painting took hold, I knew I would drop my job like a shot. If. *If* was the operative word. I needed more time for painting, but it was a vicious cycle—I needed to paint more in order to gain recognition, but I couldn't afford to spend the time painting until I made enough money from it to support myself.

One of the problems with police work was my fear of becoming hardbitten if I stayed in it too long. I had seen people to whom that had happened—decent, well-meaning, kind people, who had seen too much of the seamy side of things and been scarred by it. I didn't want to end up like that. Some people manage to skate over the rough patches without being affected: life had not always been easy for my mother, but she had done what needed doing and done it well, accomplishing it with grace and gaiety. Daddy had held some of the choice diplomatic posts, but he had also drawn some royal stinkers. I remembered one hardship post where dysentery was a way of life, plumbing a thing unknown, and constant sandstorms left minidunes in the corners of the rooms, but Mother sailed through our stay there as if we had been in Vienna or Paris, and made it bearable for the rest of us. I wanted, like my mother, the ability to accomplish whatever was necessary with a merry heart. I didn't want to grow tough. And so the time passed slowly in the long dark cold lonely nights, my uncomfortable thoughts endlessly pursuing one another, like tigers chasing their tails.

Nothing else happened on those nights while I was keeping solitary watch. Not one bloody thing. It was a complete waste of time. With Harry in L.A., I had nothing better to do with my time, I told myself sternly when it got too cold and too boring. Sometimes Alessandro went out in the evenings, but when he did he was accompanied by his wife. And they always returned home together. Their house, on the outskirts of one of the genteel suburbs of Wilmington, was backed by genuine country and surrounded by trees and undergrowth, which gave me plenty of cover; and an empty house for sale next door allowed me to park my car without being seen by them or alarming the neighbors.

I dressed in dark clothes on those night vigils, and lots of them. It was damned cold in that car in December, with no heater running. I wore my police-issue revolver in a shoulder holster under my down jacket, where I could get at it quickly. The worst of those weeks, aside from the frustration caused by my lack of results, was my constant state of exhaustion. The catnaps I found time to take now and then were nowhere near sufficient to make up for lost sleep, so whenever I could, I took a nap on my desk at lunchtime; if I have a choice between food and sleep, food invariably comes off second-best. The trouble with that strategy was, Jacko was becoming suspicious. We often had a sandwich together, and I was beginning to run out of excuses.

One evening in mid-December, I had had it. The lack of human contact was getting to me. I was out of touch with practically everybody. My friends must have all thought I was being horribly unsociable; I didn't even have time to return their telephone calls. So aside from my talks with Jacko and brief phone conversations with Harry and Janet, neither of whom knew I had been taken off the rape squad—it would have been too humiliating to admit to—I might have been living on an uninhabited planet. I could tell that Janet was hurt by my inability to work on her portrait or meet for a meal, even though I excused myself by saying the case was taking up all my time. As for the other members of the task force, except for Jacko, they were avoiding me—out of embarrassment, I suppose. And to top it all off, I was suffering the early symptoms of some horrible bug—my digestion was dicey, my bones ached cruelly—

and my eyelids stubbornly stayed at half-staff, despite all my efforts to prop them open.

"This is insane," I told myself. Absolutely zero results in nearly three weeks, and I was a basket case. If I didn't get some shut-eye soon, I was going to come down with a raging case of the flu; and then I wouldn't be able to keep an eye on Alessandro anyway. So I staggered up to bed with a thermos of tea and a hot-water bottle that was a carryover from my Left Bank days, when the central heating was nonexistent or, at best, uncertain. As it turned out, I needn't have bothered—I wouldn't have noticed if I'd been sleeping on an ice floe in the Antarctic. I was out like a light the moment I collapsed on the bed, and I didn't surface until the alarm, which I'd retained just enough wit to set before conking out, went off at seven the next morning.

When it did, I shook myself awake and sat up to take stock. Stomach okay, bone aches practically gone. As for my general condition, I could have slept for another twenty-four hours or so, but I was human again, more or less. I figured that whatever I had had must have run its course, because I could just barely remember waking in the middle of the night with a disturbing feeling of cold and panic and restlessness. It must have been a fever working its way out, I reasoned: at least I felt all right now. My improvement, however, was apparently more internal than external, because when Jacko stopped in my office later that morning for his usual chat, he gave the dark circles under my eyes a once-over.

"Hey, sweetie, what's up?" he greeted me. "You been steppin' out on your ex? You look to me like you ain't been gettin' no Zs a-tall lately, and there can only be one reason for that."

"Little you know," I snapped, and instantly regretted it.

At once he was all solicitude.

"Jeez, Kate, honey; I'm sorry. I wasn't thinking when I said that."

"Oh, for God's sake, Jacko," I told him. "Cut it out. I'm not grieving over the rape, if that's what you mean. It has nothing to do with that."

Which was true, in a way. I think if he hadn't raped me, I would have been just as intent on catching the creep for Janet's sake, not to mention the women he had killed and those he might still attack.

Jacko eyed me skeptically, but let it pass.

"Well, have I got news for you! Guess what?" he said, or, it would be more accurate to say, he crowed. "The seed report is in!"

"At last." I tried to sound excited, but I was so tired it was hard to sound anything but limp. "Does it look as if there might be a connection with DelecTable?" That point was the only one which interested me.

"None that I can see."

"Oh."

I must have drooped visibly, because Jacko said, to cheer me up, "C'mon, Kate, that don't mean your theory's gone bust. Anyway, it may help us pinpoint the area the creep comes from. But the joker is, what kind of plant one of the seeds grew into. You're never gonna guess. But try."

He gave me an expectant look, like a puppy waiting for a treat.

I was both angry and disappointed, so I opted out of his little game.

"A poppy seed," I said. "It turns out the killer was eating a kaiser roll studded with them while he stabbed Harrison."

"Naw!" Jacko was triumphant. I had failed the test, and the dog biscuit was his. "Get this. Three of the seeds were different kinds of meadow grasses, the way Layard had said, but the fourth was—" He paused for maximum effect. "Rape."

"It was?" I was interested, despite myself. "I didn't know rape was grown around here."

"You mean you heard of it?"

He sulked visibly, as crestfallen as he had been highflown a moment before.

"There are fields of the stuff in England," I explained. "They're lovely when the rape is in bright yellow flower, like fields of sunlight, even when the weather is cold and gray."

"How the hell would you know?" asked Jacko crossly, his beautiful surprise spoiled. "I thought it was Paris you lived in over there."

"We—I did cross the Channel now and then, for heaven's sake. And I lived in England when I was a kid. But seriously, Jacko, that could be a find for our side. It's an agricultural crop, and there are fields backing up to Alessandro's house. Maybe he picked the seed up there. Do they grow rape a lot on Delmarva? I've never heard it was raised here."

"That's what may turn out to be useful. The report we got says it was tried in some test fields on the peninsula ten years ago, as a substitute for soybeans; they grow it as an oil crop, like they do soy. But they gave up after about five years because soybeans do okay in this climate, and there wasn't much of a market for rape around here."

Now I was growing excited. "Where were those test fields? Could there have been one in back of Alessandro's house?"

"The report didn't say."

"Well, find out, for God's sake! What earthly use are you, anyway? Damn it," I said, "if only Rosebud would let me do some work on this case!"

"C'mon, Kate!" Jacko said, angry now. "What do you think, you're the only one around here who's any good? Give me a break!" He stamped out.

Luckily for me, Jacko never stayed angry for long; and fifteen minutes later he returned.

"No hard feelings?" I asked when I saw him. I had been feeling guilty.

"No hard feelings, kiddo," he replied somberly. "But this time I got some news you ain't gonna like. Rosebud just told me there's been another rape."

Like a pal, he had promised to keep me informed about all the details of the investigation, including the ones Rosebud said were off-limits. He had even given me an account of the Thanksgiving weekend attack up in Chester County, so I needn't have listened at the door after all. Any vestiges of tiredness disappeared when I heard him say that.

"Another rape?"

"Yeah, a doctor's wife in some fancy development in Greenville. Early this morning the doc took what turned out to be a fake phone call from the emergency room at Christiana Hospital that claimed one of his patients was sick; and while he was driving out to the hospital, someone got in the house and did the usual to his wife. Real nasty, Rosebud says. I'm on my way there now. Sorry you can't come along, kid. I tried, but Rosebud said no, *nein, nyet*. But don't worry. I'll feed you whatever we get hold of," he added, to cheer me up.

I groaned. "Oh, my God!" I said. "Why? Dear God, why? Why last night? Why, why, *why?*"

I pummeled my head with my fists.

"Jeez, Kate, what's with you?" Jacko was alarmed. "Hey, hey, take it easy!"

He grasped my forearms to stop their flailing.

"It's okay, Jacko. I haven't gone crazy." To my horror tears welled up in my eyes, a flood of them like a waterfall cascading down my cheeks. "Honestly I haven't. Let go my arms, goddamn it, so I can find a handkerchief." He did as I asked, and I searched vainly in my pockets. "Damn and blast! I haven't got one."

Jacko fled from my office, returning a moment later with a box of tissues. He handed it to me, and shut the door.

"You don't want them to see you cry," he said gruffly.

I took a wad from the box he offered and mopped at my face.

"Thanks. You needn't worry. The waterworks are over," I told him. "And for crying out loud, don't attribute them to the attack on me. Something terrible has happened."

"Sure it has. I just told you."

What an obtuse creature Jacko could be, I thought irritably.

"No, Jacko. Something even worse. I could have prevented it, and I didn't. I could have caught the creep."

That stopped him in his tracks.

"Sure you could," he scoffed after a minute. "C'mon, Kate, get real. I know you got this thing about Alessandro, but it don't mean you're right about him. What the hell could you have done to stop it anyway? Even if you sat on his doorstep, it would have happened. You couldn't have watched him around the clock by yourself. You got to face the fact that there's no hard proof the rapist is Alessandro. If there was, Rosebud would have put a tail on him. Listen, I gotta go. Rosebud'll have my balls in a sling if I don't get out there fast. You okay now?"

"Yes," I said. "Just promise me one thing. Promise you'll discuss this with me when you get back. Without prejudice. With an open mind. I know you think I must be nuts, sometimes I do, too—but I'm so *certain* about this."

"Sure thing. See you later."

He flapped his hand in my direction, and took off.

While I was waiting for him to come back, I found it difficult to concentrate on the files I was engaged in weeding out; instead I kept revolving in my mind the facts about the rapist as I saw them. It was going to be hard to convince Jacko of what I knew. I couldn't blame him; when I looked at the facts, I was incredulous myself. But I felt them in my gut. I *knew* I was right. I had a total certainty about this case that I had never before experienced in my life. Despite my rage and distress and guilt over what I had not prevented from happening the previous night, there was a core of calm, of sureness, at the center of my being. I knew. I knew so thoroughly that there was no room for doubt. I knew, and therefore I would have to act. There was no doubt about that either—no doubt about what to do, only doubt over how to go about it.

It was several hours later when, the files thoroughly pruned despite my distraction, Jacko reappeared, his normally cheerful face sober.

"I'm glad you didn't go, Kate," he said. "It was real bad. Worse than Lila Harrison. Worse than Wendy Monroe."

"How could it be?"

"Trust me. It was."

I dropped the subject for the one that was uppermost in my mind.

"Jacko, I have to tell you what's happened. Just do me a favor and don't say anything until I've finished. I know it won't be easy for you—you're going to think I've gone permanently bonkers—but hear me out. Please."

Jacko settled himself in the armchair beside my desk.

"Okay, Kate," he said. "Whatever you want."

This time I was the one who shut the door to my office. And

then I laid it all out for him, without reserve. How I had had that funny feeling on the day before Thanksgiving at the time when I was certain the girl up in Pennsylvania was being attacked; how I had begun to watch Alessandro's house at night, with no results—until last night, when I had skipped the surveillance because I'd felt lousy; how I remembered waking in the night with the same cold restless uneasy feeling I had had the other time; how I couldn't help thinking that if only I had kept up my watch over Alessandro, the doctor's wife would be alive.

When I had finished, Jacko just sat there looking at me, his face grave.

"So what are you going to do?" he asked me.

"That should be obvious. I'm not going to take my eyes off the son of a bitch. The question is, what are *you* going to do? I probably shouldn't have told you, but I had to tell someone; aside from anything else, someone needs to know where I am in case anything should . . . happen. Harry isn't around. Obviously, or I'd be fighting him tooth and nail about going out at night. He hates my work anyway, and this would be the last straw. If he weren't still out in L.A., I don't know what I'd do. As it is, I have to make up reasons why I'm never around to answer the phone when he calls—thank God for message machines! If you have any bright ideas, pass them on. The one thing I ask, no matter how nuts you think I am, is please please *please* don't tell Rosebud."

Jacko sat, reflecting, for a moment. Then he said, "I don't know, Kate. I swear I don't know whether you're nuts or whether you got something. But one thing I do know. You got to get this out of your system, or it's gonna sit inside and fester. Like a splinter I got in my big toe when I was eight. And you can't do the whole business yourself, not the way you been goin' around lookin' half-dead. So like it or not, kid, I'm with you. I just hope to God Rosebud don't find out."

I couldn't help myself. I dashed out from behind the desk, threw my arms around him, and kissed him.

CHAPTER 24

Mid-December

THANKSGIVING WAS WONDERFUL, THE WATCHER THINKS. So was the last one—it was exciting to trick her husband so he would leave her unprotected. The Watcher wants to do more like that one, to pit his skill and resourcefulness against two people instead of just one. But they didn't last long enough, he whines to himself. The knife didn't give him enough time. He has an idea about how to make the next one last longer. There are two of them he knows about. Two living in the same house. Nearby; he can walk there. The way he did once before. Not in Westover Hills, though. In Wawaset Park. They both have their hair done at Primavera. Sisters. Both blondes. Both young. One is divorced with children, but the children are living with their father. He can manage two if he does it right, he tells himself; he is getting greedy. He heard one of them say that she goes to an exercise class once a week after work, so if he does it on that day he can get in and tie up her sister, then wait for her to return home. That way the first one will have plenty of time to think about what is going to happen to her. And that way, too, one will have to watch the other die. He licks his lips at the thought.

Despite the cold weather there has been no snow, so he can watch the house safely, without fear of being silhouetted against a white background for a passerby to spot. The leaves have fallen from the trees, but the house is surrounded by evergreen bushes, behind which he can shelter while he takes note of their routine. He will begin today. He wants to be ready by Christmas at the latest. He does not think he can wait longer than that.

GRETCHEN WELBACH AND LISL O'NEILL WERE HAVING A HURRIED breakfast in the kitchen of their Tudor-style house on Fairfax Place. They were sisters. Both were fair-haired and both were divorced, but there the resemblance ended. Gretchen, the elder by three years, was middling tall, compact and well muscled, and taught tennis at the Greenville Country Club. In her heyday she had been the reigning local tennis champion, and she was still able to beat most of the nearby competition. Lisl was barely thirty, with a fragile prettiness and a tremulous lower lip. Her divorce had been very recent and spectacularly unpleasant; her husband, a hard-driving executive of the MBNA Corporation who was as ruthless in his private life as in his corporate identity, had attained custody of their two young sons, in order not to pay child support, by inducing a nervous breakdown in his wife. Lisl had a part-time job at a flower shop which was owned by a friend of her mother; fortunately, since her ex-husband had fought bitterly against any sort of alimony, she had inherited a healthy dollop of family money.

She sat, despondent, at the breakfast table. Even her naturally curly hair had a listless droop.

"Buck up, honey," said Gretchen in bracing accents. "You're going to feel a lot better soon. I promise. Remember how grim I felt just after I got rid of Alan? The son of a bitch, best thing I ever did. Wonder why I didn't shed him a lot earlier. But it takes time to get to that stage."

She loved her sister, but at the moment even her ebullient personality was somewhat dampened by Lisl's depression; not that it was her fault, poor kid. Sean O'Neill was one of the biggest bastards alive, and his action in taking the children had been a calculated coup de grâce to Lisl's happiness and peace of mind. On top of everything else, the approach of Christmas was compounding the problem. Lisl's divorce settlement only permitted her to have the boys for four hours on Christmas Day; the judge who had handled the divorce was notoriously intolerant of what he considered self-inflicted and self-indulgent feminine mental disorders.

Under the onslaught of her sister's determined optimism, Lisl wilted even more. She tried valiantly to swallow a mouthful of her coffee but choked on a suppressed sob; then she gave way to her misery and, weeping, put her head down on her arms.

"It will be the first Christmas without Tommy and Tippy. I can't bear it!" she cried.

Despite her no-nonsense attitude, Gretchen's heart was wrung by the sight of her sister's unhappiness. She, too, loved the little boys; and though she had no children herself, she could imagine what Lisl was feeling.

"Oh, sweetie," she said helplessly, incapable in the face of such emotion.

The telephone rang, and Gretchen leaped to answer it as an escape from the uncomfortable situation in which she found herself.

"Hello? . . . Oh." The change in her voice imbued the monosyllable with loathing. "Yes. She's here. Yes. I suppose so."

At the sound of Gretchen's words, Lisl had raised her head. Her sister handed her the telephone receiver gingerly, as if it were a poisonous snake.

"It's Sean," she mouthed.

Lisl made an inadvertent cringing motion, but she took the receiver.

"Sean?" Her voice was faint, tentative, colorless. From the receiver issued a sharp formless barking, all too audible in the kitchen. The sound evoked a telling portrait of Sean O'Neill as bully, Gretchen thought with distaste; but try as she might, she was unable to distinguish any meaning in the sounds.

The barking stopped, and Lisl spoke. Her voice was transformed. So, Gretchen noted with astonishment, was her face. Now her voice was glad, strong, with a lilt to it, and her face was suffused with joy.

"You are? . . . She can't? . . . Of course! I'll be delighted to! . . . Yes. Yes, that will be fine . . . The twenty-second? You'll drop them off at noon? I'll be working that day, it's a busy time for flowers, but I'll figure something out. Yes. All right. 'Bye."

She handed the telephone receiver back for Gretchen to hang up, and turned starry eyes upon her.

"They're coming for Christmas!" She gave a sob, one this time of happiness.

"Tommy and Tippy?"

Lisl nodded, for the moment unable to speak, and Gretchen put her arm around her sister's shoulders.

"That's wonderful!" she said. "It will be a real Christmas for us this year." With some trepidation she thought, I just hope the bastard sticks to it. If he changes his mind at the last moment, it will kill Lisl. "What happened?"

"He has plans to ski at Vail over Christmas. The hotel hasn't got a room for the boys, and the woman who takes care of them has Christmas off so she can't fill in, thank goodness!"

"Which, translated out of Seanese, means that his current girlfriend can't be bothered with a four-year-old and a six-year-old on their skiing trip. I told you it wasn't going to take him long to get tired of dealing with small children nonstop, even with a live-in nanny to take up the slack."

But Lisl was not listening. Her mind was full of Christmas, of what it would be like with Tommy and Tippy, of what a wonderful Christmas it was suddenly going to turn out to be. No one, thought Gretchen, looking at her in amazement, would have taken her for the same woman who had been sitting in the breakfast nook a few moments earlier; her own sister was hard put to it to see a resemblance. Lisl's expression had changed from watery sorrow to joyful expectation. Her face had a delicate and becoming flush, and even the hair on her head had acquired body and bounce.

"Oh, Gretchen. Gretchen, darling!" She was not speaking the words but singing them, and her copper-colored eyes had taken on the shine of new pennies. "It really will be Christmas after all, won't it?"

CHAPTER 25

December 21

IT IS TIME, THE WATCHER THINKS, AS HE CLICKS THE REMOTE TO TURN OFF the TV news, *for the next one.* He always enjoys watching the news when the police are interviewed about one of his rapes. He likes to listen to them pretend they're getting somewhere, when he knows perfectly well they haven't a clue. It is a game, a game which he is winning; a game they are bound to lose, though they don't know that yet. He can't help winning because he is so clever. He covers his tracks. He doesn't make mistakes. Ever. He hugs himself gleefully.

His wife is in the kitchen, making coffee. He will drink the coffee, he tells himself, and then go to bed. He does not want to go to bed yet. He wants to go to the house in Wawaset. He wants to go there more than he has ever wanted anything. The package that arrived from his mother earlier in the day has upset him. He needs to release the anger. But he can't just go whenever he pleases, not at night. His wife would notice his absence. And he must plan. He must be careful. He has to get it all right the first time. He has most of it figured out, but it will take meticulous planning to do two of them at once. Two of them. Together. So much potential. There are lots of things he can think of to do with two of them. He realizes that he is shaking with excitement.

His wife enters, carrying a tray on which there are two mugs. She sets it down on a low table in front of the sofa.

"Are you cold?" she asks him. "You're shivering."

"I must have turned the thermostat down too soon," he replies. "I'll go get a sweater."

While he is in the bedroom, the telephone rings. He leaves it for his wife to answer downstairs. As he pulls the sweater over his head, he is so wrapped up in thoughts of what he is going to do to the two women in Wawaset that he forgets about the call. On his return to the living room he finds that his wife is just hanging up the phone. She turns a grave face in his direction.

"Honey, that was Cathy. Mark has had a heart attack."

He has been so entranced by his thoughts that it is several moments before he can make sense of what she is saying.

"What a shame," he answers, a beat too late. "How is he?"

"Cathy says it's a bad one. She wants me to go down there as soon as I can. He's at Hopkins, in intensive care. Thank God Patti can manage the store. It won't be easy at this time of year; we have a lot of orders to fill for parties, but I've already arranged for extra help over the holidays. So I'll drive to Baltimore first thing in the morning." She hesitates, then says, "Any chance you could come along?"

Not a snowball's chance in hell! he thinks exultantly, but he manages to arrange his features in a suitably doleful expression.

"Afraid not, Helen," he tells her. "I can't leave the business right now. Around Christmas every broad in town has to get her hair and her face in shape for the parties, and believe me, most of them need a lot of work. If I'm not on the scene, there's no way the others will be able to take up the slack. Poor Mark. What a damn shame."

What a break for me, he is thinking. He has made most of his forays during the times his wife was away on a buying trip for the delicatessen-gourmet food shop she owns, or visiting her brother, Mark, and his family, or her sisters in San Francisco and Minneapolis and Santa Fe, her parents in St. Augustine, or her older brother in Chicago; he encourages frequent solo visits to her relations. Moreover, they often take separate vacations: he likes to snorkel, while she prefers skiing out West. In many ways it is a very modern marriage, although if he were to go out on his own late at night when she is there, she would be predictably horrified.

In her distress Helen is unable to sleep and unable to keep still. She moves around the bedroom, packing, in order to be ready to take off for Baltimore first thing in the morning.

"Why don't you take the Alfa?" he says. He feels generous, now that he is going to have his very own Christmas present after all. Very soon.

"Are you sure you won't mind?"

"No problem," he tells her expansively. "I'll have the wagon and the bike." Besides, the Alfa is too flashy, too readily notice-able. For that reason he has never used it in his attacks.

"Thanks, honey," she tells him, touched by his solicitude, and kisses him on the cheek.

"How long do you think you'll be away?" he asks casually.

"I can't stay too long. Not with all the holiday parties we do. Until Mark stabilizes, I guess. A couple of days."

That doesn't give him much time. He'll have to get moving fast. Tomorrow night or the next, to be on the safe side. He feels a pleasurable anticipatory glow.

In the midst of folding a skirt, Helen pauses. "That package that came today. From your mother. Is it a Christmas present?" It is a delicate subject, but she feels she must ask. The possessor of a sentimental side, she has not ceased to hope that someday her husband and his mother will be reconciled.

"Yeah. I opened it." A bottle of Armani For Men. Big deal.

"I was sure it must be," she says happily. "She sent me a present, too, a bottle of perfume with a note saying it's her favorite kind. An ounce of real perfume, not just cologne, it must have cost an arm and a leg. But it was that stuff you said you hate on me. Remember? Ravie. You told me it smelled like garbage. What a shame. So I thought I'd send it to Janine for Christmas. You don't mind, do you? I don't want to waste it, it's a wonderful gift."

Helen's sister Janine lives in San Francisco, far enough away to be safe.

"Sure thing. Good idea," he tells her, and smiles.

She smiles back, happy, despite her brother's illness, to see him in a good mood.

"Don't you think we might send your mother something? Flowers? Or we could get Patti to make up some kind of basket—you know, cocktail snacks, party napkins, that kind of thing—and ship it to her."

"No way," he answers flatly.

His voice has a finality that warns her to go no further. She shrugs and closes the suitcase.

Later, when they have both gone to bed, he lies awake for a very long time, mentally refining his plans for the following night.

CHAPTER 26

December 22—Morning

"TODAY'S THE DAY!" Lisl's face was lambent with happiness. Because she could not yet hug her children, she hugged herself in their place. "Do you think their room looks all right?"

"How could it possibly be improved upon?" Gretchen was amused and touched by her sister's obvious excitement. "It has more Welcome Home signs and balloons and crepe-paper streamers than a parade for a victorious army returning after a major war. Not to mention the piles of presents."

"Not piles. Only a couple for each day till Christmas. And most are just small things, stocking presents to be opened ahead of time." Lisl is somewhat shamefaced. "I know it's silly, with Christmas only a few days away, but I thought it would be fun for them to open some every morning. The presents are all things they would have gotten on Christmas morning anyway."

"It's not silly, it's charming. It will be much more fun for them to do it that way." Impulsively Gretchen leaned over to kiss her sister on the cheek. "Darling, I know how much you've been missing them. I'm only surprised at your restraint. I would have expected you to smother them with presents."

"You're sure you don't mind taking them this afternoon till I finish work?" Lisl asked.

"Mind? It will be heaven. They're dear little boys. I thought

I'd take them to Over-the-Top for ice-cream sundaes. Is that all right? Will it do dreadful things to their appetite for supper?"

"Who cares? It's Christmas—well, not yet, but almost, and Christmas only comes once a year. You're sure they won't be a nuisance? I did try to get off early, but we're doing the flowers for the Holly Ball tonight. At least Martha has promised that I can leave by six-thirty. The others will probably be working till eight or nine."

"No, sweetie, they won't be a nuisance. And I shall try not to be a bad influence and spoil them, but it won't be easy. Luckily, since I'm helping out in the country club office, there's not much except parties going on there at the moment, so we're closing up shop at twelve-thirty or so. I'll run by Bouquets and pick up the boys once they arrive. You said Sean's dropping them off at twelve-thirty?"

"That's right."

"Do you want me there for moral support?"

"N-no." Lisl knew how much her sister detested Sean, and thought it might be just as well if she were absent during the delivery. "I'll be okay, thanks."

Gretchen, who had a pretty fair idea what her sister was thinking, tended to agree; besides, their mother's friend Martha Eustis, the owner of Bouquets, would be on hand. She was a tough old bird who couldn't stand Sean either, so Lisl would be well protected.

"Okay, love, see you at one o'clock with bells on. Try to refrain from giving my love to the hellhound Sean."

She blew an airy kiss as she picked up her coat and handbag and went out toward the garage.

AT TWELVE-THIRTY ON THE DOT (SEAN O'NEILL WAS MERCILESSLY punctual) the cowbell that hung on the door of the flower shop gave a mellow clang, and Sean strode in with two small boys lined up behind him in regimental style. Lisl, who had been hovering near the door for the past ten minutes, wordlessly opened her arms and scooped up her sons, who galloped into them like twin foals who thought they had lost their dam forever. Sean frowned at this sloppy display of emotion. It was one of the reasons, he told himself, that he had insisted, despite the attendant inconvenience, on taking custody of the boys. Their mother was not good for them. All this demonstrativeness was unhealthy, particularly when bringing up boys. They needed to learn control, restraint. Currently he was on the lookout for a boarding school for Tommy; and as there were only a few in this country that took very young children, he was beginning to inquire in England. Sylvia had suggested it; a college friend of hers had recently sent her six-year-old son to a British school.

Sean stood there for a moment, tall, good-looking, immaculately tailored and barbered. He gave his ex-wife a look of strong disapproval as she clasped their sons to her breast. He was not at all sure that having them spend the Christmas holidays with her was a good idea, but there was not much else he could have done in the circumstances. Sylvia had been unalterably firm about taking them along to Vail, and he had not known what else to do with them.

"Yes, well, I must be going," he said. "Good-bye, Thomas. Good-bye, Tipton." He did not approve of nicknames.

The boys hung back until Lisl gave them a gentle push; then they went forward obediently to give him a farewell kiss.

"Merry Christmas," he said to them. "That reminds me," to Lisl. "I nearly forgot their presents."

From an inside pocket he pulled two envelopes printed in seasonal red and green, which Lisl knew from experience contained shares of MBNA stock. She could not help saying, "Is that all?" though she knew, also from experience, that almost certainly it was.

"All?" repeated Sean, with a censorious lift of one eyebrow. "It's a hundred shares apiece. How many children get that kind of Christmas present?"

Not very many, thank God! thought Lisl; and was not unpleasantly astonished at herself. Last year she would not have dared to think such a thing. She found herself wondering with fresh daring if next year she might say it aloud to him; the thought made her laugh.

Sean could not imagine what it was that had made her laugh,

and that displeased him. While they were still married he had known every thought that entered her head; not knowing what had caused her to laugh made him feel uncertain. He hated uncertainties. His life was built on a solid foundation of facts, on knowing what was going to be done and who was going to do it, because he was the one who made the decisions. Now he was no longer in a position to tell Lisl what to do, and he didn't like it. He didn't like it at all.

"Miss Weems said that the boys shouldn't have any sweets while they're with you," he instructed her. "Sugar makes them overexcited."

"Yes, Sean," said Lisl meekly. She was discovering what fun it was to feign obedience, when she had not the least intention of following his orders.

"And they've had a lot of colds this fall. She says they mustn't play outdoors for more than fifteen minutes at a time."

Fifteen minutes? When the air was bright and crisp and they adored being outdoors, and there was a pond out on the Kennett Pike where she planned to teach them to skate as soon as it froze hard enough? Two of the presents waiting to be opened early were matching pairs of double-runner ice skates.

"Yes, Sean. Don't you think you ought to be going now? You mustn't miss your plane."

"We're—I'm not leaving till tomorrow morning." But as Sylvia was waiting for him in the car, he took his leave. "Well, good-bye, Lisl. Merry Christmas," he added grudgingly.

She was looking better than he had expected, and in an obscure way this displeased him. As he drove the BMW back to his house, recently built on the Kennett Pike and designed to look like a French château oversupplied with Palladian windows, he kept clashing the gears until Sylvia was nearly ready to scream with irritation.

CHAPTER 27

December 22—Afternoon

THE WATCHER'S HANDS ARE AT WORK, BUT HIS MIND IS FAR FAR AWAY. Thinking about tonight. Thinking about this evening. It will start early in the evening, because he has to secure the first sister before the other one returns. It will start early, but then it will go on and on and on, all through the night. If only he can hold back the knife. The knife has a will of its own. But he will whisper to it, plead with it to give him time first to do what he wants to do. Because the knife is swift. Once it begins, it is eager to finish. He has tried to hold it back, but it is stronger, far stronger, than he. He is only its servant. He must do what it tells him. The knife is his God.

It lies now in his trousers pocket, demurely folded; and he touches it, caresses it, tells it silently that tonight it will have what it wants.

The Watcher is working on the coiffure of Mrs. Edmond-Hector-Marie du Pont IV. It is definitely a coiffure, and not an ordinary cut-wash-and-set: Mrs. Edmond-Hector-Marie du Pont IV has a daughter who is being presented at the Holly Ball this evening, since Mr. Edmond-Hector-Marie du Pont IV, to the vociferous disgust of his wife and daughter, is too cheap to foot the bill for a private dance at which to bring his little girl out. Mrs. Edmond-Hector-Marie du Pont IV's mouse-colored hair has been transformed by Alessandro and his minions into a miracle of scintillating highlights and seductive tendrils, and now he is deftly supplying the finishing touches to this tonsorial edifice.

"No, no, *no,* Sandro!" she cries, as he whisks the revolving chair around and holds up a hand mirror to show her the result of his labors. "It isn't right yet. It needs something. It doesn't make me look ... *je ne sais quoi.*"

She is fond of sprinkling her conversation with French phrases, although the du Pont family collectively shook the dust of France from its feet two centuries ago; and in any case she was not born into it but achieved her membership by marriage.

It doesn't make you look eighteen again, or even forty-eight, you old bat, he thinks savagely as he flashes her an ingratiating smile. His right hand blindly seeks the knife nestled in the trousers pocket of his willow green Italian silk suit, and curls possessively around it. Wouldn't she be surprised, he thinks, smiling at her in the mirror, if he were to pull it out now and start on her? How he'd like to cut her, to watch her dull cow's eyes widen in horror and her foolish slack mouth round into an O of fear. But he can feel the knife tell him through his fingers—not this one, not yet—and with an effort he gets himself under control, unclenching his hand from the knife and taking it out of his pocket to arrange a fetching curl beside her ear. He forces himself to think of nothing but the task immediately before him, to blot the knife out of his mind, blot out the delights in store for him tonight. Once more he waves the hand mirror in front of her eyes.

"Oh, yes, yes! That's much better, Sandro," she decides. "Only ... you don't think it's too young for me?" and she settles back for the expected compliment.

Alessandro sets his teeth and makes his mind, the mind which longs for the approaching night, a conscious blank.

"It suits you to perfection," he tells her. "Madly becoming. Only ... I hope your daughter won't mind having a sister beside her this evening, instead of a mother."

Mrs. Edmond-Hector-Marie du Pont IV gives a squeal of

pleasure. Like a pig having its throat cut, he thinks dispassionately.

"Naughty boy!" she exclaims, bridling at her reflection in the mirror. "But of course you don't mean it." But of course she thinks he does.

As he ushers her out of the cubicle—one of his best customers, she gets the full treatment—his mind has slipped its leash and is racing ahead toward what he will be doing later. His nerves tense in anticipation of what is to come. Scenes of blood, of violence, chase alluringly behind his eyes like clouds across the moon. Suddenly he feels that he cannot wait until tonight. He has already waited long enough.

He glances toward the big window at the front of the shop; twilight is falling. He looks at his wristwatch. Past four o'clock. Soon it will be dark. This is the evening every week that one of them stays out for her exercise class. It has all worked out perfectly. His God, the knife, has seen to that. That is the way the Watcher knows it was all meant to happen. His God wants him to kill the two blond sisters, to rape them and torture them and open them up so the sweet hot blood can be released. The knife has made everything happen the way it should: Mark's heart attack, so Helen had to go away at just the right moment; the exercise class—everything in its time. His God is good to him. Very good.

Only—why wait until seven to go to the house? Mrs. Edmond-Hector-Marie du Pont IV was his last client for the day. And now it is dusk. He can change his clothes, change into something dark, more casual, less noticeable, and walk over to the house to take a look. Maybe stay around, concealed by the bushes, till the first one comes home. He can take a bag with his killing clothes and change there before he does it. No need to disguise himself, he thinks. No longer any need for the facial pads, the skin dye, the wig and false eyebrows. This time there won't be anyone left alive to recognize him.

In his office he changes into dark gray slacks, a deep brown-and-gray tweed jacket, a brown marled Shetland turtleneck sweater, and picks up the bag that contains what he thinks of as his work outfit. As he swings past the reception desk at the front of the shop, he tells Filomena (who was christened Faye Suzanne) that he has a couple of errands to run in the neighborhood.

"You lock up, Fil, if I'm not back by closing time," he says to her. "I'll come by later to pick up the wagon."

Filomena nods her cinquecento head and returns to the bodice-ripper she is reading—the stream of clients has begun to slow down this late in the day—as he moves off in the direction of Wawaset Park.

A COUPLE OF DAYS BEFORE CHRISTMAS JACKO AND I WERE CONFERRING IN my office; he was bringing me up to date on the latest info, all the stuff about which Rosebud thought I was being kept in the dark.

At the end of my briefing, I asked him, "What about the rapeseed? Hasn't someone come up with any ideas about how it got on the creep? Have you asked the Ag man yet about the location of test fields on Delmarva?"

I had been steadily nagging Jacko about that; it infuriated me that I was not in a position to pick up the phone and check on it myself, but I knew if I did, without a doubt Rosebud would have my head.

"I told you," said Jacko.

"Told me what?" I was outraged. "You haven't said a word about it, and I've asked you every time there's been an opportunity."

"Jeez, I'm sorry, Kate. I thought I had, but don't get your hopes up. There's nothin' to tell. I guess that's why I forgot. There wasn't no test fields up around where Alessandro lives. There was one down near New Castle, and two outside Newark, and the rest in New Castle County were farther down by Middletown. So that was no go."

"What about the agricultural supply stores? Maybe some farmer is trying rape out on his own. It could even be—"

"The field in back of the creep's place? Dream on," Jacko told me. "That would be much too good to be true. Anyway, we checked it. There wasn't anything that looked like rape growing near Alessandro's place."

"How can you be sure? I bet there's at least one rape plant in that field. *I'll* go look. Somewhere in that field there's bound to be rape. I know there is! And what about DelecTable? Isn't Rosebud working on DelecTable? I still think there could be a connection there," I insisted.

"How?" he asked. "Rape ain't a fancy vegetable, like the kind they sell. Give it a rest, Kate."

"You're saying the seeds are a loose end."

"Or a dead end. We get those a lot more than we like. You know that as well as I do."

"We don't seem to have anything but dead ends in this case. Including the victims. If only we had something solid to work with. If only Alessandro would make a move. If he doesn't do something soon, I'm going to go crazy."

"Do me a favor and don't do it when we're cooped up together in that car," said Jacko.

"Speaking of which, I don't know about you, but I have every intention of waiting for Alessandro at the usual time tonight," I said.

Ever since I had begun keeping an eye on Alessandro, he had left the premises of Primavera at 6:00 P.M. sharp on every working day. I could have set my watch by him. So after six days or so Jacko was getting tired of inventing reasons for being out of the office before five.

"C'mon, Kate," he said irritably. "What's the point? The creep don't never go nowhere till six. We're just wasting that time, and right now we're short on time to waste. We're still working on the latest rape-murder, plus the usual stuff, not to mention all the jolly Christmas shoplifters and purse snatchers that are making the holiday rounds. How long do you think we can get away with leaving the office early? We could be doing this for months."

I appreciated his tactful use of the pronoun "we" when he mentioned the rape case, but whenever I was short on sleep my temper suffered.

"Why don't you just go home tonight and get some sleep?"
I said crossly. "You think this is all garbage anyway."

"Forget it, kiddo. You're stuck with me, like it or not."

"Well, I'm going straight over to Primavera to keep watch.
It's five now. And then I'm going to stay out at Alessandro's
house, the way I've been doing all by myself for the last couple
of weeks, thank you very much. If he leaves early for once so
we miss him, and then something happens tonight, I'll never
forgive myself. The creep isn't just a rapist, Jacko. He's a killer,
a really vicious killer." I gathered up my coat and gloves and
began to put them on. "See you tomorrow."

"Hey, wait up, will you?" Jacko's voice was plaintive. "If you
think I'm letting you go off by yourself, you're even crazier than
I thought. I'm your backup, whether you like it or not. I just
hope Rosebud don't get wind of this and skin us both alive."

Nice kid, I thought as I flashed him a grateful smile. He
thinks I've gone completely mental over this case, but he's standing behind me anyway. And I had to admit to myself that I
hadn't much cared for shadowing Alessandro on my own.

We left the building and got into my car. We were on our
way.

CHAPTER 28

December 22—Afternoon

THE BACK ROOM OF BOUQUETS WAS A RIOT OF COLOR. Behind the glass doors of the cooling units, spectacular blossoms flaunted their out-of-season heads—vivid yellow freesias, rose-spotted lilies scented, thought Lisl, like the Ravie perfume she customarily wore, fat orange and magenta Gerbera daisies, flights of white moth orchids, pink and apricot roses nodding on long elegant stems. The tables, where she was at work along with the owner of the shop and several others, spilled over with crimson and scarlet roses and branches of holly studded with bright berries. Loose petals were strewn over the floor looking, she thought inconsequentially, like small pools of blood. What an unpleasant idea. Why did I think of that? Lisl wondered, as she arranged the flowers and holly sprigs into tall stone urns to be transported to the Hotel duPont, where they would provide the decorations in the Gold Ballroom for the debutantes' Holly Ball that evening.

She finished work on the vase in front of her, and wriggled her shoulders to relax the muscles. Martha glanced over at her.

"Why don't you go on home now, Lisl, and get ready for the kiddies?" she suggested. "We've got everything under control here."

"But it's only a little after four," Lisl protested, although her heart leaped with joy at the prospect. Gretchen and the boys would probably not be back yet, since they did not expect her home until well after six; but it would give her time to bake the gingerbread slabs for the house she planned to make with Tommy and Tippy the next day, and she would be able to start supper. Not, she thought ruefully, that they would be likely to want much in the way of supper after the sugarplum feast Gretchen intended to provide for them at Over-the-Top.

"You get along," Martha told her gruffly. "We've done all the debs' bouquets and the flowers for the supper tables in the DuBarry Room, and the ballroom vases are well on their way. We don't need you. Sorry I couldn't let you know earlier, but I thought it was going to take us a lot longer to get this far. We've been going lickety-split. So skedaddle! And have fun with those boys of yours. They're certainly cute kids."

Lisl gathered up her things in a flurry.

"I can't thank you enough, Martha," she said gratefully. "You're sure you won't need me again before Christmas?"

"No, sweetie. It's only two days away, and I've got everything fixed up. Debbie's offered to come in if we get run off our feet. We'll be fine. You just go home and have fun."

"Oh, Martha, thank you! Thank you for everything." Lisl kissed her cheek and dashed out, turning to wave and say "Merry Christmas!" as she opened the shop door.

A few moments later she pulled into her garage and entered the house by way of the kitchen. It was growing dark, so she flicked on the light switch and went into the hall to hang her coat in the closet next to the front door.

I might as well change into something more casual to cook in, she thought, and went upstairs to her bedroom, where she exchanged her skirt and stockings and pumps for loafers and a pair of jeans.

Humming happily, Lisl returned to the kitchen, where she began to take out pots and pans and foodstuffs in preparation for cooking. It was heaven, she thought, to scrub baking potatoes and poke holes in them with a fork so the steam could escape, heaven to have two children to cook for again instead of just herself and Gretchen. It will be a terrible wrench, a small voice whispered insistently in her ear, when they go back to Sean and Miss Weems after Christmas. But Lisl refused to listen to the voice. She would think only of the joyous present. She would not, would *not* allow regrets or expectation of future sorrow to spoil this unexpected gift of a wonderful Christmas, this glorious serendipitous Christmas that had been handed to her on a silver platter.

Out of the corner of her eye Lisl sensed rather than saw what might have been a flicker of movement in one of the glass panes of the kitchen door. Gretchen and the boys back early? she wondered. But surely she would have heard their car drive into the garage. She decided that it must have been a branch of one of the bushes beside the entrance swaying against the glass. On her way home she had noticed that the weather was beginning to turn windy.

She put the potatoes in the oven and set the control back from preheat to bake. In order to do so she had to pass by the kitchen door, and she thought, *Why not leave it unlatched for the boys? They might come home early, and it seems inhospitable for them to have to wait till I open the door, or Gretchen unlocks it for them; I want to do everything to make them feel as welcome as possible. This is their home. I don't want them to have to wait for the door to be opened for them. That is what Sean would make them do.*

As she unfastened the door Lisl began to hum again, a song from *Fanny,* an old Broadway musical, and she smiled as she realized that its title was "Welcome Home." She crooned contentedly while she got out flour and spices for making the gingerbread. Moving over to the cabinet where the mixing bowls were stored, she glanced toward the door and the garage walkway beyond just in case, against all reason, Gretchen's car had driven in without her hearing it, and they were on their way into the house. To her surprise a man was standing there. In the kitchen. But she was relieved to realize that it was someone she knew, though not someone she would have expected to see there.

"Alessandro," Lisl said, bewildered. "What are—"

He slaps her hard across the face. Pain and shock cause tears to well up in her eyes. Surprise makes her reflexes dangerously slow. She does not know what is happening, why it is happening, what to do. He hits her again, to stun her, and grasps her arm with an iron grip. At this she comes alive and begins to fight like a fish hooked to a line, a fish that senses its life is at stake. But it is not only her life. Tommy and Tippy will be coming home soon. To what? What does this madman want? He must be mad to come in here and hit her without provocation. She shudders to think what a madman might do to two small defenseless boys.

He drags her across the kitchen, Lisl fighting desperately to get away from him. But it is no use. He is too strong for her. He drags her into the hall and up the stairs, as she vainly attempts to pull away from his hold. It is a grim, strangely silent struggle. She has no strength to waste on screaming; and besides, she knows that there is no one near enough to hear her. Since she realizes she is no match for him, she allows him to pull her without resistance for a moment, which enables her to fasten her teeth into the hand on her arm. He swears at her, but does not let go.

"Bitch," he says viciously, and hits her, again and again. She loses count of the number. He hits her until she is without volition, then he hauls her up the stairs, her body bumping limply on the steps.

When he reaches the second floor he takes her into the nearest room, a bedroom, Gretchen's room, and flings her onto a straight chair. She lolls there like a rag doll, her eyes closed.

I could rape her now, he tells himself. *Before the other one gets home. I could cut her now. Just a little bit.* But he knows that once he starts using the knife, he won't be able to stop. Nevertheless it is such a tempting prospect that he pleads silently with the knife to be allowed to, just this once, just a little.

JACKO DROVE US TO PRIMAVERA. I generously permitted him to do the driving; I find it gives men the illusion, however mistaken, that they're the ones in control, and who am I to burst their little bubble? As the result of our argument over when to start the surveillance, we were later than usual in taking up our post. Illogically, considering Alessandro had never in my experience left Primavera before six, that made me nervous enough to insist on checking to see if he was still in the place. Jacko was disapproving, but he indulged me nonetheless by parking the car on the street and waiting in it while I tried to find out if Alessandro was in the salon.

Filomena, seated behind the receptionist's desk, was playing with her admittedly lovely tresses; there was not much else for her to do, so near to closing time.

"I've decided to give myself a Christmas present," I told her brightly, "and schedule a cut by Alessandro for my snaky locks. What's the first year he's free?"

It must have been a question she had to answer often, because she had no need to consult the Florentine leather-bound appointment book at her elbow.

"Not till mid-April at the earliest," she replied languidly. "Want to book now?"

Her manner made it clear that whether I did or not made no difference to her. If I didn't take it, the slot would be filled by some other Alessandro idolater.

"Yes. Please," I said.

"You haven't been serviced by Alessandro before, have you?" she asked, in a superior way that indicated it was merely a rhetorical question. Her tone made me long to tell her what the verb really meant. "His fee is two-fifty for the cut. Wash and blow-dry extra."

"Yes, that's all right."

It certainly was, because I hadn't the faintest intention of keeping the appointment. By that time, with any luck, Alessandro would be locked up in the pokey awaiting trial.

"Oh," I added, as if I'd just thought of something to ask him, God knew what. "Is he still here?"

Botticelli's nymph blinked in surprise and said no before she thought of wondering why I should be asking.

Damn! He was ominously out of routine. Suppose he hadn't gone home. Suppose he was already on his way to another victim. I tried to believe that he had left work early to attend some

Christmas festivity or other, that losing track of Alessandro for one evening wouldn't make a particle of difference. *But it had, the last time.* Maybe, I told myself desperately, Rosebud was right. Maybe I was on the wrong trail entirely. Maybe Alessandro wasn't the rapist. He wasn't the only man in the world without lobes to his ears; and even if he was, I had no particular reason to suppose that tonight was going to be one of his nights to howl. But I had the bit in my teeth, and I still felt that calm assurance about the rapist's identity; so until there were definite indications that the rapist was someone else, I was betting on Alessandro. Which meant it was imperative that we kept an eye on him.

"What about April twentieth at two-thirty?" I asked Filomena at a venture, to keep her from speculating on why I wanted to know whether Alessandro was still in the place. April twentieth might fall on a Sunday, for all I knew.

Looking pained at having to make an effort, she drew the appointment book toward her and flipped through its pages.

"I can give you April twenty-fifth at three," she finally told me, with the air of one making a major concession.

"Great. The name is Kate Marbury," I said, in case she didn't remember. "Thanks, and Merry Christmas."

I left Primavera, and rejoined Jacko in the car. "No dice," I said glumly. "He's already taken off for the day."

"Well," said Jacko, starting the motor. "I guess that's the ball game. Want to try his house next?"

"I suppose we might as well."

ALESSANDRO STARES DOWN AT THE WOMAN HE HAS JUST BATTERED into semiconsciousness. A pulse beats at the base of her throat, fluttering like a small trapped creature. The sight of all that blood coursing through one small place in her body excites him. He longs to release it. He puts his hand in his pocket to touch the knife, so he will know what it wants him to do.

It is not there. The knife is not in his trousers pocket. But he knows he put it in this morning, he thinks frantically. He remembers putting it in his hip pocket before he left the house to go to work. As soon as he put on his trousers. He does not like going anywhere now without the knife. The knife is Power. What will he do if he has lost it? Suppose he never finds it? What will he do? What will he do?

He holds his hand in front of him, palm upward. Empty. His hand is empty, he thinks numbly. He stares down at it for a long moment before it occurs to him to try his other pockets. But they are all empty, too.

Panic takes control of his mind. He does not even for a moment consider using one of the kitchen knives that he saw ranged on a rack downstairs, in place of his own. He must. Go back. Find it. If he does not, it will all go wrong. The magic will not work. But it was with him that afternoon! he tells himself. When he was finishing Mrs. du Pont's hair. He remembers touching it then.

Suddenly he relaxes. Of course! When he changed from his suit, he forgot to transfer it to the trousers he is wearing now.

He must go back for it. That won't take long. He is certain he has plenty of time before the other one comes back from her exercise class. But he must make sure this one is secure while he is away. He yanks out bureau drawers until he finds a drawer full of pantyhose, which will be perfect for the job of fastening her to the chair. Stretchy and tough. She hasn't a prayer of getting out of them. Lucky, he thinks, that she came home early, that he came over here early. It doesn't matter that he has to go back for the knife. He has time. Plenty of time.

He ties her hands behind her back and to the chair, fastens her legs to the chair legs, knots a pair of pantyhose over her mouth so she cannot call out for help.

Then, as he heads for the door, he tells her conversationally, "Don't worry. I'll be back. I'm just going for the knife. My knife. The ones in the kitchen are no good."

The knife! Lisl's brain, which has been resting, trying to muster its forces to understand what is happening to her, wakens fully. *Oh, my God! This is going to be worse far worse than I thought. Alessandro? Why is he doing this? It must be a nightmare— nightmares don't make sense. That's it! I've fallen asleep and I'm dreaming that Alessandro has turned into Sweeney Todd, the Demon*

Barber of Fleet Street. He's going to cut off my hair with the knife and then turn me into sausages and sell them at that deli his wife owns. Strange what the mind can dream up while you're sleeping.

But she knows she is not asleep, not dreaming. A moment later Alessandro returns with a Vuitton bag she dimly recalls having seen beside him an eon ago on the kitchen floor.

"Before I go for the knife, I'm getting everything ready for later," he says chattily, "so I thought I'd bring this upstairs now. I wouldn't want your sister to see it when she comes home, and wonder why it was there."

He finds that he likes explaining things to her. It is pleasant to have someone to appreciate his planning and the trouble he takes over it. "I'm going to change my clothes, because the ones in here," he holds up the bag so she can see it, "won't show the blood."

Horror piled upon contemplated horror causes Lisl to black out briefly. When she comes to, he is gone. *Oh my children!* she screams silently. *My children and my sister! Oh God oh God.* But this phase does not last long. *I've got to do something,* she thinks. *I've got to save them. Somehow.* The focus of her brain seems to have narrowed and sharpened. *I must let them know,* she thinks. *As soon as they get here. So they won't come into . . . How?* She looks around the room. She flexes her wrists and ankles. Near her, very near her but not quite close enough, is a window. Window! She tries to concentrate. The window overlooking the garage and the driveway. The window overlooking the path to the kitchen door. The way—surely the way—they will be coming in.

EXPOSURE TO HER NEPHEWS WAS MAKING GRETCHEN FEEL MATERNAL, an unusual emotion for her. It would be fun to have kids, she thought, when she finally came across the right man. At least it would if they turned out like Tommy and Tippy; and the chances on that, she calculated, were at least fifty-fifty, since she and Lisl had swum out of the same gene pool. Gretchen was having a hell of a good time, and so (which was the point of the exercise) were the boys. She had driven them out to one of the malls to see Santa Claus. She hated malls, but she loved Tommy and Tippy, and the only place where she could be certain of finding a resident Santa was at a mall. Tippy, in particular, had insisted on seeing Santa Claus that afternoon with such intensity that Gretchen feared if he did not achieve this ambition, he would not have a wink of sleep that night.

"*She* don't let me wite Santy," he explained, with a darkling look on his round face.

"What is Tippy talking about?" Gretchen asked Tommy. She had long ago learned that Tippy's enigmatic utterances could always be deciphered by his elder brother.

"He means Miss Weems. She wouldn't let us write to Santa and tell him what we want for Christmas," explained Tommy. "And that we've been good boys," he added, somewhat belatedly.

"What a horrible woman!" exclaimed Gretchen.

"Ess," Tippy answered, clearly pleased with his aunt's response.

"So if we don't get to see Santa, Tippy's scared we'll just get sticks and stones like Miss Weems says bad boys do. And so am I," Tommy said as an afterthought.

"Ess." Tippy confirmed his brother's explanation. "Don't want sticks 'n stones. Want a Robot-Man and a puppy dog and a pony and a airplane and a jack ball and a—"

"Of course you do," Gretchen interjected, to break what threatened to be an interminable, and largely unobtainable, list. "We'll go see Santa Claus first thing."

Between the drive out to the mall, the wait in line to see Santa, and the enthralling inspection of the toy department's contents, it was almost four-thirty by the time they arrived at Over-the-Top for refreshments. Both boys unsurprisingly opted for the confection for which the sweetshop had been named, a miniature bathtub filled with scoops of every conceivable kind of ice cream, covered by assorted sprinkles and sauces.

Gretchen blanched when their choices were brought to the table. Oh, well, she thought in resignation, after life with Father and Miss Weems they deserve a blowout, poor little things. I only hope they won't get sick.

To her amazement, both Over-the-Tops disappeared in short order with no visible ill effects. Tippy carefully licked both sides of his spoon to ensure that he had not left anything on it, and patted it affectionately as he set it down.

"*She* don't let us eat ice cream. Bossy man don't let us eat ice cream," he told her sternly.

"Well, *I* let you eat ice cream, and you may have another just like it—in a few days," she added hastily, devoutly hoping that their digestion was up to a repetition of the experience.

"Don't like the bossy man. Don't want to go with the bossy man," Tippy informed her.

"That's what he calls Daddy," said Tommy. "I mean, Father."

"Don't you call your father Daddy anymore?" Gretchen asked him. "You used to."

"Dad—Father doesn't like it. He says it's babyish, and it's time to call him Father. But I don't always remember. He told me to call Mummy Mother. Sylvia said I should."

"Don't like the bossy man," Tippy reiterated.

"I don't like him either," said Gretchen. She glanced up behind the counter at the brightly colored clock, whose hands were shaped like ice cream cones. "Good heavens, it's after five-thirty! I'd better take you home for supper—not that you have any room left for it. We want to get back to the house before your mother does."

She wiped their faces, which their repast had decorated with a variety of sprinkles and sauces, and zipped up their jackets before shepherding them out to the car.

CHAPTER 29

December 22—Late Afternoon

"I HAVE A BAD FEELING ABOUT THIS, JACKO," I SAID. "I don't think Alessandro's going to be at home. I think he's already gone somewhere, and we haven't a clue where. We'll sit outside his house all night, and tomorrow there'll have been another killing."

"You want to cancel our watch?"

"No, I don't," I said vehemently. "Don't sound so goddamn hopeful. If he does something tonight, and I haven't even tried to stop him, I'll never forgive myself. Just don't make the mistake of thinking we're going to get anywhere tonight. Why don't you go home?"

"And leave you in that car by yourself? Forget it." Jacko scoffed. "I don't rat out on my pals."

"Thanks, Jacko." I put my hand on his arm. "And thanks, too, for not telling me how crazy you think I am. Come on, I'll buy you a drink. What the hell, we're officially off-duty."

I got out of the car and led him over to the Diamond State Brewery, next to Primavera, one of those mini-micro jobs that have been popping up recently like mushrooms. Beer isn't my tipple but it is Jacko's, and I wanted a drink like billy-o. If I got lucky they'd have a bottle or two of wine stashed away behind the bar. The place, decorated to look like a Munich *bierstübe*, was filling up rapidly now that the working day was over for the white-collar crowd, so we wound our way toward one of the few empty tables over by the front window and ordered our drinks from a nearby waiter. I asked for a glass of dry white wine, despite the frown he bestowed on me. Jacko, however, improved his mood by ordering vin de maison.

"Why'd you wanna come here if you didn't want a beer?" Jacko wanted to know after the waiter had made his departure.

"Because I thought you did. Because I was thirsty. Because I wanted a drink, any drink. It was the closest place around, and I figured they'd be able to dig up at least one cobweb-draped bottle of this year's plonk."

Our drinks arrived. I dived into mine. I needed it. The vintage wasn't, but it still tasted good to me. At that point even beer probably would have hit the spot. By now it was almost entirely dark outside, though the street and the little shopping center were well lighted. I stared absently out the large window at the buildings opposite as I drank my wine. I was feeling a shade peculiar, chilly and slightly nervous; it must, I thought, be the cold alcohol giving me a rush. Suddenly I set down my glass with a thump and sat upright.

"Hey!" I said, clutching Jacko's arm.

"What's got you?" asked Jacko, raising his face from its partial immersion in his beer. A mustache of foam clung to his upper lip. "You know somethin'? In spite of the arty surroundings, this stuff ain't half-bad."

"Forget the beer. There's Alessandro!" I hissed, shielding my face from outside view with my left hand in case Alessandro should look our way.

"Huh? What? Where?" Jacko began to crane his neck.

"Cut it out! Pretend you're not looking. Outside. Right in front of us. On his way to Primavera. In a dark sport jacket."

"Hey!" Jacko gave a long-drawn-out whistle. "Yeah. And you're right on the money. No lobes that I can see."

A cold wind was blowing outside, disarranging our quarry's hair. Jacko took another gulp of his beer.

"Of course I'm right. Did you think I'd made it up?"

"Whaddaya wanna do?"

"As soon as he goes in, we'll leave and cut back to the car. No. Wait. You get in the car, and I'll check the parking lot in back of the building, the one the employees use, in case he's left his car there. Stupid of me! I should have done that before." I patted my handbag. "I've got my flip phone, so I'll call you if he comes out that way. You call me if he leaves by the front."

"Will do."

I put some money on the table to cover our bill and we left the place, separating outside the entrance. I circled the building the long way around in the direction opposite to Primavera and found a vantage point where I could see the cars parked in back of the beauty shop, but where I was fairly certain anyone leaving Primavera by the rear door would be unable to spot me. After five minutes or so my flip phone rang and I answered it.

"Is he coming out?" I asked.

"Yeah. Get here quick. He's leaving on foot, no sign of a car."

"Okay."

I furled the phone and hurried to the front of the shopping center, where Jacko awaited me in our chariot.

"Hold on to your hat!"

The motor was already running, and as soon as I closed the door on my side the car moved off smoothly in a southerly direction.

"There he is." Jacko pointed out a figure walking fast under the streetlights. After a couple of moments Alessandro swung into a street heading west and so did Jacko, leaving a safe distance between us so he wouldn't suspect we were following him.

"This is Wawaset Park," I said after a moment.

"Yeah," Jacko responded.

"Alessandro doesn't live in Wawaset Park. He lives in the suburbs. And he isn't dressed for a party, not the kind they give around here."

"Yeah. The same thought crossed my mind. You think he's headed toward a hit?"

"Or possibly a view."

"A what?" asked Jacko, bewildered.

"He may be scoping out the ground," I said, reverting to an

argot more familiar to my henchman. "Didn't you learn that famous hunting song 'John Peel' at your dear old granny's knee?"

"Huh?"

"Obviously your education has been neglected. 'From a find to a check, from a check to a view, From a view to a death in the morning.' " I shivered. "I only hope it doesn't turn out to be accurate in this case. Step on it."

AFTER A NUMBER OF FRUITLESS ATTEMPTS LISL HAS MANAGED TO GRASP one of the curtains at the window beside her with her bound hands, and she begins painfully to pull herself toward it. Although her ankles are tightly fastened to the legs of the chair, she is able to get a little purchase with her toes, which helps impel her forward, or rather backward: since her hands are tied around the back of the chair, she is facing away from the direction in which she needs to go. She tugs cautiously at the curtain, praying that the curtain rod will hold. Fortunately Gretchen chose heavy curtains for her room, which hang on a strong wooden dowel supported by a pair of wooden cups screwed into the wall. But suppose, Lisl thinks, the dowel should slip out while she is pulling on the curtain. Suppose the cups aren't as strong as they seem, and break? She does not dare to think about that. Her questing fingers seek blindly for the footboard of the bed, which she knows stands next to the window. The bed is a heavy one, and she will be able to pull herself along its foot without fear of yanking down the curtain rod. If her bound wrists have enough freedom. She will not know whether they do until she tries.

A thrill runs up her arm. The tip of one finger has touched something. Something hard. Another fingertip, and then another, feels it. It is—it must be—the footboard. She can feel a ridge running along the top, which she remembers well by sight. As she had hoped, the wooden footboard is just the right height for her bound hands. But try as she will, she cannot twist them to the correct angle for taking hold of the top of the footboard. She weeps with anger at her own powerlessness and clumsiness.

And it is all taking so long. Too long. Soon Alessandro will return, soon Gretchen and the children will come.... Terrible scenes, unbearable scenes, play themselves out at the back of her eyes with the inevitability and finality of Greek tragedy. She must not watch them, she thinks, for they fill her with such horror that she is unable to perform even those small motions of which she is capable, motions which might save her children.

Lisl resumes tugging on the curtain, scrabbling frantically with her toes to keep from placing too much weight on the curtain rod. She must not tip over the chair; that would mean the end of even the faintest chance of saving them. She achieves a kind of working rhythm: pull, scrabble—pull, scrabble. Minute gradations of distance are crossed in this way, barely measurable stretches of floor are passed over. But the distance she must traverse in order to achieve her plan is not great, though it is only the beginning of what she must do.

Again she feels something hard against her fingers. Not the footboard of the bed; it is lower than that. The windowsill. It must be the windowsill! But now comes the most difficult, the trickiest, part. Can she do it? She must do it, she tells herself fiercely. She *will* do it.

Once more she is forced to depend on the dubious solidity of the curtain rod. By moving her hand gradually up the curtain and giving it a pull each time she shifts the position of her hand, by using her toes as a rudder, she is able to position herself and the chair to which she is tied sideways to the window. But that isn't good enough! she thinks despairingly. If she is situated beside the window, she won't be able to produce sufficient momentum to break the pane of glass. Up to this point she has been so absorbed in the task at hand that she had not considered the impossibility of breaking the windowpane. It was her only chance, and so she took it.

So little time left to her! Perhaps not enough. But she must not think about that. She takes up the rhythm again: pull, scrabble—pull, scrabble; and after what seems like hours, she is facing the window at last. Has she time? Has she time? Will she be able to smash the window? A slender thread of glimmering light on the lower pane catches her eye; and she remembers that when she and Gretchen moved into the house last autumn, they noticed that the glass was cracked. But there was a great deal to do, inside and outside the house, and they were both working, so as things go, it went; and they have not yet got around to having the pane replaced. Lisl does not permit herself to think that the fact may prove to be a blessing in disguise. By moving her neck she swathes her head in the thick curtain material—she does not care how badly she injures herself so long as she does not cut her throat, which would prevent her from screaming out and saving the boys—and butts her head forward as hard as she can.

There is no sound but a dull thump. No shattering of glass. Her chair sways and nearly turns over, sending her heart rocketing up to her throat.

ALESSANDRO'S HEART IS CALM AGAIN. It beats with a pleasing regularity, now that he has *it* in his pocket. His hand never leaves his pocket as he turns into Blackshire Road. He wants to make certain *it* won't disappear. Because he needs it. Very soon now, he will need it more than he has ever needed it before. On his face there is a wolfish grin.

As he walks briskly along toward the house in Fairfax Place, however, his content mingles with a vague disquiet. He senses something, he does not know what. Something unsettling. He snuffs at the air like a wild animal. But there is nothing nearby calculated to alarm, only the solitary drivers of automobiles heading home at the end of a day's work. His apprehensions allayed, he sinks back into his blood-splattered daydreams.

LISL REARS HER HEAD AND BODY BACKWARD INTO THE ROOM. The chair rocks ominously. She holds her breath, and hurls her head and shoulders in their tangle of curtain forward with all the force she can muster. Time is running out. So little time. So little. So ... To her joy and disbelief, she hears a crash and the tinkle of falling glass. Even with the enveloping curtain for protection, her face has been cut, but she pays no attention to her hurts.

She has not yet won. So much still to be done, if only she can. So much still to accomplish to save the boys.

She manages to shake off the curtain folds and free her face, enabling her to look at what she has done. Good, she thinks with satisfaction. Several shards of glass still fastened inside the window frame are well within her reach. If only they have not been jarred loose. If only the putty will hold.

She stretches her neck as far forward as she is able in an attempt to snag the gag that binds her mouth on one of the projecting edges of glass. It takes several tries, heart-cracking effort, dauntingly close but not quite close enough. At last, however, the nylon catches, hooked by the sharp sliver of glass. She draws her head down, pulls the gag down over the piece of glass, paying no heed as the shard slices into the tender flesh of her cheek. The gag has been tightly tied around her face, she tells herself. That is what it takes.

Too tightly tied to leave any give in the filaments. Too tightly tied for her to be able to pull it away from her mouth so she can call out a warning to Gretchen, to the children, when they come. She is sure they are not yet here, sure she would have heard the sound of Gretchen's car in the drive. Grimly she saws away at the stocking hampering her mouth. With each movement the razor-sharp glass fragment gouges her cheek, again and again.

ALESSANDRO TURNS INTO ANOTHER STREET. Ridgway Street.

"Do you think he's spotted us?" I ask Jacko. Now I recognize the feeling in the beer joint for what it was—the disturbing, unnerving sensation I've had twice before. It has me by the throat.

"Nah. There's a lot of traffic around here right now. Home-bound traffic."

He gestures at a red Jeep Cherokee with two kids, and a blond woman driving.

"They look young to have been in school this late in the afternoon," I observe, to take my mind off the terrifying panicky feeling.

"Anyone can tell you ain't got kids," says Jacko. "School's out for the holidays. They probably been Christmas shopping."

"Watch out! He's turning again."

Jacko ignores my directions and mutters something unprintable, then says, "No can do. That's a one-way street."

"Who gives a damn? Go up it anyway. Jacko, I've got that weird feeling again. I swear it's got something to do with this. I know Alessandro's on his way to a rape."

I clutch at his arm.

"I can't, Kate," he says in agony. "If I do he'll spot us."

I reach toward the door handle. "Then let me out. This instant. I'm going after him on foot. Stop the car, Jacko. For Christ's sake, stop the car!"

"No!" He turns the car to the left and into a street parallel to Ridgway. "He'll recognize you. I'm not letting you tackle him alone. Besides, you might scare him off."

"Stop the goddamn car or I'll throw myself out!"

Jacko's only answer is to go faster.

"Oh, great," I tell him. "Now you'll get us picked up for speeding."

He turns down Ridgway Street. No sign of Alessandro. A couple of husbands getting out of their cars, a couple of kids on their way home to supper, a woman in a fur coat walking a golden retriever.

"Jesus H. Christ! Don't tell me we lost him!" Jacko beats his hands on the steering wheel in frustration.

"Fat lot of good you are!" I am furious at Jacko. "I'm getting out, and I'm going to quarter the neighborhood till I find the son of a bitch. You just keep cruising around Wawaset Park till your hair turns white and your teeth fall out." As I say this I get out and start walking. "If you'd let me out when I asked you—"

"Oh, why don't you shut up? If you think I'm letting you take off alone after that guy, you got rocks in your noggin. And don't go thinking we're splitting up to look for him. The last thing I need is to have to explain to Rosebud if the creep hurts one hair of your empty head. He'd skin me alive."

Jacko is walking beside me. We are covering ground very

fast. That's great, except we haven't a clue what direction we should be heading in; for all we know, we're moving away from the creep and his destination. But what else can we do? At this point we've got more chance of spotting him on foot than we have with wheels. I pull up my coat collar in hopes he won't see enough of my face to recognize me if we do spot him, and the two of us slog doggedly on.

ALESSANDRO HAS REACHED FAIRFAX PLACE. He walks fast and with an air of purpose, as if he belongs there, as if he is a husband on his way home from work or a boyfriend coming to have dinner with one of the inhabitants. It is a comparatively risky time of day for him to enter the house. A neighbor might see him and wonder who he is and what he is doing there. But he finds that this uncertainty adds a relish, a pleasing piquancy, to his actions. When he reaches *the* house, he looks carefully around without seeming to do so in order to make certain there is no one to notice him when he slips through the kitchen door. Once inside, he stops and listens. No sound. Good. He glances around the room. It looks quiet and unalarming, since before he left he straightened up the signs of his struggle with Lisl. He does not want the other one to see anything that might alert her when she comes in.

He goes into the hall and begins to mount the stairs. He had left on the lights so that everything will look normal when the other one comes home. As he places his foot on the second step, he hears the sound of a car nearby. The motor stops. He tenses. Is someone coming here to spoil everything? His hand is still on the knife in his pocket. It reassures him silently. Nothing is going to go wrong tonight. His God will see to that. He has only to do what the knife tells him to do. When the time comes.

A SMALL PUDDLE OF BLOOD FILLS A HOLLOW PLACE IN THE WINDOWSILL. Lisl cannot tell if she is making any headway at all in slicing through the nylon pantyhose that binds her mouth. She can only pray harder than she has ever prayed before.

She keeps her eyes fixed on the driveway and the path to the kitchen door below. *Please God let me get the gag off in time. Please God make him late. Please God let them get here before he does. Please God let me get the gag off....* It is a mantra that keeps time with the sawing motion against the shard of glass.

Please God let them get here before he does.... She falters. The sawing stops for a heartbeat, then picks up pace as she sees a dark figure come up the path. If only she can get rid of the gag now, her screaming may scare him off before ...

But the nylon is tough. The strands do not part. Though she does not slow the pace of the sawing, her ears strain to hear what he is doing, where he is. She hears nothing. The house has wall-to-wall carpeting, so she cannot hear whether he is coming up the stairs.

ALESSANDRO REACHES THE LANDING. There is a window on it which provides light for the staircase. He peers out. The window, built in a vertical line with the kitchen door and the window in Gretchen's bedroom on the floor above, supplies him with a view of the garage and driveway. A car parks in the driveway as he watches, and he sees the other one get out to open the garage door. She is blond like the one who is waiting upstairs, blond like his mother. Involuntarily he licks his lips in anticipation. *It won't be long now,* he tells the knife silently. *She is early. You were right to tell me to come early. You are always right. I will pay her back for going away, won't I? I'll fix her good for leaving me behind. She'll be sorry she left she'll be sorry.*

He is about to start back downstairs when he sees two small children get out of the car. What has gone wrong? His heart begins to thud violently. He didn't expect this. But as he fondles the knife in his pocket, the contact quiets him. That is Jerry and Jenny, he thinks. He'll fix them, too. Taking his mother away from him. Just wait. They'll be sorry they were ever born. The knife nestles, warm, waiting, in his hand.

GRETCHEN STOPS THE CAR IN FRONT OF THE GARAGE. She might as well put it away, she thinks, since she won't need it again till tomorrow.

"Okay, kids, here we are. Last stop. All out." She leans over to unlock the right-hand door and unbuckle Tommy's seat belt, then unlocks the back door of the car and helps Tippy out of his child's seat. Earlier he was the one in front; at their joint request, he and Tommy have been taking turns sitting next to their aunt.

"The door's locked, so you boys wait there till I pull the car into the garage."

She watches them scamper along the path to the kitchen door. Even though it is not yet six, the lights in the house do not surprise her, as there are timer switches to turn them on at dusk so she and Lisl will return to a lighted house. But when she opens the garage door, she sees Lisl's car parked inside. Back already! Super, she thinks, pleased.

NOTHING. Not a sign of the anonymous walking figure that is Alessandro, that is the homicidal rapist we've got to find before it is too late. We haven't a clue where he's headed, but we both sense that before the night is over he will do something horrible, something unspeakable, unless we are able to find him first and stop him.

Despite myself, my eyes fill with tears. As we walk, I dash them away angrily with the back of my hand.

"A needle in a goddamn haystack," I say, my voice ragged. "We won't know where he's gone until it's too late." I take hold of Jacko's arm for comfort. "Oh, Jacko, I can't bear it! I can't bear our not being able to stop him, now that we know who he is."

"Chin up, Kate. We'll find him soon. No sweat," says Jacko jauntily, but we both know it is mere bravado, whistling in the dark to make me feel better. We trudge on.

LISL SEES GRETCHEN'S RED CHEROKEE PULL INTO THE DRIVEWAY. Her heart skips a beat. She steps up the pace of her sawing, but in her mind a voice is crying, Too late! Too late!—The children get out of the car.—*Oh dear Jesus,* the voice inside her head plains.—*Too late too late . . .*

For a split second she cannot believe it. The glass splinter has finally shredded its way through the nylon pantyhose that have prevented her from crying out. Her lips are numb from the pressure of the gag, her cheek—but she won't think about her cheek. There isn't time. She looks out the window, looks down at the path where her two sons are standing beside the kitchen door waiting for Gretchen, looks down at Gretchen striding toward them. She opens her mouth, but no sound emerges. It is a nightmare: a nightmare like the kind where you run and run and run and never get anywhere. But it is not a nightmare. It is real, and he is in the house. Waiting. They will go inside and—

She opens her mouth again and screams. A clarion scream. She strains against the bonds that fasten her to the chair, strains toward the window.

"Danger! Go away! Take them away!" she shrieks. If only Gretchen can understand her! Her voice is harsh and incomprehensible, even to her own ears. *"Go away! Go away!"*

JACKO AND I ARE CASTING ABOUT BLINDLY IN OUR SEARCH, LIKE HOUNDS that have lost the scent. Suddenly I hear a strange noise somewhere nearby, like the croak of a crow.

"What's that?" I ask Jacko.

I try to figure out if it has a human origin, and if so, whether there are words embedded in the sound. Whatever it is, it is all we have to go on; so after a quick glance at each other, Jacko and I take off in the direction it seems to be coming from. We cut over a lawn and around a fence, and find ourselves at the back of a trim brick house where a blond woman and two little boys—the ones I saw in the red Jeep Cherokee, I think, recognizing them—are staring up at a window above them. The woman has just picked up the smaller boy and is taking the hand of the elder one as we come up to them. The window on the second story is unlighted, but I glimpse what looks like a broken pane and a white smudge daubed with something dark, which seems to be a face looking out.

The blond woman looks as if she is not quite sure what to do. She steps away from the house, then turns back. The formless croaking shapes words.

"*No!* Go away, Gretchen! Get them away from here!"

The younger boy begins to cry.

Jacko and I have both drawn our guns. I have kept my hand on mine inside my jacket ever since I got out of the car. The woman sees us and looks even more confused.

"Police, ma'am," Jacko explains, since we are both in plain clothes. "Will you please get into the car with the children and lock the doors? Keep down so you can't be seen. Kate?" He turns to me. I know he is about to ask me to go with them.

"Oh, no, you don't!" I tell him. "This is my fox, remember? I'm letting you come along for the ride, but he's mine."

Together we go into the kitchen. The door is unlocked, no need to break the glass panes to get inside. An innocent-looking place, all blue-and-white checks and yellow daisies, warm and bright and smelling of cinnamon and nutmeg and ginger. I look cautiously around, keeping my gun at the ready. Nobody there. Jacko checks the doors: No one behind them, just closets and a laundry room. We move with care into the hall, and check the sitting and dining rooms. Zero. I glance up the staircase. Nothing. The noise has stopped. She has seen us, I think. She knows they are safe now in the car.

With a gesture to me, Jacko starts up the stairs, but I do not follow him. I have other ideas. I remember this house, or one very like it, in which a girl who made her debut in Wilmington the same year I did had lived. She and I became friends, and I spent a lot of time there. Now I seem to remember a glassed-in porch beyond the kitchen at the side of the house (if it is the same house), which had a door opening out into the garden. Even if it is the same house, houses are changed from time to time; but I don't want to take a chance on the creep getting out that way unnoticed while we search the rest of the place. There's no time to explain this to Jacko, who by now has made his way up past the landing and has nearly reached the second floor.

So without more ado, I sprint back toward the kitchen and turn right beyond the staircase. Bingo! Tucked away behind the stairs, just where I thought one would be, I see another door, half-open. I look through the doorway and there it is, the glass porch I remembered, with an open door that leads out to a garden beyond. No lights are on in the room, and I do not turn them on, for fear they might assist Alessandro if he is out there; but I can find my way around with the light reflected from the hall behind me.

This should be easy, I tell myself. My recollection of the garden adjoining my friend Harriet's house is of a small city garden, and what little I can see corroborates my memory. But in the dusk, shadows are strangely misleading, and it is taking time for my eyes to adjust to the comparative darkness after the light inside the house. I attain the garden doorway and take a cautious step forward. Not cautious enough. I stagger and swear savagely under my breath: I had not noticed the steps down to the lawn from the porch, because they are covered with leaves that the wind has banked against them.

In front of where I stand, something large rushes past; and I lurch backward in surprise. If that was intended as an attack, I think, Alessandro's eyes as well as mine must be confused by the uncertain light. My eyes, however, are beginning to adapt; and on some bushes in front of me and to the right I spot a blur which, it seems to me, moved just before I looked directly at it. But before I can be certain, before I can take aim, the blur vanishes. I blink my eyes in an attempt to clear and focus my vision. Did I see something there, or didn't I?

At least, I think, I have a rough idea of where Alessandro is. But the same holds true for him. I hold, however, an advantage. Literally. In my hand. My gun. If Alessandro is running true to form, he is armed only with a knife; though who knows? He got one bright idea in midstream—using a knife. Maybe he's just gotten another. Maybe he's carrying a firearm now.

Something whizzes toward me from Alessandro's general direction. Something small this time. It strikes me, hitting my left breast, and I give a grunt of surprise. *No! Oh, God, no! How could I have been so stupid? He does have a gun! And his aim was too good for him not to have spotted me!* Trembling, I bring up a hand to explore for damage. I know that I won't feel the pain for a moment or so, and I need to find out the worst. To my horror, instead of a bullet hole, I feel a knife blade sticking out of my chest. But when I fumble in my shirt pocket under the knife, I breathe a sigh of profound relief. My sketch pad, which I usually carry with me in my left-hand breast pocket, has taken the blow and contained it. I am not even scratched.

I strain my eyes out toward the darkened garden. Nothing. A sensation, as of something moving behind me. I freeze. He couldn't have managed to get behind me. He couldn't! A tickle of breath at my ear. A whisper.

"Kate? You see anything?" Jacko, catching up.

I breathe another sigh of relief; and at that instant I sense, rather than see, a darker form silhouetted against the leaves. I take careful aim. At where I think his legs must be. In case he begins to run. I don't want to kill the little bastard. I want him to suffer.

"Come out! You're under arrest." To my vast relief there is no shrillness in my voice. "Come on out." I am impatient. There is someone in the house upstairs who needs to be looked after. Stop holding us up. Let's get the show on the road. Come on, make it snappy. All the trite phrases roil in my head while we are waiting.

He must think we can't see him because he takes off, crouched like a jack rabbit. As he moves Jacko and I fire, nearly simultaneously but not quite, I think with satisfaction. My shot was a hairsbreadth faster. And placed just where I wanted it. He staggers and falls. Later I find that I had nicked him neatly in the right ankle.

As we approach the still figure, I have a moment's unreasoning terror. Surely I haven't killed him. Suppose it turns out to be a stranger? Someone I've never set eyes on? Some passerby who was lost and took a shortcut across the garden? I feel ill. I have never shot a man before.

I look at the man on the ground. It is Alessandro. He lies curled like a shrimp, whimpering. The tables have certainly turned, I think. Oddly enough, as I gaze down at him I realize that I don't hate him. I feel sorry for him.

CHAPTER 30

December 23

As Jacko and I made our way to Rosebud's office, I twitted him on the way his shot had missed Alessandro; in all the excitement, he had forgotten to compensate for the fact that his gun throws a shade to the right.

"Poor boy!" I teased him. "Hard luck for a big bad tough cop to be outdone by a mere woman."

"Sure, you must have known I missed the son of a bitch on purpose," he told me, his choirboy's eyes round with mock innocence and his tongue firmly in his cheek. "I was just trying to put the fear of God into him. I wanted you to be the one to pot him, Katie, m'dear."

"A likely tale," I scoffed. All this badinage, intended to dispel our nervousness at confronting Rosebud, was far from succeeding; and when I turned the corner with Jacko, a queasy feeling in the pit of my stomach, we found him in his office, perched on the edge of his battered desk. As usual, he had the lean and hungry look of a carrion crow. Jacko, ever gallant, had volunteered me to present the report; so I did, nonchalant without and quailing within. Lieutenant Flowerdew heard me through without interrupting.

When I had finished, he asked, "How is Mrs. O'Neill getting along?"

"Her cheek where the glass slashed it is going to need some plastic surgery, a graft I think, but the surgeon said it should look fine afterwards. Not that she seems to care one way or the other. Her children are undamaged, so she's terrific."

"And the kids?"

"A little scared, a little nervous, but basically they didn't have a clue about what was going on. I think they're going to shake it off the way a duck sheds water. Ms. Welbach was the most affected."

"The sister?"

"She told me the most horrible moment of her life was when she had to decide whether to take the boys away and leave her sister, or ignore what Mrs. O'Neill asked her to do and go in to help her."

"Lucky you showed up when you did. Which reminds me." Rosebud shoved back his chair and put his feet up on the desk. Jacko and I relaxed imperceptibly; it didn't look as if a chewing-out was imminent. When he spoke, the mild tone of his voice belied the words.

"What the hell did you two think you were doing, taking off on your own like that when Mother had told you it was no go?"

"It was my fault," I volunteered nobly, a willing sacrifice.

"No, sir, it wasn't," Jacko interpolated quickly, glaring at me.

"I don't need to be told who did what and with which and to whom," said Rosebud. He was trying to show us a stern face, but a twitch at the corner of his mouth betrayed him. "Let's just forget about it. All's well that ends well. In fact, thank God you did it. But don't do it again."

"No, sir," we chorused meekly, though I for one would do the same again in a flash, as he well knew.

"The FBI lab has assured us they'll process the suspect's blood sample soonest. Personally, though, I don't think there's the shadow of a doubt that he's our boy. As you know, Mrs. O'Neill has definitely identified him as her attacker. Good work, the pair of you. The best. But just remember to keep me posted the next time. You're not out of kindergarten yet.

"Now be off with you both. What the hell are you hanging

around for, a gold star to paste on the front of your copy books?"

Jacko was grinning as we left Rosebud's office, and from the way my face felt, so was I.

ALESSANDRO SITS ON THE COT IN HIS CELL IN GANDER HILL PRISON. His knees are bent. His arms are wrapped around them, and his head rests between his knees. His eyes are open, but he does not see the cell or its furnishings. He stares into nothingness.

He is keening, a low monotonous whine that now and then separates itself into words. A guard walking past bangs on the bars of his cell to get his attention.

"Hey, you! Cut out the noise. Shut the crap up. Ya hear me? Shut up! Cheest," the guard mutters to himself. "Gives me the creeps."

Alessandro pays no attention to him. A tray with food on it sits untouched near the door of his cell. The thin thread of sound emanating from him becomes a rude kind of language— "Mother come back. Mother don't leave me mother. Mother mother I want my mother." Then it narrows again into unintelligible mewling. He rocks back and forth incessantly, whimpering to himself like a puppy crying in its sleep.

HARRY IS BACK. Dearest Harry, home for Christmas. We are sitting—well, lying, actually—on the long sofa in the sitting room, which is dark except for the light of the burning logs of the fire. I gaze into the crimson-black-scarlet tinseled heart of it, shifting and glowing and indescribably beautiful. I want to be able to capture that in paint, I think. Like Turner at his best.

"I bet you can't find the right words to describe what that fire looks like," I say to Harry. "Really describe it. So an accurate picture springs instantly to mind. I bet paint would do a better job than words any old day."

"Done." He takes my hand to seal the bargain. "What will you wager?"

"What do you suggest?"

"Marry me if I win the bet. Quite an incentive for me."

"Again? You *are* a sucker for punishment."

For answer Harry raises the hand he is still holding to his lips. He kisses each of my fingers meticulously and delicately and precisely before he moves on to the rest of me. My body feels blazing hot, hotter than the burning wood that crackles in the fire. I suddenly realize that up to now I have been merely playing a game with Harry, a delicious, amusing, enthralling game. A game that plays out like a game of chess: one with all kinds of intricate moves that allow one player to advance while the other retreats. I have always been the one to beat a strategic retreat; I have been the one in control of the moves on the board. After Eugène, after the breakup of my marriage with Harry and the events that had led up to it, I was afraid not to keep something in reserve; and I used to enjoy playing games with Harry, used to enjoy being deliberate, detached, the one in charge. Keeping myself reined in, watching every step I took to make certain I wouldn't go too far.

But I no longer want to be cool, collected, contained. I want to let myself go, I want to shed every fiber of restraint, to let ardor consume me utterly, as if I were tinder in the flames, or the paper dancer in the fairy tale of the "The Steadfast Tin Soldier." As we lie entangled in each other, an amorous Laocoön, it is impossible to tell where one begins and the other ends. My pulse is hectic; I feel all in a glow, like a woodstove lavishly stoked with fuel. If my temperature were to be taken at this moment, it would fly straight off the chart. I am feverish with love.